D0013855

AWAKENED

As he knelt down beside her, the look in his eyes awakening a need she had never known before, she reached her hands out for him.

Boldly, she spoke what was in her heart.

"I need you," she murmured, her eyes searching his. "I…want…you."

She had never wanted a man before.

She had never met a man like him before.

She had never made love before.

Did he want her as much?

He swept his arms around her and drew her against his muscled chest. His powerful kiss was his response to her question.

As they kissed, they hurriedly undressed each other.

His heart throbbing, the heat in his loins intense, Storm spread himself over Shoshana….

Other books by Cassie Edwards:

TOUCH THE WILD WIND
ROSES AFTER RAIN
WHEN PASSION CALLS
EDEN'S PROMISE
ISLAND RAPTURE
SECRETS OF MY HEART

The *Savage* Series:

SAVAGE HOPE
SAVAGE TRUST
SAVAGE HERO
SAVAGE DESTINY
SAVAGE LOVE
SAVAGE MOON
SAVAGE HONOR
SAVAGE THUNDER
SAVAGE DEVOTION
SAVAGE GRACE
SAVAGE FIRES
SAVAGE JOY
SAVAGE WONDER
SAVAGE HEAT
SAVAGE DANCE
SAVAGE TEARS
SAVAGE LONGINGS
SAVAGE DREAM
SAVAGE BLISS
SAVAGE WHISPERS
SAVAGE SHADOWS
SAVAGE SPLENDOR
SAVAGE EDEN
SAVAGE SURRENDER
SAVAGE PASSIONS
SAVAGE SECRETS
SAVAGE PRIDE
SAVAGE SPIRIT
SAVAGE EMBERS
SAVAGE ILLUSION
SAVAGE SUNRISE
SAVAGE MISTS
SAVAGE PROMISE
SAVAGE PERSUASION

THE APACHE

His hair is so black,
Like a raven's wing,
Can make you forget everything,
Standing there, so proud and tall,
Hoping his people will never fall.
To look into his dark, brown eyes,
You would be almost mesmerized.
His bronze skin, so warm and sweet,
Would make any woman bow at his feet.
He only wants one woman,
For this you can see,
And that one woman is me.
He will be my husband, and I his wife,
So we can be together for the rest of our life.

—*Crystal Marie Carpenter*

(To Cassie Edwards—Thanks for the inspiration.)

SAVAGE COURAGE

CASSIE EDWARDS

LEISURE BOOKS NEW YORK CITY

A LEISURE BOOK®

February 2005

Published by

Dorchester Publishing Co., Inc.
200 Madison Avenue
New York, NY 10016

ISBN 0-8439-5270-9

SAVAGE COURAGE

Chapter One

You may stretch your hand out toward me,
Ah! You will—I know not when.
                    —Adelaide Anne Procter

Arizona, 1873

It was a beautiful, serene day at the Chiricahua Apache village. The mid-morning sun was flinging crimson banners across the sky. The Silent Stream band's children were laughing and playing hide-and-seek in the bushes that stood near the cluster of buffalo-hide tepees.

Mothers were keeping watch on those children as some carried water from the nearby stream, while others scraped hides outside their lodges.

Dogs were frisky this day, romping in the sun-

1

shine after the children, barking, their tails wagging contentedly.

Horses neighed in the nearby corral.

As a golden eagle soared lazily overhead in the blue, cloudless sky, a new sound was added to the normal mid-morning noises—a sound that froze everyone in place, even the children.

Then the village became frantic and filled with a cold panic as warriors ran from the council house, where they had gathered to make plans for a buffalo hunt.

One of the warriors fell to his knees, then pressed an ear to the packed dirt of the ground. Soon he leapt to his feet, his dark eyes filled with worry.

In his Apache tongue he shouted a warning to everyone that horses were approaching. His ear had picked up the sound of their pounding hooves in the vibration of the ground . . . now echoing across the land like the sound of thunder that *everyone* could hear.

A scout rode hurriedly into the village, shouting, "*Pindah-lickoyee*, white eyes! *Pindah-lickoyee*! Many pony soldiers are near! Raise the American flag! Quickly! Wave it back and forth. The pony soldiers will surely retreat! They will see that they are arriving at a peaceful Apache camp!"

A warrior hurriedly raised the flag on a pole in the center of the village, having been told by the United States Government that doing so would always keep the Silent Stream Village safe from attack by the cavalry.

But never trusting the word of any *pindah-lickoyee*, mothers dropped their water jugs to the ground, ignoring the breaking sounds and the way the precious water ran across the ground, soaking into it like water into a sponge. Their concern was their children.

Their eyes wild, their breath catching in their throats, they ran to where their children had only moments ago been playing. Other mothers grabbed their smaller babes up into their arms and ran toward the safety of their lodges.

Several warriors stood beneath the flying flag, shouting *friend* in the English tongue they had learned from friendly traders. The pony soldiers were now so close, the warriors could see the whites of their eyes, and . . . the shine of the barrels of the firearms they held in their hands.

Seeing the rifles poised now, ready to fire, the warriors knew that no American flag, or shouts of friendship, would help today.

The *pindah-lickoyee* had come to kill!

"They come as enemies today!" a warrior cried as he ran toward his lodge, his breechclout flapping, his long, black hair flying out behind him. "Prepare yourselves! Get your weapons ready to defend our people and . . . our . . . Apache honor!"

All the warriors ran in panic toward their own tepees, their eyes wildly seeking loved ones who might not yet have made it to the safety of their lodges.

In each warrior's heart he knew that today was not a good day after all, despite the fact that only moments ago they had all been bragging about the wonder of the many buffalo they had seen grazing on thick, green grass near their village.

The warriors had spoken of how many they would take today.

They had talked of who might get off the first arrow of the hunt, laughingly teasing one of the younger warriors who had not yet had a first kill.

The council house had been a place of merriment only moments ago, with its fire still burning brightly in the center of the floor in its fire pit, the smoke spiraling lazily from the smoke hole even now and into the beautiful, cloudless sky.

Everyone now felt how sharp was the edge of fate that could come on a village so quickly, taking away all hope. *Ho*, yes, too often the white man brought death and destruction to a village of the people instead of talk of peace and honor!

This was a day no warrior could save, no matter how hard he tried, or how many pony soldiers could be killed by arrows before the enemy swept through the village with their deadly firearms.

Shouting, "*Tiras*, do not fire! *Tiras*, do not fire!", the Silent Stream Band of Apache ran in many directions, sometimes colliding with each other and falling clumsily to the ground, then getting up and running again in a desperate attempt to find one last moment of life.

It was a dizzying scene; no one seemed to have any sense of direction or plan of where to go, or what to do to save their beloved families.

The horses carrying the soldiers were already galloping into the outskirts of the village.

The soldiers ignored the pleading. They ignored the looks of terror on the Apache people's faces.

Gunfire began exploding from the *pindah-lickoyee's* firearms, followed by screams of terror, and then pain.

A soldier began giving orders to those under his command. "Spare no one!" he shouted. "Kill small and big, women and children! Let no warrior come out of this alive!"

A little boy ran from a tepee, crying. A soldier saw him and stopped and took aim. He sent a bullet flying from his rifle, but missed the child.

Another soldier who saw this drew a tight rein and dismounted. He fell to a knee, set his rifle on his other knee, aimed, and knocked the boy over with one lethal shot.

Five-year-old Shoshana was with her mother, Fawn, fleeing the soldiers, as gunfire spattered all around them. She screamed as she saw her people's tepees being set afire with flaming torches.

She clung desperately to her mother's hand as

they ran onward toward the nearby ravine where they might be able to hide in the bushes that stood at the edge of the water.

Shoshana's heart raced as she heard a horse approaching from behind her and her mother. She looked wild-eyed over her shoulder as a soldier on a black steed took aim and fired.

She screamed when her mother's body lurched, then released Shoshana's hand and fell to the ground, quiet.

"*Todah*, no! *Ina*, mother! *Ina*!" Shoshana cried in her Apache tongue when she saw blood on the back of her mother's doeskin dress, turning what was only moments ago a beautiful white color to red.

Shoshana fell to her knees beside her mother.

"*Ina*! Please awaken!" Shoshana sobbed as she began shaking her mother's lifeless body. "Mother, I am so afraid. Do . . . not . . . leave me!"

But no matter what she said or did, her mother continued to lie there, her body quiet, her eyes closed.

Terror ate away at Shoshana's heart, for what she saw today on her mother's face was the same look she had seen on the day of her father's death, when an enemy renegade burst out of bushes and killed her father, only to be killed himself moments later by her father's best friend.

Now Shoshana had no one! Both her parents were dead.

Filled with despair, and a deep, gnawing need to survive this terrible day, Shoshana scurried to her feet.

Her eyes filled with the pain of loss, yet with sudden determination, she defied the whites who had brought death to her beloved Silent Stream Band of Apache as she ran onward toward the ravine. She still hoped to find shelter there.

But when she heard a horse quickly approaching from behind her and then felt an arm grabbing her up from the ground, she knew just how wrong it had been to hope for what would never be.

She gazed frantically over her shoulder and saw that the one who had grabbed her was a soldier with long hair the color of fire, and eyes the color of the sky.

She strugged to fight him off, kicking and biting him, but no matter how hard she tried, the pony soldier held her on his lap, an arm like steel around her tiny waist holding her in place against him. There was a sudden strange sort of kindness in his sky-blue eyes.

She realized that no matter how hard she tried, the soldier was taking her as his hostage as he rode away with her, leaving the fighting behind them, as well as the screams of terror and the leaping fires that were consuming the lodges.

And then Shoshana became aware of something else: the total silence behind her at the village. She

7

feared the *pindah-lickoyee* pony soldiers had done as they had been ordered to do. Except for herself, the pony soldiers had spared none of her people!

"*To-dah*, no," she sobbed. "*To-dah!*"

She then hung her head in abject sorrow as she whispered to herself, "I . . . alone . . . am . . . alive."

Yet inside her heart, she felt dead.

Chapter Two

I will not let thee go.
Have we not chid the changeful moon?
                                    —Robert Bridges

A few days later . . .

"It was a good day for a mock hunt, was it not, Little Bear?" Storm said proudly from his brown pony. He was ten winters of age and of the Chiricahua tribe of Apache, of the Piñaleno River Band.

He looked over at Little Bear, who rode at his side on his own pony, as others followed behind them. He noticed quickly that Little Bear did not even seem to have heard what Storm had said to him.

Wondering what had caught his friend's attention, Storm followed the path of Little Bear's eyes.

He grew cold at heart when he saw smoke in the distance. There was no doubt where it came from. It rose from their village which sat alongside the Piñaleno River.

And it was far too much smoke to be accounted for by the cooking fires of the village.

It was billowing and black, turning the sky dark where it had only moments ago been such a peaceful blue.

"My father ... my mother ... my sister ... our people!" Storm gasped as he sank his heels deep into the flanks of his pony. "*Nuest-chee-shee*, come! We must go and see what we can do to stop the fires and help our people!"

"We are only small braves," Little Bear whined as he came up closer to Storm on his spotted pony. "We will be riding into danger!"

"Do not cry and whine like a scared puppy," Storm said scornfully. "*Huka*, I am not afraid! We must help! We must fight if any enemies are left at our village!"

"With our tiny bows and arrows?" Little Bear whined again. "We only have what is needed for a mock hunt, not for true killing. And ... look at us, Storm. We are but a few!"

"Little Bear, we are but a few, but we are the future of our Piñaleno River Band!" Storm shouted. "Behave like a warrior instead of a mere brave! Be ready for whatever we find at our village! It takes courage, Little Bear. It takes savage courage to be what only moments ago we were not. If our people were ambushed and are no longer of this earth, it will be up to us to carry on the traditions we have been taught."

Then a thought came to Storm that made his heart skip several beats. His sister Dancing Willow had left at the same time that Storm and his friends had left. She, who was thirty winters of age, a spinster, and a Seer, had gone out into the hills to dig roots.

Dancing Willow had promised to teach the younger girls which roots to dig today. If they had returned to the village before the attack, then she, too, would be dead.

And what of his *Ina*, his mother? And . . . his . . . chieftain *ahte*, his father?

He feared his father would not have survived such an ambush, for he would have been one of the first the enemy, whether renegades or pony soldiers, would target!

To kill a powerful chief would be something to brag about.

Storm raised his eyes heavenward. "Please, *Maheo*, Great Spirit, do not let what I am thinking be true," he shouted. "Please!"

He rode harder until he entered the thick smoke. Then he slowed his horse down to a slow lope, feeling sick to his stomach at the sights that greeted him. Death was everywhere.

"*To-dah*, no!" he cried.

Tears sprang to his eyes as he dismounted and began running from person to person, checking to see if any of his fallen people might still be alive.

It was obvious that they had been shot where they stood, unable even to defend themselves.

And then Storm found his mother.

He gagged when he fell beside her on his knees and saw that whoever had shot his white-skinned mother had also taken her golden hair, her scalp!

"*Ina*, mother," he sobbed. "How could they do this to you? How? And . . . why?"

He hung his head and said a silent prayer over her, then broke away from her and turned to where his father lay only a few feet off.

Chief Two Stones, a cousin to Geronimo, was severely wounded, yet clinging to life, and had somehow been spared the terrible fate of being scalped.

When Storm fell to his knees beside his father and lifted his head onto his lap, he tried not to cry. He wanted to be a man in his father's eyes, at least while he was still alive to see him.

Storm knew what his future held for him and he had to prove to his dying father that he was worthy of the title of chief, for he was next in line after his father to lead his people.

"My son, *pindah-lickoyee*, white-eye soldiers, came and killed. I . . . witnessed . . . your mother's death. I could do nothing to help her. My son, you must flee to higher ground now, while you can," Chief Two Stones said in a voice scarcely audible to Storm. "Take the other young braves with you *ah-han-day*, afar. Lead them to safety high up in the Piñaleno Mountains."

Chief Two Stones reached a quivering hand to one of Storm's and clutched it desperately. "My son, remember to teach as I have taught you, that we Apache hold it a high virtue to speak the truth, always, and never to steal from our own tribesmen," he said thickly. "Teach the children that the Apache warrior adheres more strictly to his code of honor than the white man does to his!"

"*Ahte*, I will teach what has been taught me," Storm said, hearing just how weak his father's voice was becoming, and admiring Chief Two Stones for not thinking of death, but instead of the future of the children and what they should know in order to survive as Apache.

"Son, you have proven yourself time and again to be worthy of the title of chief," Chief Two Stones said, squeezing Storm's hand. "It is now that I hand over the chieftainship to you. Go and make a new life, a stronghold, where no *pindah-lickoyee* can ever find you. But before you go to the mountains, find your sister Dancing Willow and the girls who are with her. Take them into hiding. Keep them safe and well."

"I will find them. And I will be a great leader,"

Storm said. He swallowed hard. "I promise you that, *Ahte*."

"I know you will," Chief Two Stones said, slowly taking his hand away from Storm's. He rested his hand over his heart. "My breath will soon be gone from me forever, but I have enough left to tell you that the man who shot and killed your beloved mother, and then shot your father, was himself shot in the leg. With the last of my strength, I sent an arrow from my bow. It lodged in the evil white man's leg as he rode away."

"I shall find him one day and make him pay," Storm said softly. "I promise that I shall take revenge!"

"Storm, I know this man's name," Chief Two Stones said breathlessly. "In the middle of the massacre, just before he attacked your mother, I heard the man addressed as Colonel Whaley."

He grabbed Storm's hand once again. "Remember that name always, my son," he said, his voice now barely a whisper. "Perhaps in the future you will hear of a pony soldier whose name is Whaley. If so, you will know he is the man who tore all of your people's lives apart!"

Two Stones again released Storm's hand. He sighed deeply, closed his eyes, then gazed up at Storm again. "Leave now," he said. "But before you leave, please join one of your mother's hands with mine. I will die much more happily if I am reunited in this way with my wife."

Tears streaming from Storm's eyes, he rose and took his mother's cold hand and gently placed it in his father's. He saw how his father's fingers wrapped around his mother's hand.

"Thank you, my son," Chief Two Stones said as he gazed over at his wife, whose face was still visible to him through the blood. "Although I first knew your mother as my white captive, I fell in love with her, and she with me. We had a good, happy life, and she bore me a son of that love. That son is you, Storm. You always made us so proud."

"I have always loved you both so much," Storm said, swallowing hard. His older sister, a full-blood Apache, was from another time when his father had been married to one of his own people. She had died while giving birth to a second child . . . a child who did not survive either.

Although a half-breed because of his white mother, Storm had all of the appearance and mannerisms of an Apache warrior.

"Son, your heart is Apache," Two Stones said, coughing blood as he spoke. "Lead! Be safe! Keep what remains of our band safe!"

Storm glanced over at his mother again. He could hardly stand to think of the pain she had suffered before dying, as her lovely golden hair was removed. But at least she was at peace now, and soon his father would be joining her in the stars!

"My son, why do you hesitate to leave?" Two Stones asked. "Why?"

"*Ahte*, I just cannot leave you here like this while you still have breath in your lungs," Storm blurted out. "Mother is dead. But . . . you . . . are still among the living!"

"Storm—"

"No, *Ahte*, I must follow my heart," Storm said, quickly rising to his feet. "And it tells me to take you with me. But before we leave, it is my decision to remain here long enough to bury the dead."

"My son—"

"*Ahte*, it is the only way, or I would never get a night's rest for thinking about our people lying like this for—"

"Do what you must," Two Stones said, closing his eyes. "I understand."

"Even *Ina*," Storm said. "I must separate you two in order to bury her."

"It is truly the right thing that you are doing," Two Stones said. "But hurry, my son. Hurry. Do not take time to make deep graves. Bury the dead just deep enough so that rocks can cover them and protect them."

Storm nodded. He gathered together the young braves who were all that remained of his band. Some hurried around collecting rocks, while others began digging shallow graves.

After all were buried, a travois was made for

Storm's father and they set out, pulling him behind them.

Before long they had found the young girls and Dancing Willow and were telling them what had happened. Then together they started the long journey up the mountainside.

After going only a short distance, Storm's father passed to the other side. Storm's heart ached anew at this latest loss.

Remembering that his father had wanted to be with his mother, Storm risked returning to the place of death and buried his father alongside his beloved white wife.

Then Storm returned to the others.

They traveled onward.

Storm was filled with such grief, he found it hard to bear.

"I vow to find vengeance for my people, especially my father and mother," he whispered to himself. "Some day I shall find the man who killed them . . . that Colonel Whaley!"

Yes, when he was older and strong and ready, he would search for and kill the man responsible for the tragedy today. If he could find the man who was responsible for removing his mother's beautiful golden hair, he would bring it back and bury it with her!

His mother's hair had been so lovely . . . like golden silk.

Ho, yes, Storm might be a half-breed, but inside

17

his heart and in everything he did, he was one hundred-percent Apache!

He most certainly was not a *pindah-lickoyee*, and today he was no longer an *ish-kay-nay*, a boy.

He was a man with a man's duties and responsibilities.

His eyes narrowed angrily, he spoke a solemn vow to himself, swearing eternal vengeance against this man called Colonel Whaley.

Should Storm ever get the opportunity, he would make Colonel Whaley pay for what he had taken from Storm today!

Chapter Three

I never saw so sweet a face,
as that I stood before.

—John Clare

Arizona, 1888

A bugle blared, sounding officer's call, awakening Shoshana with a start. Her eyes were wild, her heart pounding.

Again she had dreamed of her mother, whose beloved face she now remembered so vividly, even though for many years it would not come to her.

For so long, everything about that dreadful day fifteen long years ago had been wiped from her mind.

But now, at age twenty, she did remember, and in

this recurring dream Shoshana was once again in the arms of the cavalryman as he carried her on his horse away from the death scene of those she loved.

But the dream was different this time.

In it, as Shoshana turned once again to see the body of her mother one last time, her mother was being carried away by a large and beautiful golden eagle, its huge talons gently, lovingly, gripping her.

The eagle had turned its golden eyes to Shoshana and seemed to have been telling her that he was carrying her mother to safety, that she was alive, and that she would be waiting for Shoshana to find her so that they could be reunited.

"It seemed so real," Shoshana said, scurrying from her bed. "The dream did . . . seem . . . so real!"

She pulled on a robe and slid her feet into soft slippers, then hurried from her room and went to George Whaley's bedroom door, where she knocked softly.

After learning so much about her past and George Whaley's role in it, Shoshana could no longer call him father as she had done until the truth of her background had been disclosed to her.

When she was lost in another world, when she could not recall anything of her past, she had called George Whaley father.

But not now!

Never again would she address him as father!

But she, who had had so much love and respect

for her adoptive mother, still thought of her as the woman who'd taken her in and raised her with all the love of a mother.

Although Shoshana remembered her true mother so very clearly now, she still thought of Dorothea Whaley with the same affection as always.

And even though her adoptive mother had died a year ago from a heart attack, it still seemed strange that she was not there each day with her sweet smile and hugs that always prompted Shoshana to start her own day with a smile.

Today Shoshana was too confused by the dream to smile even if Dorothea had been there.

The dream. What could it mean? It seemed so real!

When she heard a click-clack sound from beyond the door where she now stood with a pounding heart, she knew that George Whaley was coming to the door.

He had a wooden leg, from the knee down.

His right leg had been damaged irreparably by an arrow a few days after he had saved Shoshana and taken her to raise as his own with his wife, who had never been able to have children.

Shoshana and George were now at Fort Chance near the Piñaleno Mountains, a place of beauty so enchanting, it had taken Shoshana's breath away the first time she had laid eyes on it.

The mountain had a mystical, haunting quality about it, as though—

Her thoughts were interrupted when the door opened and she saw George Whaley standing there, staring down at her with his pale blue eyes. He leaned his weight on a fancy, pearl-handled cane.

Shoshana was struck again by how much he had changed since the death of his wife. His face was lean. His lips had a purplish hue from his own weak heart.

And instead of the thick crop of red hair that she had first noticed that day when he had swept her up onto his horse with him, he was now bald. His frame was no longer large, but instead shrunken and bent.

But in his eyes, Shoshana saw the same love for her that she had seen from as far back as she could remember. His feelings for her surely could not be any more genuine than if he were her true father.

And she had called him father, up until she discovered truths that made him more a stranger than a father.

Now, no matter the hurt it caused him, she only called him father when she was forced to do so.

Suddenly she was again overwhelmed by the dream that had only moments ago awakened her. She felt tears building in her eyes as George took her gently by an arm and ushered her into his bedroom.

"Shoshana, tell me what's wrong," he said, turning to gaze intently into her dark eyes.

More and more these days he was struck by her

loveliness. It would be difficult to find anyone who displayed more grace, dignity, and self-possession.

And not only that . . . she was blessed by innate good sense.

She was petite in stature.

Her hair was like her Apache people's, black and glossy.

Her eyes were very large, dark, and lustrous.

He knew that if she had remained with her people, she would have been the pet of her tribe, who were called "Stately Ones."

Almost in one breath, Shoshana told him about the dream. "What can it mean?" she asked when she had related the most intriguing part of the dream . . . about the eagle carrying her Apache mother away, then telling her that her mother, Fawn, was still alive.

"Could it be real?" she asked, her eyes anxiously searching his. "Could she be alive? You know how my dreams have often foretold things that later happen. Can this dream mean that my mother is alive?"

She went to a window and gazed from it into the distance, at the vast mountain that stood near the fort.

She had been told that a band of Apache were holed up there, high up in a stronghold, under the leadership of a young chief, Chief Storm.

She was Apache.

She was keenly aware of the silence behind her, and realized that again George did not wish to speak of the past, especially about that horrible day which she now recalled as though it had happened only yesterday.

She turned to him again. "I know that you would rather not know these things," she said, her voice breaking. "But as I told you, I felt an eeriness from the very first day of our arrival at my birthplace here in Arizona. It is as though someone is calling to me, especially when I look toward the mountain. It seems that someone is beckoning me there. Might . . . it . . . be my true mother? Can she feel my presence even now?"

She went to George. She gazed into his faded eyes. "Do you hear what I am saying?" she murmured. "Or . . . are you trying to ignore it, thinking I will soon forget these feelings and continue on with my life as I have known it?"

"It is just that I do not know exactly what to say," George said, uneasy under her close scrutiny and the questions he wished would not be asked.

He walked past her, the cane and his wooden leg making an ominous ringing sound against the oak floor, then sank down into a thickly cushioned chair before a huge stone fireplace.

In his maroon satin robe with his initials monogrammed on its one pocket, he gazed at the slowly burning fire on the grate.

"All that I do know is that I should never have brought you here," he said ruefully. "I don't know what I was thinking." He looked over at her as she sat down on a chair across from him. "I truly thought you would . . . had . . . gotten past these feelings. But now I doubt that you ever shall."

"No, I never shall, and . . . I don't want to," Shoshana said, nervously combing her long, slender fingers through her thick, black hair, positioning it over her shoulders. "Since our arrival here, I have felt many, many things. I have felt my Apache people calling to me inside my heart. I feel different from the people here at the fort, even more strongly than that day when I learned just how different I was from the children I was growing up with in Missouri."

"Yes, and what happened there was unfortunate," George said thickly. "I should have prepared you for such a situation."

"Yes, you should have," she said, recalling that day as though it had happened yesterday. "When that boy called me a savage squaw and held me down on the ground and cut off the tail end of my braids, I knew how much white people, even children my own age, despise people of any skin color but their own. It is so unfair . . . so *evil*."

"Yes, I shall never forget how you came home crying," George said, sighing heavily. "Your questions that day came so fast and furious, I found it hard to follow you. You wanted to know why those who you

25

thought were your friends treated you in such a way, and why you would be called such a name. I know how it hurt you inside when that child cut off the ends of your braids."

"And you told me that, yes, my skin was different, and to go and look in a mirror so that I would see what everyone else saw when they looked at me," Shoshana said. "I did. I looked into a mirror. I saw nothing different about myself that day than any other day when I played with those children. And I knew long ago that my skin was different from those other children's, but I was never treated differently. I knew that I was an Indian, but until that day, no one approached me with prejudice. I was happy. I . . . I . . . felt loved."

"When I first brought you home, Dorothea and I wanted you to feel loved and to be happy. We especially hoped that you could forgive the wrongs and injustices done to your people on that day," George said softly. "We always felt such love for you. We . . . I . . . especially, felt I owed you so much. You brought something into our lives that we could never have had otherwise."

"After that incident at school, I was afraid what else the children might do to me," she murmured. "I . . . I . . . was afraid to go to school the next day."

"I didn't know that," George said, feeling a sudden sharp pain in his gut to know she had felt such fear. "I'm sorry, Shoshana. I had hoped that it would never come to that."

"But you surely knew that it would," Shoshana murmured. "You were raising an Indian child."

"As I explained before, I saved your life, Shoshana, while others around you were dying," George said thickly. "I wish I could paint a better picture of that day in your mind, but I can't. What happened . . . happened. It was the way of the military back then to—"

"Please don't say any more about it," Shoshana said, interrupting him. She did know that he had saved her, yet moments before he had done that, he had been killing her people.

And, yes, it was the way of the military to do those things back then; just as now the army was forcing her people off their land and into reservation life.

After finally remembering the truth about everything, Shoshana had begun to question her loyalty to a man who had had a role in the slaying of so many people of her own kind.

That day he had come into her village with gunfire splattering all around Shoshana and her mother, she had thought that she had been the sole survivor. But now? She truly believed that her mother had somehow survived as well.

Had her mother been injured that day, badly

enough to have been rendered unconscious, yet alive, after all? Had someone found her and taken her to safety and cared for her wounds? Could she be thinking about Shoshana even now, hungering to have her in her arms as Shoshana now hungered for her true mother's embrace?

Now, so close to where it had all happened, Shoshana knew she must seek answers to the questions that plagued her.

George saw something in Shoshana's expression and eyes that troubled him. He rose from the chair and took her hands, urging her to her feet.

He did not want to feel how she tensed as he drew her into his embrace, something that happened often now that they were in the land of her ancestors.

He cursed the day he had decided to come to Arizona. He should have known something like this might happen.

But what had happened to her was so far in the past, he had thought it could not affect the present.

When she gently pushed him away from her, his heart skipped a beat, but he tried to put aside his own pain in order to reason with her.

"Shoshana, your mother couldn't be alive," he said thickly. "It is just because you are in your people's country now that you are dreaming such dreams. You are missing your past, your people, your true mother, that's all."

He stepped back from her. He gazed into her eyes.

"My darling Shoshana, my only reason for living, I know now that it was a mistake to bring you back to Arizona," he said thickly. "I wish that I had never accepted this commission from the government to come to Arizona to help find the scalp hunter who is preying on the remaining Apache. There is an evil man who is paying top dollar for scalps, Shoshana. Indian scalps, though he isn't picky as long as the hair is dark. The scalp hunter takes his grisly trophies to that man. That man pays the scalp hunter well enough to keep the fiend in business, then sells the hair for decoration, and wigs."

He stepped away from her and went to stand at a window, peering out toward the mountains. "Word is that the scalp hunter, Mountain Jack, is searching now for the most elusive half-breed of all—Chief Storm," he said, then turned to Shoshana again as she approached him, her eyes wide with horror. "To scalp Chief Storm would win Mountain Jack fame and fortune."

"Why is this Chief Storm worth so much?" Shoshana asked softly. "Why is he so elusive? Why is he even allowed to roam free when it is a government law that all Apache must live on a reservation?"

"Shoshana, I wish, oh, how I wish, that I hadn't brought you here," George said, sighing heavily. He took her by the hand. "Come and sit with me. I will explain as much to you as I can."

She sat down before the fire again. She watched

George go to a trunk, open it, then take a long-stemmed pipe from it. He sat down on the chair opposite her, the pipe on his lap.

"You know the story about this pipe. I've told you before about it," he said. "It is an Indian pipe, one that a chief brought with him to a parley when I was vital and able to lead my unit of cavalry." He lifted the pipe and held it out before him. "This was given to me by a great Chiricahua leader during the peace talks between the Apache and the whites. This was Chief Geronimo's pipe."

He handed her the pipe and watched as she studied it. "This young chief, this Chief Storm, has a reputation of being a great leader in his own way," he said. "He is kin to Geronimo, a second cousin. It is known that Chief Storm is not a warring chief, but a leader who concentrates only on keeping his people safe. He is a peaceful, noble man, who does no harm to anyone. Because of this, he has been allowed to remain free. And, Shoshana, he is not full blood. He is a half-breed leader."

"How is it that he is a half-breed yet was chosen as chief for his band of Apache?" Shoshana asked, handing the pipe back to George.

"His mother was white," George said, laying the pipe aside on a table. "As the story goes, she was taken captive. She married her captor, Chief Two Stones. This white wife bore Chief Two Stones one son, whom they named Storm. Both Storm's chieftain father and white mother were killed one day in a cavalry attack. It was said that when Storm, a mere child then, arrived at his village and found the slaughter, he became chief even though he was only ten at the time. He led what remained of their clan to safety. They reside there even now, in a stronghold in the mountains, where no one has ever been able to find them."

He knew better than to tell her the full story . . . that that day was the very day he had lost his leg . . . and that it was Chief Two Stones who had sent the arrow into it.

"Did Chief Storm ever do anything to avenge his parents' deaths?" Shoshana asked guardedly. She was thinking that if things were not so complicated, she would attempt to avenge her own people's deaths.

But to do so would mean that she would have to become a person different from who she was. She was a woman of compassion, of decency. Although she knew that George Whaley was guilty of many terrible things, she could not plot against him for the sake of vengeance.

George hoped that Shoshana wouldn't see the color drain from his face as a result of her question, for *he* was the man whom Chief Storm must hate with every fiber of his being. He was the one who had taken this young chief's parents from him. His only hope was that Storm had not been able to discover the names of those who took so much from him that day.   .

He cleared his throat nervously. He gave Shoshana a guarded look and tried to elude her question by directing her attention back to the scalp hunter. "From what our Apache scout tells us, Chief Storm knows about the scalp hunter being in the area. If Mountain Jack does find the Apache stronghold, he will be stepping into a hornets' nest, for he will cause this young chief to forget his peaceful heart," he said tightly.

"Why is the military so adamant about finding Mountain Jack?" Shoshana asked softly. "Why not let the young chief find him? Doesn't the scalp hunter deserve the wrath of the Apache?"

George cleared his throat nervously. "I would rather not talk any more about this today. Although it is only morning, I am already tired and weary," he said thickly. He got up and bent over her, running his fingers through her thick black hair. "Daughter, be careful," he said tightly. "If Mountain Jack caught sight of your hair, he would do everything within his power to have it. It . . . it . . . would bring him top dollar."

Shoshana paled at those words. She inhaled a nervous breath, for she understood the danger she could be in.

But she wouldn't let the scalp hunter get in the way of what she had planned.

George took a step away and gazed down at her, his eyes holding hers. "Shoshana, you can't leave the fort without an escort, and even then, you must keep an eye out for danger. This Mountain Jack has sandy-colored whiskers and rides a horse of pure white," he said, his voice drawn. "Do you hear me, Shoshana? Do you?"

"Yes, and I am disgusted by it all," Shoshana said, shivering.

She rose from her chair.

Again she went to the window and gazed out across the land. "I so wish that I knew where my people's village had been," she murmured. "I would love to go there."

She especially wanted to search out Chief Storm to ask if he might be harboring a woman from another band . . . one he might have found fifteen years ago.

Yes, she hoped most of all to find and talk with Chief Storm.

"Daughter, you didn't answer me," George said, moving to her side. He took her by the arm and turned her to face him. "You must never leave the fort unescorted, and even then, you should be careful . . . very, very careful."

"I hear you and I promise that I shall be careful," Shoshana said, then looked out the window again.

Her breath stopped in her throat when she caught sight of a magnificent golden eagle soaring overhead, its beauty highlighted as the sun's rays backlit its wings.

She watched the eagle until it flew from sight, then she turned to George. "I do believe in dreams," she blurted out. "My mother is surely out there somewhere, alive. I know it, for I feel her presence strongly in my heart."

"Shoshana, I know how badly you want to believe that," George said, reaching a gentle hand to her cheek. "But it was her spirit that came to you in that dream, nothing more."

Shoshana said no more about it. She didn't want to argue with him.

She was almost certain that her mother was alive. And if George Whaley didn't want to believe her, so be it.

But she would not give up her hope of finding her mother. Not now that she was in her homeland, where she had been a child running free with the wind and holding her mother's love near to her heart.

"Do not fret so much over me," Shoshana murmured as she gave him a soft smile. "I am a grown woman. I can make decisions on my own, and you know that I am very capable of taking care of myself. I learned that from living at so many forts."

She gave him one last smile, then left him alone to his thoughts and worries.

George looked out the window. He couldn't be-

lieve that this fort had no stockade. It was not fortified at all.

It was simply a few adobe houses scattered around
a dusty square.

He hadn't felt safe since his and Shoshana's arrival there. And now that Shoshana was determined
to search for her mother, he felt even more vulnerable for her. He couldn't trust her restlessness.

As soon as possible, he must take her back to Missouri, where they made their home in a huge mansion on the outskirts of Saint Louis.

Until then, he would assign someone to her.

As long as she was with a soldier, he would feel
safe enough to allow her some freedom, but he
would warn her again about wandering too far and
trusting too much in strangers.

If he lost her, he would be only half alive.

"I must get Shoshana back where she truly belongs," George whispered heatedly to himself. "Missouri, yes, Missouri. We'll be there again soon!"

His wooden leg and cane thumping against the
oak floor, he went toward the door to go and tell
Colonel Hawkins, the commander in charge of this
fort, his decision to leave.

Chapter Four

Her glorious fancies come from far,
Beneath the silver evening star.
                              —James Russell Lowell

Chief Storm stood at the entrance of his tepee, watching with much sadness as the children of his Piñaleno River Band of Apache romped and played.

He understood why they did so without smiles today. The sadness in their eyes was caused by the absence of two of their friends, a brother and sister, who were mauled yesterday by a panther while they were playing outside the village.

"The animal responsible must be found and destroyed," he whispered to himself as he doubled his hands into tight fists at his sides.

Storm, now twenty-five, a man with a square jaw

and keen dark eyes, was justly proud of his impregnable stronghold in the Piñaleno Mountains.

It was concealed in a lofty lookout where he and the warriors of their band could scan the valleys and mesas below.

He knew that all saw him as a very able chieftain, for he had kept his people out of the reservations where many other Apache were now confined.

Storm and his warriors were so elusive, the United States Government had given up on capturing them, or perhaps it was because he was known to be a man of peace that the authorities had chosen not to seek him and his people out.

However it was that Storm had kept his people out of the clutches of the white-eyes, he knew that his duties were centered on only one thing: his people's safety and freedom.

Because of those duties, Storm had not sought a wife. Besides, he remembered too well the hurt his father had felt at losing not only one wife, but two.

Ho, Chief Storm was protecting himself from such hurts. His sole reason for living was to keep his people safe.

But the young braves who were part of his band had sought out wives from the other Apache peoples before they were forced onto reservations. The children of those warriors were the hope of the Piñaleno River Band.

His thoughts strayed to someone else, causing his

eyes to narrow angrily and his jaws to tighten. He vividly remembered the name that his father had spoken before he died. Colonel Whaley!

Because of Storm's devotion to the safety and happiness of his people, he had long ago set aside his vow of vengeance against Colonel Whaley.

Storm did not see how he could have achieved it, anyhow. As far as he knew, the colonel had left Arizona after having been wounded so severely in his leg.

"I, too, see the sadness in the children's eyes," his older sister Dancing Willow said as she stepped up to Storm's side. She frowned at the lack of merriment in the children's games today.

She placed a hand on her brother's arm, causing his eyes to move to her. "You met in council with our warriors, and news was brought to me that you have proposed a plan that I see as unwise," she murmured. "You should not journey down our mountain alone. You know that I see many truths in my visions and dreams. My dreams have told me that danger awaits you if you leave the safety of our stronghold this time. If something should happen to you, all of our people's lives will change. Let someone else go. Heed my warning, my brother. This time, stay safely among our people."

She awaited his reply, afraid that she already knew what it would be. She knew that he had never backed down from anything in his life. He had always faced all danger head on, and always came away from it a victor.

Her brother was known for his wisdom in council, and all who heard him speak knew that his words came from the heart, and that what he said was to be heeded.

She was so proud of her brother, a boy on that day of their parents' deaths, who quickly stepped into the moccasins of a man. He became chief that day and had never disappointed anyone who followed him.

And he was not only a wise, powerful leader, but also a handsome warrior, with a sculpted face, noble bearing, brilliant black eyes, and smooth copper skin.

He had a large and powerful frame, corded with iron-hard sinews and muscles.

His coal-black hair hung down below the middle of his back in a broad, thick plait, wrapped in panther skin.

Today, like most days, he wore panther-skin leggings and moccasins, and a smoke-tanned buckskin shirt that was decorated with green porcupine quill-work and tassels of horse hair.

While away from the safety of his stronghold he always armed himself well. His weapons of choice were a Sharp's rifle, a bow and quiver of arrows, and a huge Bowie knife.

His bow was as powerful a weapon as a rifle,

strengthened with layers of sinew on the back, laid on with such nicety that they could scarcely be seen.

His arrows were more than three feet long, the upper part made of cane or rush. A shaft about a foot long made of light, yet hard and seasoned wood, was inserted into this. The point of the arrows was of sharpened stone.

He was able to shoot an arrow five hundred feet with fatal effect.

This younger brother of hers was a man of superior mental qualities. He showed instinct and cunning akin to those of the animals.

He was endowed with great acuteness of perception, and he was witty, quick with a sense of humor, cheerful and companionable.

His code of morals was deep-rooted, and the challenges of his life had made him vigilant, ever on the alert.

"My sister, I understand your concern, but I must go alone," Storm said, his eyes holding hers. "Too many riders would make a sound like thunder along the ground. Their horses' hooves would alert the panther that it was being stalked. I have taught my steed to travel lightly, as do I in my moccasins. Do not fret so much, my sister. What must be done must be done, and soon. Once an animal tastes the blood of a human, it hungers for more."

"My brother, what can I say to make you see the

true dangers today?" Dancing Willow said, sighing. "Must I remind you that I am a Seer, and that I know mystic arts, the power of chants, dreams, and potions? My teachers are the sun, moon, and stars. My brother, I listen to the stars at night. I study the curvature of the moon and the sun's arc across the heavens. They are my mentors. I can predict the death of a man's relative, the coming of a child. You know that, so often, what I predict comes true."

She looked past him again, but this time not at the children. Her eyes followed the slow walk of a woman whose aged appearance did not match her years. She was bent and gray, bowed down by a tragedy that had occurred near the same time that their band had been attacked by the *pindah-lickoyee*.

"Look yonder, brother," Dancing Willow said, motioning with a nod of her head to the woman who had gone to a stream for a jug of water. The weight of the jug made her shoulders bend even closer to the ground. "You do see her, do you not?"

"Yes, I see her," Storm said, now also watching the slow gait of the woman. "I have yet to see happiness in her eyes since the day we found her half-alive and wandering amid a small grove of willows as we made our escape from the pony soldiers. She has yet to speak. We have never discovered her tribe or where she came from. We have never even discovered what she calls herself."

"Had I not foretold finding the woman after the

whites had left her for dead?" Dancing Willow said, still watching the woman, whom they called No Name.

"Ho, that is true," Storm said, still in awe of the way his sister had predicted that event. It still amazed him how the woman had lived after having been shot in the back by a white man's bullet.

The bullet had still been lodged in her back when Storm had gone to her that day.

She had survived by sheer willpower, but never had she spoken since that day. It was as though the bullet had taken away her ability to speak, instead of her life.

"Storm, there is something else I must tell you," Dancing Willow said, turning to gaze up at him. "Of late, I have seen another face in the stars. The face of an *ish-tia-nay*, a woman. She is Apache born, turned traitor to her heritage: She lives as white in the white world. If you come face to face with her, your life will be changed forever. This is another reason I plead with you not to go down the mountain today. I see your face and the woman's together. This is not good, brother. Please remain in the village today. Let someone else hunt the panther and look upon the face of this woman."

"If you saw my face with hers, does it not mean that it is meant to be?" Storm asked. "Why run from a mere woman?"

She grabbed him eagerly by an arm. "My

brother," Dancing Willow said, her voice drawn. "If you go, your life will be changed forever."

"No *ish-tia-nay*, not even my Seer sister, changes my life unless I wish it," Storm said, gently easing her hand from his arm. "I will go today. I go now."

He gazed at her slowly, regretting the signs of age the years had left on his sister. But although her hair was streaked with fine strands of gray, and wrinkles radiated from the corners of her dark eyes, she was still beautiful to him at the age of forty-five winters.

He sensed her loneliness, yet she refused to consider marriage. Like him, she lived solely for her people.

Disappointed that he would not heed her warning, yet knowing that nothing else she said would change his mind, Dancing Willow went back inside his lodge with him and watched as he prepared his weapons.

When he was ready to leave, he placed a gentle hand on her face and smiled. "I love you, big sister," he said gently. "And thank you for caring so much. Had you not been with me through the years, I never would have become as strong a leader as I have. Your love and devotion made me a wise man."

He bent low and kissed her cheek. "I love you, Dancing Willow," he repeated as he stepped away from her. "But do you not think that it is time for you to let go? I must rule my own destiny, not your dreams or visions."

"Be careful," was all that she replied, then left his lodge as Storm went to his corral.

He mounted his black stallion, a beautiful animal with a white blaze on its face and white stockings. It was a wiry-looking horse, which he always rode with remarkable ease and grace.

He had chosen to arm himself with his rifle today, and it rested in the gunboot that hung at the right side of his horse as Storm kicked his steed into a slow lope from the village.

He traveled cautiously along the narrow pass and down the mountainside, troubled by his sister's words.

She *had* predicted many things that came true. Was he riding into danger?

And . . . would he come face to face with the woman Dancing Willow had seen in the stars? If so, who was she, and what would she become to him?

Again he was reminded that he had not yet looked upon any woman with favor. He could not help wondering if this woman of his sister's vision might change that.

No, his responsibilities must come first. With his chin held proudly high, he rode onward, his eyes searching constantly for the panther that had become deadly to his people.

Then the woman his sister had spoken of came to his mind again, and he wondered what she looked like. Was she beautiful?

He had to remind himself that if he did come across this *ish-tia-nay*, he must remember what else his sister had said about her. She was Apache, living as a white woman, in the white world. How could he not despise her the moment he saw her?

Yet . . . he could not help being intrigued by someone like her.

Chapter Five

Graceful and useful all she does.
Blessing and blest where'er she goes.
                                        —William Cowper

Dressed and ready to explore this land that had belonged to her people long before the white man came, Shoshana stood in George's office.

She studied him, finding it harder and harder not to look at him with contempt now that she knew what he was guilty of.

Yes, he had given her the best life any young woman could wish for. But she had been content with her world before he came with the other soldiers to kill and maim. She had never wanted anything more than to be with her family and her true people. She had never wanted anything other than to be Apache and to be raised as Apache!

But she had had no control over her destiny at that time. Now she kept the feelings that had been awakened in her quiet. She had learned how to control her feelings long ago when the white children at the various schools she had attended mocked her and called her a savage squaw.

Yes, she would work out her confused feelings for George Whaley inside her heart. There was no denying that he had tried in every way possible to make up for the wrong he had done her Apache people by treating her as though she were a princess.

But now that "princess" had come home. She ached to retrace her steps of long ago.

"Shoshana, do you hear me?" George said, bringing her out of her deep thoughts as he stepped away from his desk in his assigned office at Fort Chance.

"What?" Shoshana said, blinking her eyes as George came to stand directly before her. "Did you say something?"

"I was introducing you to this nice major, Shoshana," George said, idly rubbing his right leg above the knee. "This is Major James Klein. Shoshana, he has been assigned the duty of escorting you today since you are so stubborn about wanting to leave the fort and explore."

Blushing at her unintentional rudeness to the major, Shoshana turned to the young man who stood straight and tall beside her in his freshly pressed blue uniform.

"Major Klein, it's nice to know you," she said, reaching a gloved hand toward him.

She herself was dressed in a leather riding skirt, a long-sleeved white blouse, riding boots, and gloves that were butter soft against her flesh.

"As it is to know you," Major Klein said, blushing as he gazed into Shoshana's dark eyes. "It is my pleasure to escort you today. I shall, at all costs, keep you safe from such a ruffian as Mountain Jack."

"And anyone else who might be a threat," George said, groaning as he wheeled himself around on his wooden leg. Gripping his cane hard, he went and sat down behind his desk again.

Shoshana smiled into Major Klein's green eyes, finding him handsome with his square jaw and long, straight nose.

He was muscled beneath his uniform, and surely drew female attention whenever he entered a room back where there was civilization and women.

She would have singled him out with her own eyes at one time, but the world had changed for her when she arrived in Arizona.

She had only one thing on her mind now, and that was to familiarize herself with this land that she had roamed as a child. She hoped to run across one of her people. She wanted to speak her mother's Indian name and ask if anyone had heard of her.

"Young man," George said, drawing Major Klein's eyes back to him. "I can't stress enough the importance of keeping an eye on my daughter at all times. And listen well to me when I say you must not travel far from this fort. Don't let anything happen to Shoshana. Do not let her out of your sight. Don't you ever forget the cunning of Mountain Jack, and most of all, why he is in this area. He would surely enjoy getting his hands on such beautiful hair as Shoshana's!"

"How ghastly," Shoshana gasped. She straightened her shoulders and tried to put from her mind that terrible reminder of what Mountain Jack did for a living.

She must, for nothing would dissuade her from what she planned to do.

If only her father would not treat her like a child. To have a soldier escort her at a time when she wanted to explore the land of her people was an insult, most certainly a bother.

While riding on land where her mother surely had been, she wanted to feel her mother's presence. She wanted to have the opportunity to follow the vision she had had in her dreams. She wanted to believe that her mother was alive, and that she would somehow find her.

"Major Klein is not needed," Shoshana suddenly blurted out. She placed her hands on her hips and lifted her chin stubbornly as she turned to the major. "You are excused. I apologize for having taken up your time, which could surely be put to more valuable use elsewhere."

"Shoshana!" George said, pushing himself up from his chair. He placed the palms of his hands flat on the desk and leaned over to glare into her face, then turned to Major Klein. "Ignore her. She's just showing her stubborn side. You've been brought here to escort my daughter. So be it."

"Yes, sir," Major Klein gulped out, now stiff as a board at Shoshana's side.

Shoshana was not to be dissuaded. She glared into George's angry eyes. "You know that I can defend myself if necessary," she said tightly. "Must I remind you that I am a crack shot with a rifle?"

She had become a tomboy early on, especially after she realized just how different she was from the other children.

She was Apache, and that name had seemed a brand of sorts.

The taunts had gotten mean. She had felt the need to learn how to protect herself.

She had learned how to shoot from a young man who became smitten with her when she was ten and he was twelve.

He had seen the Apache in her as intriguing and thought her beautiful.

He would have done anything to get a kiss from her. That something was to teach her how to shoot his father's rifle.

She smiled at the recollection of how many kisses she'd given him in payment!

It saddened her to realize that he had been killed on his very first outing when he got old enough to enlist. Ironically, it had been an Apache that had killed him.

Because of his lessons, she didn't need any escort today, or ever.

Yet she knew just how stubborn George Whaley was when he made his mind up about something; she knew she had no choice but to go along with what he demanded today.

If she refused to agree with him, she would be stuck at the fort.

And there was so much about this Major Klein that reminded her of that younger boy . . . of that sweet Paul Breningmeyer.

She forced a smile, and made certain it was as sweet as possible as she gazed at George. "All right," she said. "I know that you are doing this because you feel it is right. I understand. Now can we go? I'm anxious to be on my way."

Colonel James Hawkins, the colonel in charge of

the fort, sauntered into the room at that moment. He was in full uniform, with shiny gold epaulets, and several medals pinned on his chest, his brown hair resting on his shoulders.

He had a lean, pockmarked face and a thin mustache. "Are you two ready to leave?" he asked, stopping and smiling from Shoshana to Major Klein.

"Yes, sir," Major Klein said, stiffening and saluting the colonel.

"Yes, they're ready, and I've given them both a lecture," George said as he stepped around the desk, his wooden leg and cane thumping against the oak floor, his hand reaching out for the other colonel's.

They shook hands, then Colonel Hawkins turned to Shoshana. "Young lady, I want to assure you that you are in good hands and will be absolutely safe with Major Klein," he said, clasping his hands behind him. "The scalp hunter has been laying low, anyway."

He slid a slow smile over to George. "I'm sure Mountain Jack has got wind of a certain Colonel George Whaley being in the area, and why," he said. "George, the sandy-whiskered varmint'll probably stay hidden as long as you're here, not realizing that he'll be sniffed out real soon *by* you."

George gave the colonel an uneasy glance, for in a matter of moments Hawkins would not be feeling as chipper as he did now. After George told him that he was returning to Missouri as soon as possible, that confident smirk would be wiped off the colonel's face.

"Shoshana, I've got something to give you," George said, going behind his desk and opening a drawer. He took a red bandanna from it, then handed it over the desk to her. "Honey, it's a hot day. Use the bandanna to tie your long hair back from your face."

"Thank you," Shoshana said, taking the bandanna and doing as he suggested. She knew that the bandanna was meant to serve a dual purpose. It *would* keep her hair from her face, and it might also distract attention from her long black hair just in case Mountain Jack was in the area.

She turned to Major Klein. "I'm ready," she said, and together they left the room.

George watched from a window as Shoshana mounted her assigned steed, while the young major mounted his own. George followed them with his gaze until they rode out of sight.

Then he turned to the colonel. "I have something to tell you that is sure to rankle," he said, his voice tight.

"And that is?" Colonel Hawkins asked, lifting a thick brown eyebrow.

"I have no choice but to step away from this opportunity to track down the scalp hunter," George blurted out. "My Shoshana comes first, and by damn, I plan to take her back home to Missouri where she will be absolutely safe."

"You are going to do what?" Colonel Hawkins demanded. "You can't do this, George. I personally chose you for this assignment. If you fail, it won't look good for me in Washington."

"I'm sorry about that," George said. He sighed heavily. "Truly, I'm damn sorry about that."

"I've gone to a lot of trouble and expense to bring you to Arizona!" Colonel Hawkins shouted. "And now you're telling me that you're walking out on me? George, I won't have it. Do you hear? I won't have it!"

"You won't have it?" George said, his eyes narrowing angrily. "Must I remind you that I retired long ago from the military and am under nobody's thumb anymore? You can't dictate to me. No one can. I came to help. But now I see the mistake in doing so. No ranting and raving you do will make me change my mind. Do you hear? Nothing will change my mind. I'm Missouri-bound with my daughter tomorrow." He lifted his wooden leg from the floor and banged it down hard. "Do you hear? Tomorrow!"

Colonel Hawkins's face was red with anger. His eyes flared.

Without a word he turned and left the room in a hurry.

George wiped his brow free of sweat with the back of a hand. "Now that's that," he whispered to himself. "I guess I told him a thing or two, didn't I?"

Frowning, he went to the window and gazed into the distance.

He knew that he had just won a victory over the famous colonel.

But he didn't feel all victorious. He was too aware that many things could happen between now and tomorrow!

He knew that no one was safe in this area. Especially a woman as beautiful and alluring as his Shoshana.

Chapter Six

Oh, could the Fair, who this does see,
Be by this great example won.
                    —Richard Leigh

Many feelings overwhelmed Shoshana as she and
Major Klein rode along a river that flowed into a
broad, marshy valley. She was having occasional
flashes of recognition that made her think she was
near the spot where her village had stood, where she
had run and played with friends . . . where she
helped her mother fill her large jug with water. . . .

"Come autumn, this valley will be full of elk and
deer that will have moved down from the higher elevations," Major Klein said, interrupting Shoshana's
train of thought. "The first time I saw them, I was
stunned at how many there were."

Shoshana looked quickly over at him. "How long have you been stationed at Fort Chance?" she asked, wondering if he had been there long enough to know the places where the Apache villages had once been.

"A year," Colonel Klein said, smiling over at her.

"A year?" Shoshana said, her heart filling with hope. "Then you surely know much about the land and—"

Major Klein's smile waned. "No, not much at all," he said, interrupting her. "My duties until only recently were menial and kept me at the fort."

"Oh, I see," Shoshana said, feeling foolish at having thought she would get answers so soon after arriving at her homeland.

"I've been in charge of feeding the horses and grooming them," Major Klein said, fondly patting his horse's sleek neck. "Yeah, Colonel Hawkins ordered me to care for the horses but very rarely allowed me to enjoy riding them. Today is the first time I've been away from the fort on a horse in weeks."

"So you haven't had much opportunity to learn anything about the area, or where the Apache villages might have been?" Shoshana asked, surprised that the colonel would have chosen him to see to her safety today.

Suddenly she didn't feel all that safe.

"No, not much," Major Klein said tightly. He

gazed over at Shoshana. "I have you to thank for my being away from the fort today. If you hadn't needed an escort, I'd still be in the stalls seeing to the horses."

"Don't thank me," Shoshana said dryly. "I had nothing to do with it. The colonel chose you."

She wanted to add that she had no idea why he'd been chosen. Surely an older soldier with more knowledge of the land would have been better suited for the job.

If George Whaley knew just how vulnerable she was with this young major at her side, he would most certainly have reason to worry, just as she was now worrying.

She decided she would turn back soon. With someone so unfamiliar with the land, she was afraid of possibly getting lost, or worse yet, riding into the face of danger.

"I can tell that you don't feel comfortable about my escorting you today," Major Klein said ruefully. "I'm sorry about disappointing you. Do you want to turn back?"

"Not quite yet," Shoshana said, nudging her steed with her knees and riding on ahead of the major.

She didn't want any more small talk with him. She wanted to inhale all of this loveliness without interruption.

This valley was the province of butterflies and lovely dragonflies.

The crystalline body of water was full of caddis flies.

The air was alive with hummingbirds and magpies.

A colony of otters flourished in the river, and she saw badgers, too.

She was only five on that terrible day long ago when her life had changed forever, but things were coming back to her again—her laughter as she ran through the tall grass and flowers where her mother had bent low to pluck a bouquet, Shoshana's baby brother on her mother's back in his cradle board . . .

She was remembering a day when she had sat dangling her feet in the river while her mother stopped to nurse Shoshana's baby brother . . . a brother who had died from an illness unfamiliar to Shoshana only days before the massacre that took her mother from her, as well.

This could be the exact place where she had shared those precious moments with her mother and brother. It did seem so familiar.

Then her breath was stolen away when she saw the remains of tepees a short distance from the river. The poles were like the bones of skeletons sticking up from the ground.

Could this be . . . ?

A groan behind Shoshana caused her to turn quickly in the saddle.

She went pale and gasped when she saw a hatchet lodged in the young major's chest, his eyes wide with disbelief.

She cried out when he suddenly tumbled from the horse to the ground, dead.

Frozen with fear, Shoshana remembered her father's warnings about Mountain Jack, the scalp hunter! Could he have done this terrible thing to the kind young major?

Was . . . she . . . next?

With a pounding heart, and a fear so keen she felt cold all over even though the day was miserably hot, she grabbed her rifle from her gunboot, but dropped it in the next instant. A voice shouted at her from a nearby stand of aspens, telling her not to do anything foolish or she would be the next to die.

"Dismount," the killer shouted at her in a gravelly voice. "And stay away from that rifle."

Her knees trembling with fear of who might come out into the open, and horrified by Major Klein's death, Shoshana slid slowly from the saddle.

She eyed the rifle. It was only a footstep away.

"Kick the rifle away from you," the hidden man told her.

She did what he said, although reluctantly.

Then she watched as a sandy-whiskered man on a white horse rode out into the open, his rifle aimed at Shoshana. It didn't take much thought to realize that this was the scalp hunter.

This was Mountain Jack! There was no doubt that it was he.

He'd been described as having sandy, bushy whiskers and a white horse. She observed that he also had steely cold gray eyes.

From even this distance, she could smell the stench of the soiled buckskin attire he wore.

"You murdering bastard," Shoshana found the courage to say.

"You just shut up," Mountain Jack growled out. "For now, I only want the major's scalp. But if you say anything else to rile me, I'll also take yours and be done with you."

The realization that the man was going to scalp the young major made Shoshana turn her head away with the need to vomit.

She recalled George telling her that the scalp hunter not only killed Apaches for their scalps, but also white people who had dark hair. The young major had hair the color of an Indian's, and it was almost as long.

"You are Mountain Jack, aren't you?" she asked guardedly. "You're the scalp hunter that everyone is talking about."

"Yep, I'm that famed man," he said, riding closer on his white mare. "But like I said, shut up or I'll scalp you to shut you up."

Shoshana fought the fear that was building within her.

But she had to pretend to be strong, even though every bone in her body was weak with fear of what this evil man might decide to do to her.

"You'll never get my scalp," she said bravely, defying him, her eyes again on her rifle.

"Just you try to grab that rifle and you'll see how quickly your scalp can be loosed from your head," Mountain Jack growled out. "I don't want to be forced into doing what I don't want to do. I have other plans for you first."

"What . . . plans?" Shoshana gulped out, her courage waning. "You aren't going to rape me, are you?"

"I don't reveal my plans before doin' 'em," Mountain Jack said sardonically as he dismounted his steed. "You'd best get back on your horse and turn your head if you don't want to see the soldier lose his hair."

When he bent to a knee beside Major Klein, his knife drawn from its sheath, Shoshana felt a strange, rubbery weakness in her knees.

"Please don't do that," she begged, pale from knowing that nothing she said would stop him.

"Get on that horse and turn your eyes away," Mountain Jack shouted. "I don't like making a woman faint, and, sweet thing, if you watch me scalp the young man, I swear you'll faint dead away."

Her heart pounding, a sob lodging deep within her throat, Shoshana quickly mounted her steed.

She inched her horse away from the death scene.

She was tempted to sink her heels into the flanks

of her steed and try to escape, but she knew that Mountain Jack wouldn't allow it.

Her own rifle, which lay only a few inches from his knee, might even be used to kill her.

"I need to ask you somethin' before scalpin' the lad," Mountain Jack said. "I figure you're Apache, but why is an Apache squaw like you dressed as a white woman? Why did you turn your back on your people to live in the white world?"

Shoshana refused to answer him.

She sat stiffly in the saddle, awaiting her fate; poor Major Klein's was already sealed.

She cringed and covered her ears with her hands in order not to hear Mountain Jack cutting the scalp from Major Klein.

Tears splashed from her eyes when she remembered the young man's kindness. Then Mountain Jack told her she could open her eyes and turn around, that the scalping was done.

"It's time now to hurry back to my hideout," Mountain Jack said, ignoring how Shoshana still refused to look his way.

He slid the scalp into his saddlebag, grabbed up Shoshana's rifle and secured it with his other firearm in his gunboot, then mounted his steed and rode over to Shoshana.

"Did you hear me say it's time to ride to my hideout?" he snarled. "Do as I say, pretty thing, or else.

Follow me and don't try and escape. You're nothing to me, so it would not mean anything to me to shoot you."

He shrugged. "Either you cooperate with me or your scalp will join the young major's real quick like," he said tightly.

Swallowing hard, Shoshana gave him a quick glance, then snapped her reins and rode alongside him as he made a wide swing left and rode toward the mountain.

Shoshana thought about how her life had changed so many years ago in her homeland; now she was home again, and tragedy had struck once more.

She lowered her eyes and prayed that someone would come soon and save her, for she feared what was going to happen to her now more than she feared actually being scalped.

She would rather be dead than to have that filthy man touch her in any way!

Chapter Seven

Is there within thy heart a need
That mine cannot fulfill?
　　　　　　　—Adelaide Anne Procter

His eyes ever searching for the elusive panther, Storm had traveled halfway down his mountain, yet he had seen no trace of it or its den anywhere. He was ready to turn back, but decided to take one last look with his spyglass.

He had found the spyglass along the trail many years ago and had discovered just how useful it was. Things he saw so distinctly through the glass could only be dimly perceived with the naked eye.

He drew a tight rein and reached inside his parfleche bag. With one sweep of his hand he had his spyglass up to his eye and was slowly scanning the mountain from side to side.

Still he saw no sign of the panther.

From his horse he could see farther below him, where some time ago the land had been scarred by lightning. He would never forget seeing the huge billows of smoke from the lookout at his stronghold, and then the flames.

Far down away from his stronghold, where the land stretched out away from his mountain, fire had spread in leaps and bounds, continuing until rain began falling in torrents, soon killing the flames.

But the rain had not come soon enough. There had been much damage done to the vegetation.

That had been two winters ago. The cycle of rebirth had soon started afresh.

Through the burned stubs of broken conifers, toothlike and stubbed, came the spears of grass and the shoots of shrubs. From the charred logs came curled ferns. Under the warm earth, the hot seeds cracked open and life began anew.

Today he admired the gleam of willow branches bending in the breeze far beyond the area cleared by fire.

He looked even farther, where the river's roar turned into tireless lapping, where dipping out of the sunlight it slipped into the ground, whispering quietly.

Even now as he watched, herons lifted off, big-winged, from the water.

Then he moved his spyglass so he could see the adobe houses at Fort Chance. When he had watched the fort being built so close to his mountain not long ago, he had feared an eventual confrontation with the white pony soldiers.

But his scouts, who were clever at watching and learning things, discovered that the main purpose for this fort had nothing to do with the Apache who made their homes in his stronghold.

The pony soldiers were there to protect the arriving settlers, and the white-eyes who were already there. One of the dangers they guarded against was scalp hunters who preyed on white-eye and red skins alike. Mountain Jack was the worst of these. Thus far, he had successfully eluded the soldiers, as well as Storm and his warriors, who also wanted to stop the evil man.

Despite their familiarity with all the haunts of this mountain, Storm's men could not find him. Mountain Jack remained free to kill.

Just then his eyes widened and he held the spyglass steady as it picked up some movement down below, far beyond the fort. Off in the distance he spotted the tiny mounted figures of a man and a woman.

"The scalp hunter!" Storm gasped out, his heart

thudding in his chest as he recognized the white horse.

He could not believe that the scalp hunter had come out into the open. Storm shifted his spyglass so he could see who was riding with the scalp hunter.

It was a woman, a woman of Storm's own skin color!

Ho, she was Indian, but dressed as a white woman.

Had the scalp hunter taken a bride? Was he taking her to his hideout? It caused a bitter bile to rise in Storm's throat to think that a red-skinned woman would lower herself to marry the evil man who had taken the scalps of so many Apache.

"She must pay in her own way for deceiving her race," Storm whispered heatedly.

His jaw tight, he put his spyglass back in his bag and continued downward on the mountain pass, but this time as rapidly as possible. The narrow pass was dangerous; one slip of a hoof and both the horse and Storm could fall to their deaths.

But he could not waste time. He could not let the scalp hunter get away. Finally. Finally he had a chance to stop the man's evil ways.

He rode on and on, then stopped long enough to take his spyglass from his bag again to take another look.

His heart sank when he saw no signs of Mountain Jack, or of the woman. But now at least he knew where to look for them.

The scalp hunter had become careless, and surely because of the woman.

And the woman had also been careless. Choosing a man such as Mountain Jack had sealed her doom.

Then his sister's warning came to him. Was this possibly the woman she had seen in the stars?

If so, he understood why his sister had warned him. This woman was surely a traitor to her own people.

He rode onward. He would not stop until he found the sandy-whiskered man's hideout.

He would stop the man's evil ways. But what of the woman? What would he do with her once he had her in his possession?

"She, who is a traitor to her people, will be my captive," he said, his jaw tight, his eyes narrowed with angry determination.

Chapter Eight

I will not let thee go!
I hold thee by too many bonds.
—Robert Bridges

"It's been too long since Shoshana left," George said as he stood before Colonel Hawkins's massive oak desk. "I told both her and Major Klein not to be gone for long. I most definitely made it clear to them that they weren't to go far. I shouldn't have put my trust in that major. He's too young."

"The major might be young, but when assigned any duty, even as simple as being an escort to a lovely lady, he is more reliable than most men your age," Colonel Hawkins said reassuringly. "Go back to your quarters. Relax. If they don't return soon, I'll send several of my most trusted men to find them and bring them back."

"As simple as being an escort to a lady?" George spat out, stunned that the colonel was taking Shoshana's safety so lightly. "You know the dangers out there."

"I'm sorry if you're unhappy with my choice of escort, but they weren't going far enough to worry about and Major Klein had finished his chores yesterday. He was to be idle today," the colonel said.

"What kind of chores?" George asked between clenched teeth. He immediately saw how uneasy that question made the colonel. He held his hand out, palm side toward the colonel. "No. Don't tell me. I might be too tempted to floor you."

"It's good you're having second thoughts before doing something so asinine, George," the colonel said tightly. "As I said, I'll send out several soldiers to find them and bring them back to the fort."

"Don't wait too long," George said angrily.

He swung around and walked out of the room, his wooden leg seeming to be twice as heavy today since the burden he was carrying on his shoulders was so great.

His daughter.

How stupid he'd been to allow her to leave the fort at all!

But as headstrong as she was, he knew that had he

not given her permission, she would have set out on her own, without an escort, and that would have been even worse.

He went back to his house and to the window in the living room, where he stared at the open land stretching away from the fort. There was still no sign of Shoshana or the major.

His eyebrows lifted when he saw a huge contingent of blue-coated troopers ride from the fort on their big chargers.

"Why, he's as worried as I am," George whispered to himself. The colonel had gone ahead and sent the soldiers out to search for Shoshana without waiting any longer.

George watched the dust scatter from the hooves of the horses and continued to follow the soldiers' progress until they rode from sight. He felt hopeful that the soldiers would find Shoshana and the major because he had seen two Apache scouts at the head of the search party. If anyone could find two lost souls out there in the wilderness, those scouts could do it.

All Apache were well acquainted with this country that their ancestors had inhabited since the beginning of time. These scouts surely knew every spring, water hole, canyon, and crevice.

George was beginning to feel better about the situation now. All he had to do now was practice patience.

"I won't think the worst," he mumbled. "I won't."

He got out the long-stemmed pipe. He gazed at it for a long time, remembering the very moment he had gotten it. He had been torn with conflicting feelings since he had already slain a good number of redskins before attending the peace talks.

Sighing heavily, he sprinkled tobacco into the bowl of the pipe, lit it, then sat down before a slowly burning fire in the fireplace. His eyes watched the flames rolling over the logs in a slow caress.

Oh, how often had he sat before a fire with Shoshana, popping corn in the flames, munching it as they shared a game of chess?

"She's always been so smart," he whispered, tears shining in the corners of his eyes. "Too smart to allow anything to happen to her, especially in this land of her ancestors. Shoshana, honey, come back to me. Do you hear? Come . . . back . . . to me."

He sat there for as long as it took to smoke the tobacco in his pipe, then turned when he saw the reflection of a bright sunset paint the wall above the fireplace.

He paled when he realized how long he had been sitting there, reminiscing. The sun was lowering behind the mountains. Soon it would be dark and Shoshana had not yet been found and brought back to the fort.

"Good Lord," he mumbled as he pushed himself up from the chair.

He laid the pipe aside, then left the house.

Just as he got halfway between his house and the colonel's, he heard the thunder of hoofbeats arriving.

His heart thumping, he turned and saw soldiers returning to the fort.

His heart skipped a beat when he got a glimpse of something that turned his insides cold. The body of a soldier was draped across a horse, his . . . scalp . . . removed.

Unaware that the colonel had come to his side, George jumped when he spoke.

He turned to Colonel Hawkins and saw his deep frown at the sight of the slain soldier.

"I was afraid of that," the colonel said, sighing heavily. "After you came to me worrying so much about your daughter and Major Klein, I sent the cavalry out to search for them. It seems they found the major, but not Shoshana."

"The major . . . ?" George gasped out, turning and once again gazing at the slain man. He turned back to the colonel. "How do you know it's him?"

"A scout came ahead and told me," Colonel Hawkins said, his eyes wavering as they gazed into George's. "George, someone apparently ambushed them. The major was killed and your daughter . . . abducted."

"Lord . . . Lord . . ." George said, feeling light-headed as he thought about Mountain Jack and how surely he was the one who had done this horrible, heartless thing.

"Most of the search party is still out there trying to find Shoshana, but the scouts lost the tracks early on," Colonel Hawkins said. "They won't give up, at least not until darkness makes tracking impossible. Then they will have no choice but to return to the fort or become victims themselves, of either the scalp hunter or hungry animals . . . or even renegades."

As the soldiers drew rein a short distance from George and the colonel, George went to one. "Where did you find the major?" he asked thickly. "How far from the fort?"

"Quite a distance, sir," the young soldier replied. "I'm sorry, sir, but there was no sign of your daughter anywhere. The tracks had been covered up. The one who is responsible for this killing is a clever man who is skilled at being elusive."

George felt a burning rage enter his heart. He glared from soldier to soldier, then flailed an arm in the air as he shouted at them. "Get back out there! Find her! Don't come back until you have my daughter with you!"

A strained silence ensued as the soldiers looked past George and stared at their colonel.

Colonel Hawkins stepped up to George's side. "Must I remind you that I'm in charge here, and that I am the one who gives out the orders?" he said tightly. "For now, we must lie low. We have a dead soldier to bury. As we speak, there are soldiers out there risking their lives to hunt for Shoshana. You can't expect the whole fort to go."

"I can't believe my ears," George shouted at the colonel. "You, and those who returned without my daughter, are yellow!"

Although it had been some time since he had mounted a horse because of his wooden leg, George yanked a soldier from his steed. He shoved his cane in next to the rifle in its leather case at the side of the horse.

Then after groaning and grunting, he finally managed to get himself in the saddle. He glared at the colonel, as if daring him to allow a crippled man to leave the fort alone, with darkness coming on.

"Oh, very well," Colonel Hawkins grunted. "We'll ride out together to find the rest of the search party. We'll camp overnight and begin the hunt again as soon as it's light. I don't need two missing people on my hands."

Chapter Nine

My face in thine eyes,
Thine in mine appear,
And true plain hearts do
In the faces rest!

—John Donne

Shoshana was made to travel in front of Mountain Jack up a steep, narrow pass that climbed from the valley floor up a rock-walled canyon.

She knew now that she was at the mercy of the sandy-whiskered man, for the only escape was down the narrow passageway, and he had made sure that she wouldn't get the chance to flee by forcing her to ride ahead of him.

Her only hope now was that whenever they

reached their destination, however far it was up in the mountain, there would be a moment of inattention when she could turn her horse around and escape back down the mountain pass.

She had hoped that soon he would have to take a break to relieve himself in the bushes. She felt the need to do that, herself, but would not ask permission of him. After she escaped she would take care of her personal needs.

He had taken a drink from his canteen often. She knew there was whiskey in the canteen because she had gotten a sniff of it when he handed it to her, asking if she wanted a swig of firewater, as he had called it.

He had laughed when she declined, then told her that most Indians would kill for a drink of firewater. Then he'd scowled, saying that she was different, though, wasn't she? She was a civilized savage!

Refusing to allow what he said to upset her too much, she had refused his offer. She hated alcohol, even the vile smell of it. And if she didn't drink any, there would be more for him.

If he drank himself into a stupor and lost all sense of what he was doing, it would not take much to escape from him.

She saw even now out of the corner of her eye that he had taken another drink, then rudely burped and laughed raucously when she turned her head quickly so that she didn't have to look at his disgusting face.

"So you think you're too good to share firewater with me, do you?" Mountain Jack said, sliding his canteen back into his saddlebag. "What else do you think you're too good for, squaw? Don't you know that those white clothes don't really make a civilized person outta you? You're a redskin through and through, no matter how you dress or talk. I'll have a lot of fun with you, squaw. But first things first. I have business to attend to."

Shoshana wondered what sort of business he was talking about. What was he going to do with her while taking care of this other "business"?

And where was he taking her?

A thought came to her that made cold dread swim through her. Had he spared her life in order to trade her as a slave to some depraved man?

If that was his plan, was he taking her where he was going to trade her, instead of to his hideout as she had originally thought?

No matter where he planned to take her, or why, she *must* find a way to escape, and soon. If not, she was doomed to a life far different from any she had ever known.

As the sun lowered in the sky and shadows fell all around her, she knew that George Whaley would be concerned about her not having returned to the fort with the young major.

Tears stung her eyes as she thought of Major Klein and how he had died. But she could not dwell on that. Her prime concern now must be herself.

Somehow, some way, she must find a way to flee this horrible man and whatever horrible fate he had planned for her.

She guessed they were near their destination, for she doubted that Mountain Jack would want to travel along this steep, narrow pass at night, especially without a moon to guide them.

She glanced up at the sky. It was cloudy. There wouldn't be a moon tonight. There might even be a storm.

The temperature had dropped with the setting of the sun. She began to tremble. She ached to be near a comforting fire.

She ached to be safe back at the fort. Or even back home in Missouri. She could not deny missing Missouri and the friends she had left behind there.

But she longed even more to find traces of her true people, perhaps even her mother, here in Arizona. This was where her life started. She wondered if it would end here, too.

She gazed farther up the mountain in the direction of the setting sun. Not long ago, she had seen the sun reflecting from something in the higher elevations above her.

Perhaps it was an Indian. It might even have been Chief Storm, sending a message to another Indian with a mirror instead of smoke, which could attract too much attention.

Upon learning that she was going to Arizona, where her Apache people lived, Shoshana had read as much material on Indians as she could find. She had read about smoke signals and learned that it was a swift way to send messages to friends.

She learned that "smokes," as the smoke signals were called by the Apache, were of various kinds, each one communicating a particular idea.

A sudden puff, rising into a graceful column from the mountain heights, indicated the presence of a strange party upon the plains below.

If the column was rapidly multiplied and repeated, the signal served as a warning that the travelers were well armed, and numerous.

If a steady smoke was maintained for some time, the scattered bands of Apache would congregate at some designated point.

She hadn't seen any smoke signals today, but she might have seen a mirror being used to send similar signals. If it *was* an Indian watching her and the scalp hunter, should she hope that he might save her? Or should she be even more afraid of an Indian than the scalp hunter?

"Make a sharp right turn," Mountain Jack suddenly growled out to her. "We're leavin' the pass now. Just keep on ridin' and doin' what I say and you've got a good chance of surviving."

Good chance? Shoshana thought to herself. She didn't know how to interpret that.

They rode for a long time, the darkness like a shroud around them. Mountain Jack seemed not to have need of any light. He knew where he was going, guiding Shoshana down first one pass and then another, leveling off to a flat stretch of land, and then climbing higher again.

But finally the way grew wider and Shoshana began to believe that she was going to at least survive the journey to wherever he was taking her.

The murky clouds suddenly split apart to show shiny, blue-white stars, and the moon now silvered the crest of distant spruces.

Shoshana could see much around her, for everything was splashed by the white reflection of the moonlight. It was such a clear, bright night now, it was as though night had turned to day.

"Here we are," Mountain Jack said, interrupting Shoshana's thoughts as he rode up beside her. "Cast your eyes yonder, squaw, and you'll see my hideout."

She gazed at a newly built log cabin well hidden in a narrow canyon, trees on each end hiding the entrance and exit.

Unless one knew that it was there, it would not be found.

"Especially by the cavalry," she whispered to herself dismounting and being forced to enter the cabin first.

After he lit a kerosene lantern, Shoshana gasped and felt bitter bile rise into her throat as she fought back the urge to vomit. The cabin was filled with stacks of scalps, as well as three hanging from hooks in the ceiling, with fresh blood on them.

"Come here, squaw," Mountain Jack said as he dropped his saddlebag to the floor.

Shoshana hesitated, then felt her insides tightening when he came to her with a long chain.

"What are you going to do with that?" she asked faintly.

"What do you think?" Mountain Jack said, chuckling. "You're my prisoner, ain't you? Well, let me show you how I treat my prisoners."

He twisted the chain around her waist, locked it in place, and then attached another part of it to her wrist.

"See how long it is?" he said, smiling at her as he stepped away from her. "That's so's you can be free enough to roam outside. I know a woman has private duties to tend to. I'd rather you do them outside, not here on my floor."

He threw his head back in a fit of laughter, then sobered again and glared at her as he stepped closer and yanked the red bandanna from her hair. "Mighty fine hair, squaw," he said, his eyes gleaming as he dropped the bandanna and moved his hand toward her head again. "Yep, that's mighty fine hair."

With her free hand, Shoshana grabbed his wrist

and thrust his hand away just before he got a chance to touch her hair. "As long as my hair is still mine, I'd rather your filthy hands aren't on it," she said tightly. She shoved his hand away. "But I doubt that you want to scalp me just yet. Surely you have other . . . other . . . sordid plans for me first."

"Rape?" Mountain Jack said, walking away from her. He removed Major Klein's scalp from his bag and held it out before Shoshana.

She turned her head away, again fighting not to vomit.

"You have me all wrong," Mountain Jack said, placing the scalp on another hook in the ceiling. "I don't want your scalp, nor do I want to rape you." He chuckled. "Not yet, anyways."

He stepped around so that she was forced to look at him. "I've chores to do," he said. "Chores I've got to take care of before decidin' what to do with you."

When she turned away from him again, he stepped directly in front of her. He glared into her eyes. "I only wish I could get pleasure from your body as I used to get pleasure from squaws before I scalped 'em," he said thickly. He leaned his face into hers. "But you don't have to worry about me fornicatin' with you. Some time back, when I went by my real name, Jackson Cole, I was a major in the cavalry. I was injured in the worst possible place by an Apache brave. Because of that injury, I can no longer function as a man in that particular way. But

84

it doesn't keep me from enjoyin' the company of a beautiful squaw, now does it? I've been terribly lonely. 'Cept for my pen of wolves, which I breed and raise for their skins, I'm totally alone."

He stepped away from her. "While you're here, you're going to behave like you're my bride," he said. He laughed a strange sort of cackle, then again gazed into her eyes. "You're gonna cook and clean for me. You're gonna care for my wolves. That's the other reason why the chain has been left purposely long. You're to feed my wolves when they get hungry."

"I won't do anything for you," Shoshana said bitterly. "I won't clean. I won't cook. And I most certainly won't go into a pen of wolves and feed them."

Mountain Jack shrugged. "Then you'll starve," he said. He walked away from her and began placing logs on the grate in his fireplace. "It's up to you."

After he got a good fire going, he went to Shoshana and again spoke directly into her face. "I'll be leavin' real soon to take my scalps to the buyer," he said stiffly. "While I'm gone, by God, you *will* feed my wolves. If you don't, and any of 'em die, I'll kill you immediately when I return. And I'll be movin' my hideout again as soon as I return. That's how I've been successful at eludin' everyone, by stayin' on the run, by buildin' new hideouts in the most remote places."

Seeing how insane this man truly was, Shoshana ran from the cabin, but she got a rude reminder that she wasn't going far, not as long as the chain held her prisoner.

Mountain Jack ran after her. He grabbed her by the wrist and swung her around to face him.

"You do as I say, squaw, or by God, your scalp'll join those that I'm takin' to sell tonight," he warned. "Promise that you'll obey me. Promise me now! Tell me you'll feed my wolves. Tell me now that when I return you'll cook a good meal for me."

Knowing she was risking her life, yet feeling that she was a dead woman anyway, for she doubted that anyone could ever find her so far up in the mountains, she spat at Mountain Jack's feet.

He raised a fist, but didn't hit her.

He lowered his fist to his right side. He laughed.

"You're an Injun squaw all right," he said. "You're full of spunk and sassiness."

Then he glared at her. "I want to know why you're wearin' white woman's clothes when it's obvious that you're a full blood," he said tightly. "You're an Apache, ain't you? I ain't never seen any Apache squaws wear duds such as you're wearin' today."

Shoshana proudly lifted her chin. "Yes, I am full blood all right," she said. "I *am* Apache. And it's none of your business why I'm wearing the clothes of one people while my blood is of another."

He slunk away from her, pale at the knowledge of the tribe she belonged to. It was an Apache that took his manhood from him.

He grabbed his pistol from his holster.

Breathing hard, his eyes glittering in the moonlight, he aimed at Shoshana. "The Apache are the worst of all Injuns," he said, his voice drawn. "I loathe 'em all. It is always a pleasure to remove their scalps. And it will be a pleasure to remove yours now that I know for certain you are Apache."

Her heart pounded and her knees went weak at the realization that she was going to die at any moment now. Yet, being strong-willed and proud, as proud as her Apache mother and father had been, Shoshana held her chin high and challenged him with her sparkling black eyes.

Seeing that Shoshana showed no fear, and intrigued by her courage, Mountain Jack lowered his pistol and slid it back in his holster. "For now you're safe, but you'd better watch yourself," he warned darkly. "Too much insolence on your part will send you into an early grave."

He took her elbow and forced her back inside the cabin.

Shoshana stood back from him as he gathered up the scalps, took them outside, and prepared to place them on his horse. He hid them in blankets, then tied them securely behind his saddle along with several skins of various animals, wolves the most prominent.

Shoshana stepped aside as Mountain Jack came back into the cabin and got his saddlebag. Again he spoke directly into her face. "There's plenty of grub," he said solemnly. "Help yourself."

He nodded toward the wolves in the pen. "And don't forget to feed them," he flatly ordered. "There's fresh meat outside in a shack. It's for the wolves."

Laughing gruffly, he left.

Shoshana stood still, scarcely breathing, until she heard Mountain Jack ride away into the night.

She felt as though she was in a state of shock over everything that had happened to her. She was the prisoner of a crazy man!

Dragging the chain behind her, Shoshana began searching the cabin for something she could use to cut it off. She guessed that her search would be fruitless, for surely he wouldn't have left anything for her to find.

"A key?" she whispered. "Could there be a key?"

She searched in the cabin until she lost hope of finding one, then went and sat down on the floor before the fireplace.

She hid her face in her hands.

"Please come and find me," she whispered, uncertain whom she was imploring. "Anyone . . . please . . . ?"

She shivered when the wolves outside in the pen began howling at the moon.

It was an eerie, lonesome sound.

It made Shoshana feel even more alone . . . and afraid.

Chapter Ten

> There is a garden in her face
> Where roses and white lilies grow,
> A heavenly paradise in that place
> Wherein all pleasant fruits do flow.
>   —Thomas Campion

Almost ready to give up the search for both the panther and the scalp hunter, knowing that traveling at this hour on the mountain was full of risks, Storm began wheeling his horse around. He stopped halfway when the moonlight revealed something he had not seen before while traveling up and down the mountain.

But his travels had never brought him to this part of the mountain before. He had never expected Mountain Jack to be daft enough to hide on the very mountain that was home to a proud Apache chief!

But perhaps Mountain Jack was more clever than anyone gave him credit for. Cleverness and cunning had to have played a role in his elusiveness.

Storm gazed at length at a thick aspen forest, and through a break in the trees he saw a canyon beyond, where the moon worked its light into every crevice: the shine of silken trees, moon-bent grass, and gray-blue cliffs.

Ho, yes, in all of Storm's ventures, he had never seen this canyon, yet his exploring had never brought him so far from the pass in this direction.

The mountain was huge. It would take a lifetime to explore all of it.

Determined to discover what was in the canyon, forgetting the dangers of the night, of the panther that stalked the darkness, Storm sank his heels into the flanks of his horse and rode through the aspen forest and into the canyon.

He stopped to allow his eyes to scan the area. Nothing escaped his piercing glance.

He had to make sure this wasn't a trap. He wasn't ready to lose his scalp!

When he was sure no enemy lurked nearby, he rode onward. Before another minute had passed, he saw a cabin nestled in the canyon.

"This is a clever hideout," he said to himself as he paused to again check for any sign of movement.

When there was none, he rode onward, but more cautiously now. He wasn't sure whether the scalp hunter worked alone, or whether he had sentries guarding him. He didn't even know if this was the scalp hunter's lodge.

As the moon poured its silver light down onto the cabin, Storm saw that the logs were newly cut. No doubt the scalp hunter moved from place to place often in order to avoid capture.

Next Storm noticed a pen of gray wolves close to the cabin. The sight angered him, for no wolves should be penned up. They were meant to run free!

At that moment several of the wolves began to howl at the moon.

Dismounting, Storm tied his horse's reins to a tree. After taking his rifle from its gunboot, he crept toward the cabin, his moccasined feet falling noiselessly on the ground like the velvet paws of a cat.

He circled around to a far side of the cabin. He stayed in the shadows and downwind from the wolves so that they would not be startled by his presence and make a commotion.

Now that he was so close, Storm realized that only one horse was reined at the hitching rail. One horse meant only one person was there.

His hand tight on his rifle, Storm crept slowly to a window. He looked through it. His heart skipped a beat when he saw who was in the cabin.

It was the *ish-tia-nay* he had seen traveling with

Mountain Jack . . . the one he had seen through his spyglass! She was sitting on the floor in front of the fireplace, unaware of his observation.

He turned his eyes left, then right, making sure that Mountain Jack was not in the room. Storm realized that the scalp hunter had left the woman alone.

Again he gazed at her. Even though her back was to him, he could see the same long, sleek, black hair that he had seen earlier.

He wondered why she sat with her head hung, as one who was despondent might hold it.

Was she sad? Or was she dozing?

Needing answers from this woman about why she was there and where the scalp hunter had gone, Storm crept around to the front of the cabin.

Again he was so noiseless that the wolves did not sense his approach.

When he reached the front door, which was ajar, he boldly opened it the rest of the way, then moved quietly to stand just inside the door.

Again he gazed at the woman. She was still unaware that he was there.

Then he noticed something else that made his heart skip a beat as she moved an arm. A chain was attached to it. She was a prisoner, not the evil man's wife!

And up this close, he could tell for certain she

could not be anything but a full-blood Indian. Yet she wore the clothes of a white woman.

Now that he saw she was being held captive, he supposed the scalp hunter had made her wear a white woman's clothes instead of her own in order to keep her people from recognizing her at a distance.

But where had he found her? Which band did she come from?

For many moons Storm had searched for the scalp hunter. Now he had finally found his lodge, but this woman's safety must take precedence over his desire to catch the scalp hunter.

It was important that she be freed.

And because she was so beautiful, Storm could not help wanting to know her better and discover where she made her home. In his many travels between Apache strongholds, he had never seen her.

But he knew that there were bands that he had not yet found. *Ho*, this woman must have been stolen from one of them.

Had Mountain Jack killed many in order to have her?

Storm's eyes widened and he felt his pulse race when suddenly the woman lifted her head and turned her eyes to him.

Now that he saw her up close, he knew that he would never find anyone else in his entire life who could match her beauty.

When he saw fear leap into her eyes, Storm took a step closer, then stopped as she gasped and cowered in his shadow.

"I am a friend," he said tightly. "Do not be afraid."

Chapter Eleven

Do! I tell you, I rather guess
She was a wonder, and nothing less!
    —Oliver Wendell Holmes

As soon as Shoshana saw the stranger, she was frightened. Although she was glad that someone besides Mountain Jack had arrived, she wasn't sure what to think about this tall and muscular Indian, who carried in his left hand a seventeen-shot Winchester rifle.

She guessed that this must be the Indian who had been high in the mountain earlier, possibly sending signals to his warriors.

Was . . . he . . . Apache?

Although she still felt fear like the cold blade of a knife in the pit of her stomach, she could not help noticing how uniquely handsome he was with his high cheekbones, his well-formed nose, his black eyes that blazed with fire and energy, and his strong jaw.

He had firm lips. His hair, which he wore in a thick braid, was black, thick, and coarse. He had a lean, supple, sinewy body . . . a broad chest and slender waist.

"Still you say nothing?" Storm said as he took one step closer to the maiden. "I spoke in English when I said I was a friend. Again hear me well when I tell you that I pose no threat to you."

Then he recalled the powerful weapon that he held in his left hand and knew that it, alone, could put fear into the heart of any man or woman.

"I am armed thusly because there are others who pose a threat to me, as well as animals that I must protect myself from," Storm explained. "While on a hunt for a panther that killed two small ones from my stronghold, I saw you with the scalp hunter. Since I have been searching for the scalp hunter for many moons now, I could not give up tonight until I found him."

His gaze swept down to where she was held prisoner by the chain at her wrist, then slowly looked up at her again. "When I first saw you with Mountain Jack, I thought you were with him of your own choosing, yet I found it hard to believe that any woman would want such a man for a husband, especially . . . especially a woman who is of my own Apache blood," he said guardedly.

He stooped and lifted a portion of the chain in his free hand, gazed at it, and then again at the woman. "Now that I see you are a prisoner of the whiskered scalp hunter, I realize how wrong I was in my first impression of you. Let me help you. Let me release you. I will take you to safety."

No longer so afraid, Shoshana moved slowly to her feet, her gaze holding his as he rose to his full height.

Yet he *was* a stranger, and she could not put her full trust in him just yet. Since the day she had been taken away from the horrible ambush on her people, she had never been around Indians except for those who worked as scouts for the cavalry.

She knew the name of only one Apache in this area; she wondered if this could possibly be he.

"Are you Chief Storm?" she blurted out without any more hesitation.

"Ah, so you do know of me," Storm said thickly. "How have you heard of me? What is your name, and where do you make your home? I have never seen you before this day with Mountain Jack."

His gaze swept slowly over her again, then he looked intently into her eyes. "You are of Indian blood, yet you wear the clothes of white people," he said, his voice tight. "Why is this?"

"It's a long story, but I will tell you this much . . .

yes, I am Apache," she murmured, her heart beating loudly at the knowledge that he was Chief Storm, the proud, elusive Apache chief who made his home high on this very mountain.

She gazed more intently into his midnight-dark eyes. "My home?" she murmured. "For many moons I have lived with white people as a white woman. You see, long ago I was taken from my true people. I was only five on that terrible day when my village was attacked by the cavalry. For so long I was not able to remember anything about that day. And then . . . and then . . . a dream came to me that told me of the tragedy. When I awakened, I recalled most of what had happened; slowly the rest came to me in more dreams."

"Do you dream often?" Storm asked, amazed by her story.

This beautiful woman had suffered the same as he, yet he had been able to flee those who had killed so many that day.

Although her life had been spared, she had been forced to live apart from her people. He didn't know which was worse, being slain by white-eyes or taken and made into one of them.

"Yes, I dream often," Shoshana murmured. "I dream of my mother, who I'd always believed was killed that day. Now, I'm not so sure. The dreams give me hope that one day I may find her again."

"Why are you here in Apache land now?" Storm

asked softly. "Where have you made your home since the age of five?"

Shoshana felt the tension between them lessening as she explained about having lived at various forts, and then mainly in Missouri.

"I was treated like a princess," she murmured. "But after discovering my true heritage, I have never forgotten who I really am, and where I belong."

"And you are in Apache land now for what purpose?" Storm asked, stepping closer, lifting the chain again and examining the spot where it was attached around her wrist. Soon he would have her free.

"The man who adopted me, who once was in the cavalry, himself, has returned to my homeland to help the cavalry find the scalp hunter. He has accepted this commission even though he has been slowed down, not only by age, but by his wooden leg," Shoshana said.

At those words Storm's eyes shot up and stared strangely into hers.

"This man," Storm said, his heart pounding at the mention of a man with a wooden leg who was in the cavalry. "What is his name?"

"His name?" Shoshana asked, seeing his eagerness to hear her response. She wondered now if she should tell him. Could Chief Storm somehow know about George's past atrocities against the Apache?

Might he want vengeance if he knew what

George Whaley had been guilty of those long years ago? Might Chief Storm not understand how she could have continued to care for him after learning of his role in the attack on her own band?

"Yes, his name," Storm said thickly. "What . . . is . . . his name?"

"George Whaley," Shoshana said, tightening inside when she saw a strange light enter the handsome chief's eyes.

"Chief Storm, do you know the name?" Shoshana murmured. "Do you know the man?"

Although Storm prided himself, like all Apache, on speaking the truth, he knew that a lie was necessary now in order to give him time to decide what he must do.

Ho, fate was working in his favor today. It was unbelievable but true that this woman was the adopted daughter of the man he had despaired of ever finding. This woman must be the joy of George Whaley's life. Without her, surely he would be half a man.

If she was taken from him, would he not be devastated? Would he not know the true heartache of suddenly losing someone he loved so dearly?

It was hard to see how a man could kill so many Apache, then take one to keep for himself, to raise as his own beloved daughter. Yet it seemed she had not known anything but the love of this evil white man since the day of her capture.

Ho, he must lie to this woman, in order to finally

achieve the vengeance he had promised his father so long ago.

Yes, he would promise that he would take her back to George Whaley, but he never would. He would keep her in his stronghold. Instead of killing the man, Storm would deprive him of his daughter. Whaley's loss would be a heartache that he could never get over; he would experience a loss such as the Apache had known due to the evil of this man.

Heartache could bring a man down quickly . . . especially an older man.

Realizing that Storm was finding it difficult for some reason to answer her question, Shoshana decided to change the subject. There was another question she was longing to ask him.

"Will you take me to your stronghold?" she blurted out, surprised that she trusted a stranger enough to ask such a thing of him, especially a stranger who surely hated all whites with a passion.

But she wasn't white!

She was Apache!

"You see, I ache to be among my Apache people," she explained. "Please? Will you take me?"

She desperately wanted to mention the name Fawn; to ask if he knew her, yet now that she could, she was afraid to know. If she discovered that her search had been for naught, that her dreams meant nothing and that her mother wasn't alive after all, she would be devastated.

As long as she had hope, she felt she could go on. But if she discovered that her mother didn't exist, it would break her heart.

Yes, she would delay the knowing awhile longer.

Storm was stunned by her request. What courage she possessed! It made him admire her beauty all the more, but nothing would change the plans he now had for her.

Not even the fact that he felt something for her even though they had just met.

No woman had raised this sensual heat in him before. This daring beauty was the first.

But he must remember why he was taking her with him. It was for vengeance, not to have someone to fall in love with!

"*Ho*, I will take you," he said, hiding his smile of victory.

"Thank you, oh, thank you," Shoshana said, her excitement causing a hot blush to rush to her cheeks. She gazed down at the chain as he studied it. "But how can you free me?"

"A key must be somewhere in this cabin," Storm said, turning and wincing when he saw the bloody scalps still hanging from the rafters.

"I already searched and didn't find one," Shoshana said wearily. "I hope you can."

"I will look until I find it," he said, giving her a look over his shoulder. How fortunate it was that her scalp had not joined the others. Her hair was as black and as thick and beautiful as any he had ever seen.

Surely upon Mountain Jack's return, he planned to rape, then scalp her.

Realizing that lingering at the cabin for much longer might endanger them both, Storm looked high and low for the key.

He didn't find it inside the cabin.

"I shall look outside," he said, walking toward the door. "He would not leave it where you could find it easily."

Shoshana sat back down on the floor before the fire as Storm stepped out into the moonlight.

His gaze swept slowly over everything, then fell upon a small shed that hugged the cabin not far from the front door.

He went there. It was dark, so he could only feel with his hands.

He smiled victoriously when he found several keys on a ring which hung from a nail on the wall beneath a layer of old pelts.

Smiling, he took the ring of keys into the cabin.

"Perhaps the one we are looking for is here," he said, setting his rifle against a wall.

He knelt before Shoshana.

One by one he tried the keys, then smiled into her lustrously dark eyes as the chain finally fell away from her wrist.

"Thank goodness," Shoshana sighed. She rubbed

her raw wrist and smiled at Storm as he unwrapped the chain from around her waist. "Thank you so much. Had you not came along, I . . . I . . . am not certain what my final fate would have been."

"But I *am* here and you *are* free," Storm said as he grabbed his rifle, amazed that the lie about her being free slipped across his lips so easily . . . lips that never lied.

He felt guilty over what he was planning to do with her, when she was so sweetly sincere about thanking him for having freed her.

But he must block everything from his mind except the vengeance he had waited so long to achieve.

"You did not tell me when I asked what name you go by," Storm said, stepping out into the moonlight and looking guardedly around them for any sign of the scalp hunter's return.

"Shoshana," she murmured. "It is the name I was given as a child by my mother. The man who took me from my mother allowed me to keep the name, but only because his wife, who has long since passed away, loved its prettiness."

She paused, then took his free hand in hers. "It was destiny that brought us together tonight," she said, her eyes searching his. "The scalp hunter unknowingly led me to the very man I was searching for."

"You were searching for me?" Storm asked, raising an eyebrow.

His flesh felt hot where her hand held his. He could not help feeling so much for her that he wished to deny.

But when she was so close, her hand in his, her eyes so hauntingly beautiful, her body so enticing, he suddenly remembered his sister's warnings. She had told him about a woman . . . an Apache woman who had betrayed her people by living as white.

But Storm now knew that Shoshana was not a woman guilty of betrayal. She had been forced to live with the white-eyes. She had never had a role in her own destiny . . . until now.

From the moment George Whaley had abducted Shoshana, he had had full control of her life.

Well, now that had changed. Storm had just made Shoshana's destiny his.

He put his sister's warnings in the farthest recesses of his mind. This woman had come to Arizona for a reason. She was sent to him by *Maheo*, the Great Spirit, to help Storm finally achieve the vengeance that he had sought since the day of his people's massacre.

"Your name is known well among whites," Shoshana said, interrupting his thoughts. "I was told of your courage and how you have kept your band safe high up the mountain in your stronghold. You are admired for your dedication to your people, and for the way you have kept peace between them and the whites."

She paused, then said, "You *will* take me to your home, won't you?" she asked, her eyes wide. "It has been so long since I have been among my own kind. I have ached for such an opportunity as this."

"Yes, I will take you," he said quietly. Little did she know that she would be taken not as a free woman, but as a captive.

"We must hurry now," Storm said as he gently took Shoshana by the arm, ushering her away from the cabin.

Shoshana felt no fear, only hope, and something even more. She was intrigued by everything about this man. She had never felt such a strong attraction to any other man. Chief Storm made her come alive inside where she had never known such feelings existed.

She hoped that she was right to trust him, as well as her feelings for him.

Chapter Twelve

Does there within the dimmest dreams
A possible future shine?
                    —Adelaide Anne Procter

"The wolves," Storm said, stopping beside their pen. "Gray wolves should never be imprisoned. They are the spirit of the wilderness."

"Mountain Jack mates them and raises their young for pelts that he sells to the same people who buy scalps from him," Shoshana said. She watched the younger ones romp and play in the moonlight. Except for one. It stood apart, much thinner than the others, trembling visibly. "It looks like one of the pups isn't all that strong, or well."

"I shall release them, all except for the one that is

not strong enough to be set free," Storm said, already stepping toward the gate.

"What are you going to do with it?" Shoshana asked, taking a step away from the pen. "And . . . and . . . is it safe to set any of them free? How do you know they won't attack us?"

"They are smart animals," Storm said, slowly lifting the latch that held the gate closed. "They will take advantage of their freedom. They will not take the time even to look at us, much less attack us. They have been penned up for a long time. They are as anxious to taste freedom as you were when you were chained up in the cabin."

Shoshana heard what he said, but, still unsure whether to trust his judgement about the wolves, she took another step away from them.

She watched as one by one they ran to freedom.

Shoshana marveled how one grown wolf stayed with the weak one and tried to nudge it with its nose to get it to leave the pen.

But the tiny one was not convinced. Its legs wobbled. It gazed wistfully into the eyes of the older one, which Shoshana now assumed was its mother.

"The mother won't leave the pup behind," Shoshana said, amazed at the dedication and love the mother had for its pup, especially when freedom beckoned.

"It must," Storm said. He went inside the pen. He looked directly into the eyes of the older wolf.

It seemed to Shoshana that they were communicating in some mystical, silent way.

She gasped with awe when the wolf stepped closer to Storm, nuzzled his hand with its nose, then gave its pup a long, last look and left the pen, yapping as it ran to catch up with the others.

"You seemed to be communicating with one another," Shoshana said, moving to Storm's side. "And . . . and . . . she actually left her pup behind, apparently in your care."

"I have talked often to animals, as they talk to me," Storm said. He bent low and gathered up the tiny, weak pup in his arms, cuddling it close to his chest.

"Will you take the pup to your village to care for it?" Shoshana asked as Storm carried it away from the pen.

"Yes, it will be a part of my people until it is well enough to be released back to the wild," Storm said. He nodded to the horse tied at the hitching rail. "Mount the steed. We must not delay any longer."

Overjoyed to be leaving that filthy cabin behind, Shoshana didn't hesitate to mount the horse.

After Storm secured the wolf pup in the bag at the side of his horse, where only its face was exposed, he mounted his own steed and, together, he and Shoshana rode from the cabin.

"How far do we have to travel before reaching your stronghold?" Shoshana asked, suddenly realizing just how tired she was, and hungry.

She was also beginning to feel guilty for not having asked to be taken to the fort so that George Whaley would know she was all right.

Yet part of her rejoiced in her freedom from him. In a very real way, his love had kept her a prisoner. She was free for the first time since that day when her entire world had been torn apart.

"It is quite a distance, but if you grow too tired along the way, we can stop and rest. It would be best to continue onward until we reach the safety of the stronghold," Storm said.

They traveled through the narrow canyon, then through the thick aspen forest, and started up a narrow pass, with a steep drop-off at one side.

Shoshana didn't feel the danger of the drop-off. In fact, she felt as though she were home. She felt completely safe with this man.

Staying close by his side, she glanced over at him. She admired his splendid panther-skin saddle. She admired him. He had such poise . . . such dignity of character!

"Are you married?" Shoshana suddenly blurted out, then blushed when she saw his stunned expression.

She was surprised at herself for being so inquisitive. She started to apologize, but didn't, for she truly did want to know if he was married or not.

"No, I am not married," Storm said slowly. "My life is too full of responsibilities. I have not wanted any others . . . until today."

"What do you mean by that?" Shoshana dared ask. "What is different about today?"

He looked over at her. Her eyes met his in the soft moonlight.

"You," he said thickly.

She was taken off guard by his answer, and wondered if she should be afraid.

"Why . . . me . . . ?" she murmured, knowing that he must be able to see the blush on her copper cheeks, with the moon's glow rendering the night so much like day.

"Because I must see to your safety," Storm said, lying again.

Trying to hide her disappointment, Shoshana turned her eyes quickly away from Storm. She had been foolish to think that she might be something more than a responsibility to Storm.

They had only just met!

But Storm was thinking to himself that until today he hadn't wanted such a responsibility as a wife, nor the sadness of losing one.

But now? He was attracted to Shoshana in ways he had never felt before.

But he must keep reminding himself that she was there for only one reason. To achieve a vengeance that had eaten away at his gut since that day he had buried his mother and father.

Suddenly the screech of a panther split the still night air.

Only now was Storm reminded of why he had left his stronghold this morning.

It was not to take a woman captive.

It was to search for a dangerous panther.

He yanked his rifle from its gunboot and searched both sides of the trail.

"*Ish-tia-nay*, stay close by me," he said.

The wolf pup let out a tiny growl, as though even it sensed the panther's nearness.

"Silence, Gray Wolf," Storm said, releasing his reins long enough to drop the flap down over the pup's head and curious eyes.

"I'm so afraid," Shoshana said, visibly trembling. "I have never seen a panther before, but I know they are killers."

"Not always," Storm said quietly. "But once a panther has tasted human blood, it does become a killer that must be dealt with."

"You seem to be very wary of this particular panther," Shoshana said, edging her horse even closer to Storm's.

"I was on a hunt for the panther when I spied you and the scalp hunter earlier in the afternoon," Storm said. "That is how I knew where to search for you."

"So it was you making that reflection in the sun," Shoshana said, then gasped and looked quickly upward.

She froze when she saw the panther.

It was on a limb directly above her, gazing down at her with piercing green eyes, its sleek body covered by a beautiful bluish-black coat. It was whipping its tail back and forth against its sides and clawing great pieces of bark from the limb.

It screeched again, and before Storm saw it and could take aim with his rifle, it leapt away to a higher bluff, the action causing Shoshana's horse to bolt. Snorting, the horse slipped and lost its footing, throwing Shoshana from the saddle.

She screamed in terror as she felt herself being thrown over the side of the cliff.

Chapter Thirteen

If ever any beauty I did see,
Which I desired and got,
'Twas a dream of thee.

—John Donne

Storm's heart leapt with fear when he saw Shoshana thrown from her horse, and then fall out of sight, down the side of the cliff.

His pulse racing, he slid his rifle back inside the gunboot at the side of his horse, then dismounted and fell to his belly so he could lean over the side of the cliff. He found Shoshana hanging from a limb, her legs dangling.

The moonlight revealed her wide eyes gazing in desperation up at him.

Suddenly Storm saw something else. Far below him, so far away they looked like tiny ants, were soldiers making camp around a huge, blazing campfire. Should they look up, would the bright light of the moon reveal Shoshana to them?

But knowing that saving her life was the most important thing now, he looked back into her eyes. "Hang on a moment longer," he said reassuringly. "I will save you."

"My hands . . . hurt . . . I'm not sure how long I can last," Shoshana cried, her heart pounding so hard, she felt as though her chest might burst.

Storm quickly got a rope from his horse and tied it to his steed, then handed the other end down to Shoshana. "Grab the rope," he said, holding it fast.

After a moment of paralyzing fear, she dared to grab the rope with one hand and then the other. She held on with both hands as Storm pulled her to safety with the aid of his horse.

But just as she got on solid ground, stretched out on her back, breathing hard, she felt as though the earth was rocking and heaving beneath her.

It gave a sharp turn, and seemed to keep right on turning. When she looked around, everything seemed to be upside down, the sky under her.

And then she fell into a black void of unconsciousness.

"Shoshana?" Storm gasped when he saw her eyes

suddenly close. It was then that he saw a large lump on her brow and realized that she had apparently hit the rock face as she fell.

Fortunately, she had managed to remain conscious long enough to help in her rescue.

Forgetting the soldiers down below and even the panther, Storm swept Shoshana up into his arms and carried her away from the edge of the cliff. He laid her down on the path where they had been riding.

The moon's glow provided enough light for him to inspect the wound on her brow more carefully. It was a nasty lump, oozing blood.

He tried to get her awake. But she didn't respond.

Afraid to leave her for long, with the panther still nearby, yet wanting to find an herb that his people used for restoring consciousness, Storm went into the edge of the thicket a few feet away and searched until he found what he was looking for.

With the hope of arousing her, he took the plant back to her. Slowly, he waved it back and forth beneath her nose.

To his utter disappointment, it didn't work. She was still unconscious.

Deciding to forget about the panther for now, so that he could take Shoshana to his stronghold where the shaman could see to her wound, Storm hurried away from her and tied her horse's reins to his own, thankful that the animal had settled down and not run off.

Before getting Shoshana, Storm checked the wolf pup and found that it was in a deep sleep. He lifted and carried Shoshana to his horse, soon having her positioned on his lap as he settled himself in the saddle.

He rode onward.

He was disappointed that he had lost the chance to finally kill the deadly panther; he had also given up the opportunity to finally stop the evil of the scalp hunter.

But there would come another time for both. He was more concerned about Shoshana now than anything else.

He was worried that she was still unconscious. He hoped that once he got her in the hands of his shaman, the medicine man would know how to revive her.

He saw the wolf pup stirring in the bag. He reached a hand down and stroked its wiry fur. "You will be all right," he reassured it. "But you must learn to live without your mother. Do not fear, I will protect you. No man will ever get near enough to harm you!"

With Shoshana's horse trailing behind his, Storm rode onward up an even narrower pass, past a series of waterfalls that cut through ponderosa pine and aspen.

As the night wore on, clouds marred the face of the moon, and lightning played among the mountain peaks. Soon thunder heralded the arrival of a black-walled rainstorm.

Almost blinded by the rain, and deafened by hailstones ringing on the rocks, rocketing about in all directions, Storm trundled down to safety, to a cave where he had found dry shelter many times before.

He secured the horses just inside the cave entrance, hung his bag with the wolf pup in it over his left arm, then carried Shoshana to the back of the cave where he had left equipment, blankets, and wood for fires.

Storm set down the bag with the wolf pup, glad that it had slept through the storm and rain, protected by the lid of the buckskin bag.

It still slept soundly, and Shoshana was still unconscious.

Storm made Shoshana as comfortable as possible in her wet clothes on blankets, then built a fire, the smoke escaping through a fissure in the cave's ceiling.

Storm made another pallet of blankets and carried Shoshana to them so she could be closer to the fire. He knew it was best that her clothes dry quickly to keep her from getting chilled.

He sat down beside her, already feeling the warmth of the fire through his own wet attire. He wanted the warmth of a blanket around his shoulders, but knew that he must endure the wet coldness for a while longer in order to get his clothes dry.

He checked the bag and saw that the wolf pup was still sleeping soundly. Then he looked again at Shoshana, his heart skipping an anxious beat when he saw her stir, and then awaken.

Shoshana raised herself up on an elbow.

She looked slowly around her, but she had such a terrible headache that everything she saw was a fuzzy blur.

But she knew she was beside a fire. She felt its warmth against her flesh.

"How are you?" Storm asked, kneeling down beside her.

Shoshana recognized the voice as Storm's, then gazed up at him. "My head aches so," she murmured, reaching a hand to her forehead, wincing when she felt just how large the lump there was.

She squinted as she again tried to focus on Storm, then looked slowly around her. "Where are we?" she murmured. "I see you . . . and everything else . . . as only a blur."

"When you fell from the horse you hit your forehead," Storm softly explained. "After it began to rain, I brought you to the safety of this cave. Once the storm passes by, we will resume our travel to my stronghold. When we arrive, my shaman, White Moon, will care for you. Soon you will be well."

"I . . . I . . . feel ill," Shoshana murmured, tasting a strange bitterness in her mouth.

"Sometimes one does feel that way after a blow to the head," Storm said softly. "*Ish-tia-nay*, close your eyes. Rest. Soon you will be at my stronghold in the care of my shaman."

"Thank you. . . ." Shoshana murmured as she slowly drifted off to sleep again.

Storm sat down beside her.

He studied her as she slept.

He had never seen such a beautiful woman.

He wondered what her life had been like while she had lived among whites. She had been raised by a man who had the blood of many Apache on his hands. Had Shoshana possibly caused this man to change for the better?

The man was in the area to help find the scalp hunter who was the enemy of all Apache. Why would the wooden-legged man care enough about the scalp hunter's evil to help track him down?

Guilt for his past sins against the Apache? Was he trying to atone for those sins?

Well, none of that meant anything to Storm. He would still take his vengeance. He would still make the wooden-legged man pay!

He gazed at Shoshana again. *Ho*, her absence would cause the wooden-legged man much distress.

When Shoshana knew of Storm's plans to take vengeance against George Whaley, how would she react? Would she care?

He ran a finger softly across her lips. They were

made to be kissed. She was born to be loved, and not by *pindah-lickoyee*, but by an Apache!

He knew that even if it stopped raining soon, he should not move Shoshana until tomorrow. He must give the mountain pass time to dry, otherwise it would be too slippery for travel, and there was always the chance of a mud slide.

Yes, he would take Shoshana then, and she would be well soon.

Ah, finally he had found a woman who made him want more than to be the protector of his people. With every beat of his heart he wanted to protect Shoshana.

She had been apart from her true people long enough.

He wondered about Shoshana's Apache mother. Could she have survived that ambush even as Shoshana's dreams had revealed to her? Might she even be among the older women at his own stronghold? Had her mother been among those who had been found wandering alone through the years and brought to safety to live among his people?

If so, and Shoshana could find her among the many older women, would Shoshana be content to remain with him? Would she be happy to live with her mother again, and allow him to court her?

"I will make it so," he whispered.

Smiling, he stretched out on a blanket beside Shoshana.

He was still smiling when he drifted off to sleep, Shoshana's beautiful face and sweet voice filling his dreams.

He awakened with a start when his sister's face came to him in his dreams, and he remembered the warnings she had given him about the woman he would meet.

He gazed at Shoshana. Was this the woman of his sister's dreams?

If so, what did they truly mean?

Chapter Fourteen

To lose thee were to lose myself.
—John Milton

The next morning, after Storm felt that it was dry enough along the mountain pass, he left the cave with Shoshana, again holding her on the horse with him. She was still too dizzy and sleepy to ride by herself.

Storm gazed down at her, snuggled contentedly against his chest. It was as though she belonged there. He felt attached to her even though he knew that when she was awake and able to understand that she was no longer free to leave his stronghold when she wanted to, she would probably hate him.

When the stronghold was only a short distance

away, Storm sent up a signal of his nearness, imitating the howl of a coyote.

The same type of howl came to him in response; his sentries were aware that their chief, not an enemy, was approaching.

He had to smile when he heard a small howl come from the bag at the side of his horse; the gray wolf pup had heard the mock coyote sounds.

"You are aware, that is good," Storm said, reaching to flip back the cover so that the pup could see things around him.

Up until now, he had mostly slept.

The pup's blue eyes gazed trustingly up at Storm; then the tiny thing gave what sounded like a bark.

"You soon will be at my stronghold and fed something nourishing," Storm said, reaching a hand to the wolf's gray, wiry fur and stroking it. "Gray Wolf, when you are fully grown and have the strength of an adult, you will be sent out to find those who are kin to you. You will mate one day, Gray Wolf."

The sound of an approaching horse drew Storm's attention from the wolf. He smiled and waved when he saw one of his favored warriors riding toward him.

Four Wings returned the wave, then drew rein beside Storm. He looked questioningly at the woman, and the wolf pup.

"I will explain later how I have the woman with me, and the pup," Storm said calmly. "Ride ahead,

Four Wings, and alert White Moon that I am bringing an injured woman to him. Tell him that the woman received a hard blow to her brow and she cannot stay awake for any long period of time."

"I shall do this for you," Four Wings replied. He wheeled his horse around and rode back in the direction of the stronghold.

Storm made his way through a canyon, a rough, rocky, and very dangerous defile, and then arrived at his stronghold, where there were a mixture of homes built for his people.

There were many tepees made of buffalo skins tanned white.

There were also some circular wickiups, built from saplings and brush. Ordinarily four or five of these shelters were built in close proximity to each other.

"Storm!"

Storm saw his sister leave her tepee and run toward him. She stopped abruptly when she noticed the woman on his horse with him. She stood stiffly as Storm rode onward, then drew rein beside her.

When Dancing Willow saw the face of the woman, she gasped, then looked questioningly up at Storm. "This is the very *ish-tia-nay* that I have seen in the stars . . . in my dreams and visions," she said ominously. "This is the woman that I warned you about, Storm."

Dancing Willow folded her arms angrily across

her chest as she glowered up at Storm. "You have just brought trouble into our people's lives by bringing this woman here," she scolded. "Why did you bring her? Did you not recall my warning?"

"I found this woman being held prisoner," Storm said, his eyes meeting and locking with his sister's. "While her captor, Mountain Jack, was gone, I released her. It was my decision to bring her to our stronghold. She will bring satisfaction into my life, not trouble to our people."

"Satisfaction?" Dancing Willow said, her dark eyes widening. She ignored the people mulling around them, watching and listening. "It is not like you to think of . . . 'satisfaction' . . . instead of what is right for our band."

Knowing what must be said to make his sister understand, yet not wanting Shoshana to hear their dialogue, he gazed down at Shoshana.

He studied her eyes to see whether there was movement behind the closed lids. When he saw no signs of movement, Storm felt that it was safe to speak freely.

His sister had one trait that rankled him more often than not. Although he was a proud chief, his older sister had a tendency to speak up and argue when she should only listen.

He had forgiven her this weakness, for she had never done anything to hurt him, although some-

126

times she had embarrassed him. She did seem to forget that he was chief, and she only a sister!

In time surely she would realize that it was best not to enter into these arguments with him, especially while their people were listening.

"You misinterpret the word 'satisfaction' and how I use it today," Storm said, keeping his voice as quiet as possible since he did not want Shoshana to awaken at this moment.

He tried to control the anger that was rising within him at the way his sister openly questioned him.

"I do not care how I misinterpreted anything," Dancing Willow snapped back at him, then realized that she was treading on thin ice with her brother by questioning him in front of their people.

"My chief, my big brother," she said more softly and respectfully. "It does not matter who this woman is, or why you feel the need to bring her to our stronghold. You must take her away while she is still unconscious and is not aware of where our stronghold is."

"Big sister, do you not want the same vengeance that I want, the vengeance we have talked about so often since the deaths of our parents and people?" Storm said, controlling his anger and frustration. "When she was only five winters of age, this woman was taken from her people and raised by the wooden-legged man who brought so much sadness and heartache to our people those many moons ago. Our very own father shot an arrow into this white man's leg. By taking this woman whom the wooden-legged man has raised as a daughter, we will be shooting an arrow into his heart. We must keep her at the stronghold. We must deny this man the opportunity to ever see or hold this woman again!"

"But, brother—"

"Listen and do not question what I have done and plan to do," Storm said tightly. "This woman is here to stay. Finally, you and I, and our people as well, will achieve a measure of vengeance. I would rather do this than kill the wooden-legged man. It will be good that he suffers, alive. Death comes too quickly and ends sufferings, especially sufferings of the heart. And if I should kill George Whaley, who was once a powerful colonel, it would anger the United States Government so much, those in charge would send out the cavalry to search until they finally found our stronghold. We would all be doomed then. Under my plan, the colonel will be made to pay for the wrongs done to our people. He will never know if his daughter is alive or dead. That alone will make his heart ache as it has probably never ached before."

He smiled cunningly at his sister. "But best of all, George Whaley will never know whom to blame," he said. "It is enough for me just to know that I have done something to inflict pain on him. It is not important to me that he should know who caused it."

"Storm, I will say just one more thing and then I will be silent about what you have done," Dancing Willow said. "Vengeance should be the last thing on my mind or yours. You are a peaceful man. You have always protected our people from misfortune. They have suffered enough at the hands of the *pindah-lickoyee*. Please, brother, if you must keep this *ish-tia-nay*, let us leave even now for Canada with our people while the white-eyes are not aware of our stronghold. But I say, leave the woman here for them to find. She has lived as a white-eye. She does not deserve to live among we Apache!"

In truth, Dancing Willow could not help feeling jealous about her brother's obvious feelings for this woman whom he held so gently in his arms.

She could tell that Storm did not see this woman as a captive. He saw her as a beautiful woman.

It was in his eyes as he looked at her. It was in his voice as he talked about her.

Dancing Willow had been the most important woman in his life since the death of their mother. She would be less important if another woman crowded her way into their family. He would no longer come to Dancing Willow for suggestions . . . for advice; instead he would go to the other woman.

Dancing Willow *must* find a way to discourage him.

"Brother, you have always stood for good, not bad," Dancing Willow said. "Forget the evils of the past. Forget your hunger for vengeance. If you continue down this road that you have begun to travel today . . . this road to vengeance . . . then you will become bad, yourself."

She saw how his eyes narrowed angrily, and how his lips pursed tightly as he glared at her. And she understood. But although she had promised not to say anything else, she could not get past her uneasiness and jealousy over this woman.

"Enough, *enough*," Storm said, then looked past his sister toward Four Wings, who was dismounting nearby. "Four Wings, come and help me with the woman."

Dancing Willow stepped aside, bitter that her brother wouldn't listen to reason and see the evil that this *ish-tia-nay* would bring into all of their lives.

An Apache-born woman who lived the life of a white woman could never mix among the Apache again as one of them. That this woman had come to their stronghold as a captive made no difference to Dancing Willow. She knew by her brother's behavior that she would not remain captive for long.

Gradually, he would bring the woman into their lives. Eventually, he might even marry her.

That would be the worst of all evils, as far as Dancing Willow was concerned. She had to find a way to put a halt to all of this.

Four Wings took Shoshana in his arms as Storm lifted her down to him.

Then Storm dismounted and handed his reins to a young brave. "As you see," he told the boy, "there is a young wolf pup on the side of my horse in my bag," he said. "Take him home with you. He will be hungry. Feed him. I call him by the name Gray Wolf."

"I will care for Gray Wolf for you," the young brave said, smiling at Storm. Then he walked away with the horse toward Storm's personal corral at the back of his lodge.

"I will take Shoshana now," Storm said as he held his arms out for her. "Thank you, Four Wings. Now go for White Moon. Send him to me."

Four Wings nodded and walked briskly away. All others turned and went their separate ways to their own lodges.

Dancing Willow still stood watching as her brother carried the woman into his large tepee; then she turned and stamped away to her own dwelling. She sat down before her fire and began softly chanting, her dark eyes gleaming in the fire's glow. "She is bad," she whispered over and over again. "She . . . is . . . evil. . . ."

131

* * *

As soon as the women of the village had been warned that he was about to return, a fire had been lit in Storm's firepit in the center of the floor. He placed Shoshana gently on a pallet of furs beside the fire that he used at night for sleeping.

He knelt beside her and slowly ran a hand along her lips, and then gently touched her cheek. "You are more beautiful than all the stars in the heaven," he whispered. "How can I be anything but good to you? Yet . . . you are here for a purpose other than what I would want you for. I must remember that."

"My chief, I have come to offer my medicine," White Moon said as he came into the lodge, wearing his artistically ornamented medicine shirt of buckskin. It was decorated with various designs symbolic of the sun, the moon, the stars, rainbows, and clouds.

Next to the chief, the medicine man was the most powerful and influential member of their band.

"Come," Storm said, nodding. "I shall sit on the other side of the fire as you care for Shoshana."

"Her name is Shoshana?" White Moon asked, sinking to his knees beside her.

"She is Shoshana of our Apache tribe, but not of our band," Storm said. "She was taken long ago by whites and raised as one of them. She has returned to her homeland to search out her true Apache heritage, but she had not planned to stay. It is my decision that she will."

"I heard you and Dancing Willow from my lodge," White Moon said as he burned sweet grass over Storm's lodge fire, then cleansed his hands in the smoke.

He leaned closer to Shoshana and placed his hands on her wound. "I have seen you and your sister disagree before, but this time your differences seem worse," White Moon said as he took from his bag some *hoddentin*, a powder made of the tule plant. He took only a pinch of it and sprinkled it across Shoshana's wound.

"Yes, like many a brother and sister, we do argue," Storm said, nodding. "Especially on this matter, my sister does not agree with her brother."

"All who know you, even your sister, know that you do not take any action without thinking it through thoroughly," White Moon said.

He took more of the same plant and others from his bag and mixed them with water in a small pot that he placed over the fire.

He found this plant often as it grew along creeks. It was used in every medicine he made. He could not make medicine without it. It was like a grass. It had no flowers, but a root like a small carrot, and it was the root that he used for his medicines.

Now, after the mixture in the pot grew thick and warm, he began slowly drizzling it into Shoshana's mouth from a narrow wooden spoon.

At first she choked on the mixture, then began to swallow it freely.

White Moon fed it all to her slowly, then replaced his things in his bag and gazed at Storm.

"She will be well soon," he said. "And so will the feelings between yourself and your sister. Your love for one another is strong enough to sustain any hurts caused by loose-tongued words."

"Yes, I know," Storm said. "Thank you for your wisdom and medicine."

White Moon rose slowly to his feet, hung his bag across his left shoulder, then left the lodge.

Storm continued to watch Shoshana, hoping she would awaken soon. He would like to know more about her . . . about her Apache band . . . especially about her mother.

"Perhaps I can help you, pretty woman," he whispered. "But you must awaken. Please . . . awaken."

Chapter Fifteen

Let us hope the future
Will share with thee my sorrows,
And thou thy joys with me.
—Charles Jeffreys

George Whaley glared at the flames of a newly built fire where a rabbit cooked on a spit and coffee brewed in a cup in the hot coals. He cursed the one who had taken his daughter, placing him in this terrible position out in the middle of nowhere, where first one minute he was sitting comfortably beside a roaring campfire beneath the moonlight, then the next soaked to the bone by a sudden storm.

This storm had not only made things uncomfortable for everyone, but had delayed the search for Shoshana.

Everyone's clothes were finally dried, and after they shared a morning meal of cooked rabbit and hot tin cups of coffee, they would move onward.

Several complained that this was a waste of time, that they should turn back. There had been no sign of Shoshana anywhere.

But George would not give up yet. There was one thing that might change his mind, though. His "invisible" leg, the amputated part below his right knee, ached unmercifully as though it were still there.

During damp weather, George's pain worsened, and after his thorough soaking the night before, the pain was almost unbearable.

He would never understand this mysterious pain. There was nothing there to hurt. There was only a piece of wood where his flesh had once been.

But the pain was real enough. At this very moment, the ache felt like icy stabs going up his leg.

Because of this pain, George was beginning to doubt whether he could continue the search. If he was in such pain after just one night on the trail, how would he feel once they climbed to higher elevations, and then had the entire journey to make back down on their return to the fort?

"Damn bad," he whispered to himself.

Yes, his misery was real enough, and it was doubled because he missed Shoshana so much and was so concerned about her welfare. Anyone who would kill a young soldier and scalp him in such a way had no heart.

Had her abductor already killed Shoshana?

Then another thought came to him that made him almost vomit: Perhaps by now the man had raped her. If so, George would have no mercy for the culprit. He would make sure the man died slowly and painfully.

He looked over his shoulder and upward at the steep mountain pass they would soon be traveling. He was not sure if he could make it with the awkwardness he felt now while riding a horse. Having only one leg made it difficult to stay in the saddle.

More than once yesterday he had almost slid off his horse.

He stared into the fire once again. He hadn't been aware of how his age had caught up with him until he had come back to the land of the Apache.

Missouri was tame compared to Arizona.

He hated himself for being so daft as to think he was young enough to help find the damnable scalp hunter. He must be crazy to have brought Shoshana back to her roots. And he never should have allowed her to leave the safety of the fort.

Oh, Lord, he thought wearily to himself, *who has taken her?*

He wondered if it might be an Apache. If so, would she be safe with her own people?

Or was it the scalp hunter? He wasn't sure which

would be better. The Apache or Mountain Jack.

With such thoughts racing inside his head, George decided he must find the strength to climb the mountain. Shoshana came first. If he had to, he would die trying to find and save her.

With his mind made up, George rose and went to sit beside Colonel Hawkins.

"I think we should focus on finding Chief Storm's stronghold," George said, bringing the colonel's eyes quickly to him. "There is a strong possibility that he has her . . . don't you think?"

"I certainly do not think that Chief Storm has anything to do with this," Colonel Hawkins said flatly. He accepted his second cup of coffee from a young lieutenant, nodding a silent thanks to him. He took a sip, then glared into George's eyes. "And I will not search for his stronghold. I am proud to have such a peaceful relationship with the young chief. I don't want to stir up problems. Must I remind you, George, that my fort is not fortified against attacks?"

"Yes, I realize that," George grumbled. "And I think the army was insane to build such a fort in Indian country. Not all the Apache practice peace. Most don't know the meaning of the word."

"Well, George, I can definitely say that we don't have anything to fear from Chief Storm," the colonel said, nodding. "Most of the other Apache are on reservations now, and harmless. Those who are not, are walking a straight line, for they know that one wrong move on their part will make them lose their freedom."

George pushed himself up from the ground.

He placed his hands on his hips and glared down at the colonel. "My daughter has been abducted, and you won't even listen to reason!" he spat out.

He leaned down closer to the colonel's face. "I see where this is coming from," he growled out. "Your reluctance to go up against the young Apache chief proves only one thing to me. You're scared. You are damn scared. How can such a young chief put fear in the heart of a powerful colonel? It's true that most Apache are living on reservations. You're scared of Chief Storm, or he'd have joined the others long ago and you know it."

Colonel Hawkins moved slowly to his feet. He leaned his face into George's.

"Get hold of yourself, George. If you want any more cooperation from me and my men, get . . . past . . . this."

George sighed and, leaning heavily on his cane, limped away from Colonel Hawkins. He knew now that he had no choice but to do as the colonel said. George was only one man, and his damn "invisible" leg was like a huge, throbbing boil.

"It's all in your imagination," the doctor had told George over and over again.

He had also told George that it was his guilt over

killing so many men, women, and children that made him feel a pain that was not possible.

Suddenly George turned and went back to the colonel. "Let's get off our asses and get going before I have to admit that I don't have the strength to go on," he said dryly. "Once I give in to my pain, that'll be the end of me. Come on. Let's get going. Now. Not later."

"Are you certain this is what you want to do?" Colonel Hawkins asked, his eyes searching George's. "You aren't looking so good. You are so pale."

"Like I said, let's move on," George said, turning away. He did not want Colonel Hawkins to see how weak he felt, how difficult it had become to breathe. He started violently when he heard a rustling in the nearby bushes.

His heart skipped a beat when he saw green eyes and heard a small hiss, then a crashing sound as the animal leapt away.

"We've just been visited by a panther," the colonel said as he came to stand beside George. "That might change your mind about going on."

George turned to the colonel. He glared at him. "Nothing, not even a panther, will stop me from finding my daughter," he said tightly. "Nothing."

"All right, then, we'd best get going now," Colonel Hawkins said. "I'd like to get as much space between us and that damn panther as possible."

George's heart thumped wildly inside his chest at

the thought of having come so close to such a deadly animal.

He shuddered at the thought of Shoshana not only being at the mercy of a madman scalp hunter and a renegade Apache, but also animals that might enjoy the taste of human flesh.

Chapter Sixteen

I believe love pure and true,
Is to the soul, a sweet immortal dew.
                    —Mary Ashley Townsend

The aroma of food and a feeling of warmth came to Shoshana as she slowly opened her eyes and found Storm sitting across the fire from her, his midnight-dark eyes gazing back at her.

"Did you sleep the night comfortably enough?" Storm asked as she drew a blanket around her shoulders, then sat up. "Does your head still pound?"

Shoshana reached a hand to her lump and was stunned to find that touching it no longer hurt, nor did it pound any longer.

She no longer had blurred vision. She could see Storm perfectly now.

She had heard about the magic that Apache medicine men could do, and it seemed that this handsome young chief's shaman had worked magic on her.

"I did sleep the night," she murmured. She lowered her hand from her brow. "And . . . and . . . like magic, my pain is gone."

"That is good," Storm said, leaning to slide a log into the fire. Sparks rose quickly from the flames that soon wrapped their fingers around the log. "It is good that you slept. It is good that you no longer feel pain."

"But the lump is still there," Shoshana said, again running her fingers over the injury.

"That, too, will be gone soon," Storm said.

Shoshana felt a certain tension between them. This man stirred delicious feelings within her that she had never known before.

The sensations seemed to begin down at the very tip of her toes and worked their way up her slender legs to that place at the juncture of her thighs that had never before felt the stirrings of desire.

When she'd first laid eyes upon Storm's face, it had been as though something began twining between them, like a vine wraps itself around an object, taking possession of it.

She felt this bond with the Apache chief even though she was not sure if he saw her in the same light. At times, though, when he let down his guard, he gazed at her with a soft look that seemed fueled by passion.

Breaking their intense eye contact, Shoshana spotted a black pot hanging on a tripod over the fire. She felt a gnawing at the pit of her stomach and knew it had nothing to do with her infatuation with Chief Storm.

She was hungry.

Since her accident, food had been the last thing on her mind. But now that her head no longer ached, and her stomach no longer felt queasy, she wanted to eat whatever was in that pot that smelled so tantalizingly rich and delicious.

Storm noticed how her gaze suddenly fell on the pot of food. He saw the sudden hunger in her eyes and was glad that she had regained her appetite.

He wanted to know her, truly know her, and now that she was well on the road to recovery, they could become better acquainted.

"Food was brought to my lodge while you slept," Storm said, reaching for two wooden bowls and spoons and placing them beside him. He ladled out stew into both bowls, then took one to Shoshana.

"It looks and smells so good," Shoshana said, allowing the blanket to fall away from her shoulders as she took the bowl from him with both hands.

She suddenly became aware of the clothing she now wore. While she had slept, someone had dressed her in a clean, soft doeskin gown. It had no decoration, but felt wonderful against her skin.

Storm reached for a spoon and placed it beside Shoshana, then moved back to his own pallet of blankets and furs and began eating. As he did so, he watched Shoshana dig into the food, almost ravenously.

He gazed at the gown that No Name had brought for her, and then at her hair. Both were in disarray.

But nothing could take away her loveliness.

The more he was with her, the more he wanted her as his woman, not his captive. He had finally found a woman who spoke to that corner of his heart that had been closed to the love of a woman. But how could he even think of taking her as his wife? Once she was aware of why he had been so eager to take her to his stronghold, she would hate him.

"You aren't eating," Shoshana said, pausing to look up questioning at Storm.

She saw that he was lost in thought; if his bowl tipped any more, it would spill the hot stew on his bare legs.

Today he wore only moccasins and a breechclout that bared his body to Shoshana, making her realize that he was more muscular and virile than any other man she had ever seen.

Both the moccasins and breechclout were made of dressed deerskin.

The breechclout was a strip of buckskin that passed between the legs around the loins and was adjusted so that the ends fell to just above the knees, both in front and behind.

The moccasins reached halfway up the thighs, the soles extending and curving up at the toes, terminating in a sort of a button the size of a half dollar. The tops were pushed down below the knees, and the folds looked as though they might be used as pockets for small articles the wearer might want to carry.

Today Storm didn't wear his hair in a braid. Instead, he wore it long and free to his waist with a beaded band of buckskin tightly bound about his head to hold his hair back from his face.

Her heart skipped a beat when she allowed her eyes to wander lower, where only the cloth of his breechclout covered that part of his anatomy that—

"I am not all that hungry," Storm said, shaken from his deep thoughts by her voice.

He realized that he had almost spilled the stew on himself, and felt embarrassed that she had caught him being so distracted.

If she knew what he'd been thinking, she wouldn't be sitting there so at ease.

Knowing how determined she was, he guessed that once she discovered why he had brought her to his stronghold, she would try to find a way to escape. He dreaded the moment when he must reveal the truth to her—that she was not the scalp hunter's captive, but instead the prisoner of a powerful Apache chief.

"The food was so good," Shoshana said, pushing the empty bowl aside. "It brought nourishment to my body, but now I need something else to bring back my full strength. I would like to take a walk to strengthen my legs. While doing this I can see your village and people."

She gazed down at herself again. Although the robe was wonderfully soft and comfortable, she had wrinkled it terribly as she slept. After everything she had been through, she longed to freshen up.

"Before I do anything else, Storm, I need a bath," she blurted out. "If you could point me to a place where I can bathe, and . . . and . . . even supply me with a clean dress, I would appreciate it."

"I would enjoy showing you my home and introducing you to my people," Storm said, rising. "I will fetch one of our older women, who will bring you a change of clothes," he said. "She will then take you to a pool of water where you can bathe in full privacy."

"Thank you," Shoshana said, smiling up at him. "You are so very, very kind. I hope one day I can find a way to repay you."

She was puzzled when her words made him look uneasy. That look made her wonder if there was a reason why she shouldn't be so eager to thank him.

Something seemed hidden behind those beautiful dark eyes.

But she had always been teased by her friends back in Missouri about her vivid imagination. They had said that she saw things nobody else saw. She had always believed that was true; she had inner vision that came of her Apache heritage.

As he walked out of the lodge, she shrugged off her momentary concern about his behavior.

"This is no time to begin doubting him," Shoshana said, rising and testing her ability to stand. She was glad when she discovered that her knees weren't wobbling and she didn't feel any lightheadedness.

Yes, she was on the road to full recovery!

And once she'd recovered, she would begin a serious search among these people for a woman who might have been brought here fifteen winters ago, a woman who could be her mother.

Suddenly the entrance flap was brushed aside and an elderly woman with snow-white hair and a bent back entered the lodge. She had a very lined face, and eyes that were sunken in their sockets. A beautiful dress was lying across her outstretched arms.

The woman did not speak. She only motioned with her head.

Shoshana realized what the woman wanted. She wanted Shoshana to take the dress, which she did. Before she could thank her, the woman had stepped outside the lodge again and just as quickly came back inside with moccasins and a towel.

Through all of this, Shoshana could not help staring at the elderly woman. She was startled to see something familiar in her features, especially the eyes.

Yet she was so old, it was hard to see beyond the wrinkles and the pursed, tight lips. Her mother would not be this old. No, this could not be her mother.

Shoshana turned her eyes quickly away and gazed down at the lovely dress that lay across her own arms. It was snow white with bits of bright metal or glass sewn onto it that shone and twinkled in the fire's glow.

The elderly woman nodded toward the door. Shoshana took that to mean that she wanted Shoshana to go with her.

Shoshana nodded and with the towel draped across one arm, the dress across the other, and carrying the lovely moccasins, she left the tepee in her bare feet and gown and followed the elderly, stooped woman to a beautiful pool of water some distance from the village. It was surrounded by lovely weeping-willow trees, whose fronds hung around the water like a huge blanket.

Shoshana wondered why the elderly woman couldn't speak. Was it a physical or an emotional injury that caused her muteness?

Again the woman nodded, this time toward the water, which Shoshana interpreted as a sign that this was where she was to take her bath.

She nodded and so began to disrobe as the woman turned her back to give Shoshana privacy.

When Shoshana stepped into the water, she sighed with pleasure. It totally relaxed her. She wanted to wash her hair but was afraid to get her wound wet, so she just concentrated on bathing the rest of herself.

After she was out of the water and dressed, she was shaken by a sudden, vivid memory of the day her world had changed forever: her mother gripping Shoshana's hand desperately as they ran toward the ravine for safety.

It was as though Shoshana was there now.

She could hear the gunfire and screams behind her.

She could feel the pounding of her heartbeat and her mother encouraging her, saying they would be safe soon, not to be afraid.

And then Shoshana gasped as she heard the sound of a closer volley of gunfire behind her. She still ran, hand in hand with her mother, then her mother dropped Shoshana's hand; looking behind her, Shoshana saw the blood on her mother's back as she fell to the ground.

Then Shoshana suddenly recalled her recent dreams, how her mother had been in the talons of a golden eagle.

Suddenly Shoshana was aware of something else. This was no dream.

It was happening now, at this very minute!

She gasped as she gazed heavenward and saw a golden eagle even now circling low overhead, its huge shadow falling over her.

Shoshana trembled as her eyes and the eagle's met and held.

In the eagle's golden eyes she saw the same look as she had seen in her dreams.

The eagle was flying away from her now, and as Shoshana followed its flight with her eyes, she saw how it stopped and circled above the old woman's head.

Shoshana gasped as again she recalled the dream. The eagle! Her mother!

She gazed with a thudding heart at the older woman, whose back was still turned to her. Could it be? Could her tragic life have aged her so much? Had it robbed her of her voice?

Yes, oh, yes, surely this was her mother. Why else would the eagle have come to her like this, in truth, instead of in a dream?

"Is your name Fawn? *Ina* . . . mother?" Shoshana asked, her voice trembling. "*Ina*, it is I, Shoshana. Do you hear me? It is I, your daughter!"

Her heart stood still as the old woman turned and their eyes met. In the woman's was the shine of tears.

Then her mother held her arms out for Shoshana and softly spoke her name.

"Shoshana . . . Shoshana . . ." Fawn said, tears streaming from her old eyes.

"It is you!" Shoshana cried. "And you *can* speak!"

"I have not talked since the day I lost you," Fawn cried. "This morning I saw you brought into the village but I did not ask who you were. I did not think it was my business."

"But I am your business, *Ina*," Shoshana murmured, tears rushing from her eyes. "I am your daughter."

Shoshana ran to her. She fell into her embrace. They clung and cried, and then Shoshana gazed heavenward and watched the eagle make a few more circles above them before flying away.

"Mother, I have had so many dreams," Shoshana murmured. "Dreams of you. Dreams of me and you being together. Dreams of the eagle . . . and . . . you . . ."

"It was fate that led you to me," Fawn said, wiping tears from her eyes. "I prayed so often to *Maheo*, Shoshana. Oh, so often. And I never gave up the hope of seeing you again. I knew that you did not die that day. I searched among the dead. You were not there."

"No, Mother, I am *here*," Shoshana murmured. "And it was not fate that led us to one another. It . . . it . . . was the eagle! It has brought us together again! Come and sit with me. Please tell me what happened after I was taken away that day. I . . . thought . . . you were dead."

Hand in hand, they walked to the pond and sat down beside it. They started talking, Fawn's words tumbling over each other as she poured out her story.

"I was shot by the white man's bullet, but it was not a mortal wound," Fawn said, reaching a quivering hand to Shoshana's face and slowly running it over her beautiful features. "After the pony soldiers left, I became conscious. I looked around and you were gone. My heart broken, but not my spirit, I managed to get to my feet. I . . . I . . . checked to see if anyone else was alive. I was the only one . . . apart from you . . . who survived that tragedy."

"And then where did you go?" Shoshana asked, not able to get enough of looking at her mother. She could look beyond the wrinkles and see her mother as she had been on that day they were separated.

Beautiful.

Entrancingly beautiful.

"I wandered alone, getting weaker each day as I lost more blood from my wound," Fawn said, her voice breaking. "And then one day a young brave found me. He brought me here, where I have made my home ever since."

"That young brave was Storm," Shoshana said, her voice breaking.

"Yes, it was Chief Storm," Fawn murmured. She reached for Shoshana and hugged her. "But my voice would not come to me. I could not speak. I could not tell him about your disappearance." She hung her head. "I did not want to think of what might have happened to you. I . . . I . . . made my home with Chief Storm and his people, but I never forgot you."

"Mother, Mother," Shoshana said, again embracing Fawn.

"You kept your Indian name although you lived with whites," Fawn said. "How can that be?"

"I was allowed to keep my name because the woman who raised me thought it pretty," Shoshana murmured. "Just as you were unable to speak, for many years I was unable to remember anything but my name. But when I did begin to remember, it became my goal to return to the home of my ancestors. I . . . I . . . had seen in my dreams that you were alive. I had to try to find you."

"I want to know everything about where you have been, and how life has treated you in the white world," Fawn said softly.

"I shall tell you everything," Shoshana murmured. She took her mother's bony hands and began the long tale that had brought her finally to this place with her beloved mother.

"*Ina*, I was treated like a princess," Shoshana murmured. "But, *Ina*, this princess has come home . . . home to *you*."

Chapter Seventeen

Last night, ah, yesternight,
Betwixt her lips and mine,
There fell thy shadow.

—Ernest Dowson

Storm knelt beside the bed of blankets and pelts upon which Shoshana had slept. He saw the distinct outline that she had left there before rising. In his mind's eye, he could still see her tempting body with its lovely, delicious curves.

His heart beat faster as he slowly reached a hand out to touch the imprint. Then, feeling foolish that he had let this woman affect him so much, he quickly drew his hand away.

But his heart would not stop its fierce beating. Nor would his mind wander elsewhere.

He had watched her sleep. He had hungered to kiss her lovely, full, voluptuous lips. He had even ached to kiss her closed eyelids.

He had successfully fought off those temptations. But now?

He could not help himself. He reached his hand again to the bed and slowly ran it across the imprint, somehow feeling as though he were touching her.

"No!" he said aloud, jerking his hand away. He knew that what he was doing was foolish, yet he had feelings for Shoshana that he could not ignore.

But he also knew that succumbing to temptations like this would cause his people to lose faith in the strength they had always seen in their leader . . . their *chief*.

His jaw tight, his hands doubled into fists at his sides, he rose quickly from the blankets, and then kicked at them as frustration got the best of him.

He gazed toward the closed entrance flap. It dawned on him that Shoshana and No Name had been gone too long. What if they had met with some danger?

Grabbing his rifle, he left the tepee at a run.

He ignored the people who stopped and stared as they saw him leave in such haste with a worried look on his face.

He ignored the young brave who always stood ready to bring him his steed. The boy scurried out of the way when Storm ran past him without even a nod of hello.

He ran on until he caught a glimpse of Shoshana through a break in the trees. To his astonishment, she and No Name were sitting beside the water, their hands clasped as they talked and smiled and even sometimes cried.

"What is this?" he whispered to himself. "What has happened?"

And No Name was talking! What had brought her voice back to her?

He moved stealthily onward, making sure that the women did not hear him. A little distance from the clearing he stopped to observe them.

He was truly puzzled by No Name's behavior. Since the day of her rescue, she had never spoken, not even enough to say her name.

What she was saying now warmed his heart, though. She was telling Shoshana that he, Chief Storm, was kind and considerate, that he and his young friends had been so brave that day when they found her wandering alone and thirsty and hungry. They had saved her, when it would have been so much easier to leave her to die beneath the hot rays of the afternoon sun.

Then his heart skipped a beat and his eyes widened when he heard No Name call Shoshana her daughter. He heard Shoshana address No Name as Fawn in the Apache tongue.

Then he gasped quietly when he saw Shoshana suddenly embrace No Name, whom he now knew as Fawn.

He was absolutely stunned. Somehow fate had reunited mother and daughter.

His heart was warmed by the sight, and it was at this moment, as he watched the heartfelt reunion and witnessed Shoshana's sweetness, that he knew he could no longer deny the deep loving feelings he had for her.

He wasn't sure what to do now—turn and leave them undisturbed with their sudden happiness, or . . .

When he stepped closer and his moccassined feet broke a twig in half, Shoshana turned and discovered him standing there.

He did not have time to say anything. Shoshana leapt to her feet and ran to fling herself into his arms.

"Thank you, oh, thank you," she cried as she clung to him. "Thank you, Storm, for allowing me to come to your stronghold." She stepped away and gazed at him with tears streaming from her eyes. "Storm, oh, Storm, remember how I said that my dreams had told me my mother was not dead?" she said, a sob catching in her throat. "Oh, Storm, my dreams were right." She held a hand out toward Fawn. "This is my mother. I am her daughter!"

Again she hugged him.

As she clung to him a moment longer, Storm

wrapped his arms around her. Her body felt so good against his, so *right*, and her eyes were so beautiful as she gazed into his, her voice so sweet, he was speechless for a moment.

Then he took her by the hand and led her back to her mother. He smiled at Fawn. "I heard you addressed as Fawn," he said gently. "It is good to know your true name at last, and even better to see you with your daughter."

Fawn rose shakily to her feet and smiled up at Storm. "For many moons I dreamed and prayed to *Maheo* that this moment could be possible," she said, her voice breaking with emotion. With tears shining in her eyes, she turned to Shoshana. "My dreams told me that I would see and hold my Shoshana again. Today those dreams became reality."

"I am glad to have had a part in this reunion of the heart," Storm said, stepping between Fawn and Shoshana, placing an arm around each of their waists. "It is a good day."

"It is a day I shall never forget," Fawn said, wiping tears from her eyes. "I knew that *Maheo* would not let me down. I knew that, somehow, this day had to happen. I . . . could . . . not die without first seeing and holding my daughter once again."

"*Ina*, my dreams kept me close to you always," Shoshana murmured as she gazed past Storm, her eyes holding her mother's. "You came to me, ah, so vividly. It was as though we were never parted."

They sat down and talked and talked as Storm enjoyed seeing the happiness in both women's eyes.

But then a disquieting thought intruded. He remembered his sister's premonition . . . her warning about a woman becoming involved with him and his people.

That woman had to be Shoshana! Should he still be wary?

Should he mistrust these feelings he had for her, and those she seemed to have for him?

And what of his plans for vengeance? If she asked to go back to her white world for any reason, and he refused to allow it, she would discover his ulterior motive for bringing her here. How would she feel about him then?

His only hope was that now that Shoshana would wish to remain in his stronghold now that she had found her mother. He knew Fawn would never want to leave the people she had grown to love.

He hoped that Shoshana would gladly live among his people, too. That would mean that he and she would be free to love one another; to eventually marry.

Ho, he did want a wife after all. But only if he could have Shoshana.

Chapter Eighteen

I love your eyes when the
lovelight lies lit with
a passionate fire.

—Ella Wheeler Wilcox

Still in a state of awe that she had found her
mother, Shoshana sat beside Fawn's bed of blankets
and pelts and watched her sleep.

It was only now that Shoshana realized her
mother was not well. She was frail. She was weak.

The excitement of having found her daughter
had drained her of what little strength she seemed
to have had.

After arriving at her tepee, Fawn had fallen
asleep almost immediately.

161

Sitting on beautifully dressed deer, bear, and beaver skins, Shoshana realized that her dream had come true almost exactly as she'd envisioned it.

Except for the most mystical part of the dream. No eagle with golden talons had brought her mother back to her. Yet an eagle *had* shown itself in the sky at the very moment of mother and daughter realizing they had found one another.

"It is a miracle, *Ina*," Shoshana whispered softly as she reached a hand to her sleeping mother's frail cheek and gently touched it. "Mother, Mother. How I have missed you." Tears welled up in her eyes. "Yes, it is a miracle," she said, her voice breaking. "A miracle created by Storm."

If he had not brought her to his stronghold, Shoshana would never have known the blessing of being with her mother again.

"Thank you, Storm," she whispered, seeing in her mind's eye his handsomeness, the gentle look in his midnight-dark eyes. "I love you. I did from the moment I first saw you. And I shall always love you."

"As I will you," Storm said from behind her, startling Shoshana so much she leapt to her feet.

She turned to him. "I . . . I . . . didn't hear you come in," she said, blushing as she remembered exactly what she had just said.

Ah, but he had heard; he knew now how she felt about him.

And had she heard right? Had he just confessed to loving her?

Could it be true? Did . . . he . . . love her?

"I wanted to come and see how your mother was faring after the excitement of finding her daughter," Storm said.

He gazed down at Fawn and saw how soundly, how peacefully, she slept. He could even see a slight smile on her lips.

The reason she had lived this long, despite her weakness and illness these past months, was there. Her daughter had come to her!

He turned back to Shoshana and took her hands. "*Nuest-chee-shee*, come with me," he said thickly. "Your *Ina* will be asleep for a while. Come to my lodge and sit with me beside my fire as you wait for her to awaken."

"Yes, I would love to," Shoshana murmured, the touch of his flesh against hers so warm, so wonderful.

She thought over what he had heard her confess, and again recalled how he had responded.

Had he really said he would always love her? Could any of this truly be happening?

She felt as though she were floating on clouds as, hand in hand, she walked with Storm from her mother's lodge to his. And once they were inside and out of the view of his people, it seemed almost magical to Shoshana how they were drawn into one another's arms.

163

When he brought his lips down to hers and gave her a soft, yet passionate kiss, everything within Shoshana melted. She was scarcely aware as he swept her fully into his arms and carried her to his bed of plush pelts and laid her there.

As he knelt down beside her, the look in his eyes awakening a need she had never known before, she reached her hands out for him.

Boldly she spoke what was in her heart.

"I need you," she murmured, her eyes searching his. "I . . . want . . . you."

She had never wanted a man before.

She had never met a man like him before.

She had never made love before.

Did he want her as much?

He swept his arms around her and drew her against his muscled chest. His powerful kiss was his response to her question.

As they kissed, they hurriedly undressed each other.

His heart throbbing, the heat in his loins intense, Storm spread himself over Shoshana.

As they continued to kiss, and to touch, and to feel the wonder of each other's bodies, Shoshana's head spun with a rapture she knew she would never be able to describe. She clung to him as for a moment his dark, stormy eyes gazed into hers. It was as though he still questioned whether this was what she truly wanted. He seemed to know that she was a virgin.

"Yes, yes," she murmured, without his actually saying anything. "I can hardly stand the waiting, Storm. Please, oh, please do make love to me."

"*With*, not to," he said huskily. "When we make love, it will be both of us who will enjoy it."

She smiled, nodded, then drew a ragged breath and closed her eyes when she felt the strength of his manhood against her thigh, and then at her private place where no man had ever been before.

She had heard tales of how it hurt the first time.

She was prepared, for she had also heard that after the hurt came exquisite pleasure.

"I shall be gentle," Storm whispered against her cheek, tamping down the raging hunger inside.

"I know you will," Shoshana said, reaching a hand to his cheek. "You could never be anything but."

Again he kissed her.

His hands slid down and reached around to her buttocks, where he splayed his fingers against her soft, copper skin.

In that way, holding her in place, he began filling her softly yielding folds with himself. Gradually, the heat within her blended with his.

And then when he reached that barrier inside her, he paused, gazed into her eyes, and leaned slightly away from her.

She smiled sweetly at him and nodded.

He returned the smile, then kissed her pain away as he thrust deep inside her.

Shoshana withstood the pain, for she knew what came next. And it was even more incredible than she had ever imagined. She gave herself up to the rapture.

The wondrous bliss that swept through her made her moan repeatedly against his lips. She felt his hands move upward now, then cup her breasts.

She sighed as his thumbs circled her nipples; his lips soon found their way there, his tongue replacing his fingers.

"It is all so wonderful . . ." Shoshana said, twining her fingers through his thick black hair. "Please . . . please . . ."

With each stroke came more heat for Storm. Again he kissed her lips, his arms sweeping around her to draw her body even more closely against his.

His mouth scorched hers, and they groaned together as he moved faster within her, his movements sure and quick.

Overcome by a feverish heat, Shoshana sighed and seemed to float above herself as his steely arms enfolded her even more tightly. Their bodies strained against each other.

And then he thrust more deeply within her, over and over again, and a euphoria filled her entire being.

It overwhelmed her as the pleasure spread through her. The quaking of his body against hers proved that he had found that same pleasure.

When they both lay quietly beside one another, with the fire's glow on their gleaming bodies, Shoshana thought of the miracles that had come into her life this day.

First she had found her true mother.

And now she had known true, passionate love!

"Is this real?" Shoshana asked, turning to gaze at Storm, not even feeling bashful that she lay there nude beside a man for the first time in her life.

"Yes, it is real," Storm said, turning toward her. He reached out to cup one of her breasts, his thumb slowly circling the nipple.

"I have had many dreams in my life about things that came to pass, but never could I have dreamed anything like this," Shoshana said, slowly running a hand down his flat stomach.

Daringly she touched the part of him that had given her pleasure, surprised that it was no longer as large as before.

Her eyes widened as she touched him there and found that part of him growing again, as though it had a life of its own.

"You are good at giving pleasure," Storm said, closing his eyes and gritting his teeth as he felt ecstasy approaching again.

"Do you want me to stop?" Shoshana asked, seeing how he was gritting his teeth as though he were in pain.

He reached down and touched her hand, then twined his fingers through hers and showed her how to give him the most pleasure.

"*To-dah*, which in our Apache tongue means 'no,'" he said huskily. "Continue, but know that soon you will see the seed that is the result of your pleasuring me."

She watched him, mystified that a man should be so different from a woman in this way. Then she sucked in a wild breath of wonder when his body shuddered and he spent himself in her hand.

He smiled at her, sat up, and reached for a buckskin cloth to clean her hand.

"You had best not do that again to me tonight, or I might not be able to walk from my lodge," he said, laughing throatily. "You will have drained me of my energy."

"I don't want to do that," she said as he laid the cloth aside. "But I do wish to talk awhile before returning to my mother's bedside."

She hung her head, then looked at him again. "Then I must return to the fort so that everyone will know that I am all right," she said softly.

She wondered why her words caused Storm to look wary, but brushed her curiosity aside when he sat up and fetched a soft pelt from his stack of many.

He placed it around her shoulders, and then took the end of the very same pelt and brought it around his own shoulders so that as they sat before the fire, their shoulders touched beneath the pelt.

"Tell me about *your* mother," Shoshana said, seeing a strange haunted look enter his eyes.

He turned and gazed into the fire and did not respond right away; then he looked at her again. "My mother was white," he said, drawing a soft gasp from Shoshana. "Yes, Shoshana, my mother was white. And she had such golden hair. I remember that when I touched it as a child, I thought it was made of silk. She was a golden-haired Apache princess after she was taken captive and fell in love with her captor, who was my father."

He gazed into the fire once again. "I have always longed to find my mother's hair so that I could give it back to her," he said, his voice breaking.

"Your mother was scalped?" Shoshana gasped, drawing his eyes back to her.

"Yes, scalped," Storm said thickly.

"I . . . am . . . so sorry," Shoshana gulped out, imagining renegades coming into his village, killing and scalping.

"You have lived the life of a white person, as my mother, who was white, lived the life of an Apache," Storm said, his voice drawn. "How do you feel about it?"

"I grow weary thinking about these things,"

Shoshana said, sighing. "Especially thinking about the man who allowed me to live that day instead of killing me like all the others. But there is one thing about him that you must know. He spent his lifetime trying to make me happy. I know now that it was surely to help ease the guilt in his heart over all the wrongs he had committed against innocent people."

"Is that man truly regretful of what he did?" Storm asked guardedly as he stood and dressed while Shoshana put on the lovely beaded dress that was made by her mother's own hands.

"He says he is," Shoshana murmured, running her fingers through her hair to remove the tangles from making love. "And, yes, I truly believe he is sorry," she murmured. "Don't you see, Storm? That is why he came here to Arizona to help find the scalp hunter who preys on the Apache."

"I, personally, do not believe that any man who killed as Colonel George Whaley killed could ever truly be sorry about it," Storm said. "He killed with too much ease, too much authority."

"How do you know so much about him?" Shoshana asked.

"How?" Storm repeated. "The man who brought death into your life also brought it into mine. He . . . killed . . . my parents."

"How do you know this?" she asked, her pulse racing. "You were so young. Surely you were not present when your parents were slain or you would not be alive."

"I arrived almost immediately after the massacre," Storm said thickly. "My *ahte*, my father, was alive long enough to tell me what happened, and the name he had heard that day—the name of the man who had murdered and scalped my mother."

"Lord," Shoshana gasped, remembering that only moments ago Storm had said that his mother's golden hair had been taken by the man who murdered her.

And he knew that this man was Colonel Whaley!

She stumbled to her feet. She stepped slowly away from Storm, then turned and ran from the tepee.

Storm followed and caught up with her. He grabbed her around the waist and turned her to face him. "Why did you run?" he demanded as his eyes searched hers.

"I'm not sure," she said, swallowing hard. "I just can't accept that George Whaley, the man who raised me with such love and tenderness, had a role in killing not only my people, but also yours . . . and that he could actually scalp someone." She lowered her eyes. "Oh, surely you are wrong," she gulped out.

He placed a gentle hand beneath her chin and raised it so that their eyes could meet. "*To-dah*, I am not wrong," he said, his voice drawn. "My father spoke the man's name to me. He told me that Colonel George Whaley was the one who took my mother's scalp. My father shot his last arrow into Colonel Whaley's leg. Had my father not sunk back to the ground as though dead, your father would have came back and killed my father, too. As it was, Father lived long enough to tell me the truth about the tragedy that day, and who was responsible."

"It's so horrible," Shoshana said, her heart sinking.

"And you still respect the man after knowing this?" Storm asked, his eyes again searching hers.

"I'm not sure if I ever truly did respect him after the truth was revealed to me in bits and pieces in my dreams," she said softly. "But the fact remains that I am alive because of him."

"Are you well enough to ride?" Storm asked, reaching a hand to her cheek. "I would like to take you somewhere tomorrow."

"Yes, I am well enough, and, yes, I would love to go with you," she murmured.

They embraced; and then he walked her back to her mother's tepee. "I shall see you tomorrow then?" he asked, framing her face between his hands.

"Yes, tomorrow," she said, then flung herself into his arms. "I do love you so. And . . . and you make me feel safer than I have ever felt before in my entire life." She gazed up at him. "You . . . you . . . make me whole," she murmured. "You make me feel Apache again!"

He smiled at her, gave her another kiss, then walked away from her as she disappeared inside her mother's lodge.

As she sat down beside the fire, she tried to come to terms with what she had just learned. Now that she knew so much more about George Whaley and the evil he had committed, she felt sick at having ever considered him her father.

Had she allowed herself to forget too easily through the years? Surely she never should have given that man her love and respect.

Tears filled her eyes as she gazed at her old, bent mother, who was not as old in years as she appeared in the flesh. Oh, how that terrible day had changed her.

A part of Shoshana now detested George Whaley more than she could have ever thought possible. How would she behave when they came together again after she left this stronghold?

Would he see that she could not help detesting the very ground he walked upon?

"The wooden leg," she whispered to herself.

An even more disturbing thought came to her. He had gotten that injured leg *after* he had taken her into his home. Even the act of saving an innocent child had not changed his mind about killing more Apache.

Suddenly she felt a loathing for George Whaley she had never known was possible. She was now

173

more determined than ever to return to the fort, for she had a few things to say to this man she now knew was a demon.

She hung her head and tears fell from her eyes as she realized how much she had allowed herself to forget. She knew that her mind had shut out the past because she was a child who needed love just as any child did. She had just accepted it from the wrong person.

Thank heavens Dorothea Whaley had also been there to love and nurture her as she was growing up.

"But you are gone now," she whispered as she wiped tears from her eyes. Her jaw firmed. "But your husband, Colonel George Whaley, is still alive and I have a score to settle."

Chapter Nineteen

Not as all other women are
Is she that to my soul is dear.
                    —James Russell Lowell

On his steed, his hands tightly wound around the reins as he traveled with the soldiers in single file up the small mountain pass, George could not stop worrying about what their Apache guide had said just before he headed back down the mountain, alone. The guide had warned everyone that they should return with him to the fort, not go farther into the mountain.

His eyes and voice frantic, he had said that all who traveled on this mountain today were in danger of being attacked by "ghost sickness." He'd explained that ghost sickness overwhelmed a person with extreme nervousness and fright. He said he had already been struck by it. That was why he was retreating.

He claimed that this ghost sickness was often brought on by the hooting of a nearby owl at night. The whole camp had been disturbed by an owl all night after the storm had passed. It had not ceased its call until daybreak.

George had awakened just in time to see the owl flutter away, higher up the mountain. It had been huge and white, its wingspan even larger than any eagle he had ever seen.

George had further questioned the guide about this ghost sickness. The guide had said that the Apache had an excessive dread of owls, and that if an owl hooted near one's camp, it was an omen of the most frightful import. The Apache believed the spirit of the dead entered into the owl and came back to warn or threaten them.

Not believing in such superstitious hogwash, George had ignored the guide—even when the man refused to travel onward.

"We must travel on foot until the pass widens again," said the soldier who had taken over the duties of the guide. "Let's head toward that growth of aspen trees over there. There seems to be a path worn in the grass that leads to those trees. We may just find something interesting."

They followed the path, leading their horses behind them, and when they came to the aspens and made their way through them, what they found on the other side made George's heart skip a beat. From this vantage point he could see a well-hidden, newly built cabin nestled on the floor of a canyon, with a cluster of trees on each end standing like sentinels, guarding whoever lived there.

"Surely it's the scalp hunter's cabin," George said, his heart pounding.

He struggled up into the saddle again and rode with the others until they reached the cabin and surrounded it.

"Come out with your hands in the air!" Colonel Hawkins shouted. "Don't try anything funny. You're surrounded."

"I don't think anyone is there," a soldier said as he sidled his steed close to George's. "I see no horse, and there isn't any smoke coming from the chimney."

George gazed at the chimney and saw that the soldier was right. There was no smoke.

He looked cautiously around the cabin and saw no horse. What he did see was a pen that had been built near the cabin; it was empty.

He was close enough to it to get the scent of animals and guessed that whoever lived in the cabin usually had some sort of animals locked in there. The gate, however, was open now.

"Let's go inside the cabin," George said, dismounting. "I think it's safe enough."

Well armed, George and the others crept to the door. George took it upon himself to open it, anxious to see if there might be any sign of Shoshana inside.

Squinting his eyes as he stepped into the dark room from the bright sunshine out doors, George could not make out anything at first. But as his eyes adjusted, what he saw made his stomach turn. There was blood in more than one place, and hanging from the rafters were several fresh scalps.

"Are you thinking what I'm thinking?" Colonel Hawkins asked as he stepped to George's side. "That we've found Mountain Jack's cabin?"

"Yes, I believe so, but we haven't found him, or my daughter," George said, sighing heavily. He began walking slowly around the room, limping as he leaned on his cane, his eyes not missing anything.

His heart seemed to stop dead inside his chest when he stepped on something that was very familiar to him.

"Lord . . ." he gasped, paling.

He knelt and grabbed up the red bandanna, the very one that he had given to Shoshana right before she left with Major Klein.

"What is it, George?" Colonel Hawkins asked as he came to his side. "What have you got there?"

George held it out for the colonel to see. "This is mine," he said thickly. "I gave it to Shoshana right before she left the fort."

He gulped hard as he brought the bandanna up to his nose; his daughter's scent was on it. He would recognize the smell of her soap anywhere. She and her mother had used it to wash their hair for years.

"There is no doubt whatsoever that Shoshana was here," he said, his eyes flashing angrily. "But . . . where . . . is she now?"

"Come and look at this," a soldier said, lifting a chain as George turned toward him. "This was used to imprison someone. I wonder if—"

"If it might have been Shoshana?" George said, completing the soldier's words.

He thrust the bandanna in his rear pants pocket and gazed at the chain as the soldier held it up for his inspection.

A cold stab of fear mixed with repulsion filled George's being. He looked quickly away from the chain. Seeing it and the bandanna gave him thoughts he did not want to think.

His Shoshana had been chained by this madman scalp hunter?

If so, where was she now?

He lowered his head so that the others wouldn't see the tears that came to his eyes at the thought of possibly losing her forever.

He suddenly remembered the very first day he had seen her, how sweet and tiny she was, how alone and frightened, after so many around her had died.

He thought of how she had clung to her mother,

crying over her. He had felt an instant love for the child that day, and even a strange sort of pity for those she had lost.

He had raised her with all the love he would have given his own daughter.

He had always regretted that he had been forced to leave on another attack against the Apache the very next day.

He had already decided to head back for Missouri, where no Indians could take Shoshana away from him. But he had had second thoughts about leaving for Missouri right away when he was told that he risked losing his status as colonel and being court-martialed if he did not ride that one last time with the military. Afterward, he was promised, he could be transferred to a quieter, more peaceful place.

"George?" The colonel's voice broke through George's thoughts.

"What do you want to do?" Colonel Hawkins asked. "I can see the dread in your eyes . . . the fear. I know what you're thinking."

"No, I don't believe you do," George said tightly.

"George, I think we should get back to the fort and send troops out immediately in all directions to try to find Mountain Jack before he goes into hiding again," Colonel Hawkins said. "I believe he's on his way to where he sells scalps."

"And what about Shoshana?" George asked, his voice drawn.

"Hopefully, the scalp hunter has spared her life," Colonel Hawkins mumbled.

George went pale and felt sick to his stomach at the various possible fates that might have befallen Shoshana. If Mountain Jack hadn't already taken her scalp, he might be planning to sell her as a slave.

"Damn him to hell," George gulped out, then rushed outside as fast as his wooden leg would take him. There he vomited, the thought of what his daughter might be enduring devastating him.

"George, we'll find her," Colonel Hawkins said as he handed George a cloth to wipe his mouth with. "Be brave, George. Come on. We've wasted enough time here."

George wiped his mouth clean, tossed the cloth into the brush, and then, with a tight jaw and angry fire in his eyes, mounted his steed.

When he found that damn scalp hunter, there would be no mercy showed him, especially if he had harmed Shoshana in any way.

George had not saved that small, helpless child so long ago only to lose her to such vermin as Mountain Jack and those who aligned themselves with him.

"You'll regret the day you left the military to take up scalp hunting," George growled between his clenched teeth.

Chapter Twenty

And this maiden, she lived
With no other thought
Than to love and be loved by me.
                        —Edgar Allan Poe

Shoshana was glad she felt up to riding again, her lump having faded to a slight yellowish discoloration on her brow.

She was especially happy to be riding with Storm, on their way to see something he had said he wanted to show her.

Just as they were ready to ride from his village, she noticed something that intrigued her. It was a huge pen of turkeys.

She glanced over at Storm. "I see that you raise turkeys to eat," she said, recalling the turkey dinners she had eaten every Christmas, no matter where George had been stationed.

She could even now smell the delicious aromas wafting from the kitchen as the cook prepared the special meal while Shoshana sat beside the tree, unwrapping gifts.

That seemed another lifetime now, but she was content to be who she had become. She had no wish to return to that other life.

"We do not eat turkeys," Storm said. "We use their feathers for many things. Did you know that *Chiricahua* was taken from the word *Chiquicaqui*, which means mountain of the wild turkeys?"

"No. There are so many things I do not know about my people," Shoshana said somberly. She gazed intently into his eyes as they rode onward. "I so want to know what I have missed learning. I've read as much as I could about our people, but that is not the same as living it."

"You are still young," Storm said gently. "You have time to learn all that you wish to learn."

"For a while, after Mountain Jack captured me, I doubted that I had even another day to live," she murmured. "It is a miracle that you came when you did and set me free." She smiled radiantly at him. "I know that I have thanked you already, but I want to do it again," she said softly. "Thank you, Storm. Thank you so much."

"I feel grateful, too. If I had not found you, I

would not know the wonder of these precious moments with you," Storm said.

He noticed that she gazed slowly around her, absorbed in the beauty he had grown to love when he first escaped to this place where no white man had yet come.

He gazed at it, too, as awed by its beauty as the first time he had seen it. From this high place the valley was visible spread out below, surrounded by a scallop of weathered crests. Peregrine falcons soared overhead, and lynx could be seen romping here and there, as well as otters as they came and went from the river.

Wolf howls pierced the air, reminding him of the pups that he and Shoshana had set free. He wondered if the sounds he heard today were made by those animals as they tasted freedom now instead of captivity?

He smiled when he thought of the wolf pup that he had saved. The young brave he had given it to loved animals more than anyone he had ever known. Storm had entrusted the pup to this child, who understood that in time the wolf would have to be released to the wild.

They rode onward down one mountain pass, then another, until they reached the valley where Storm had once made his home with his family.

"It is such a beautiful, serene place," Shoshana said as she, too, gazed at the valley where trees of all kinds grew tall and beautiful, and where the Piñaleno River meandered across the land, fed by melting snows from the mountain high above.

"Lovely, yes, in a way," Storm said tightly. "But ugly in another. Many deaths occurred here."

Shoshana heard the somberness of his voice and saw pain in his eyes. It had been a long journey down the mountain. She knew they had arrived where his village had once been, for he stopped and dismounted and now led his horse slowly across the land, his eyes studying the ground on which he walked.

Shoshana dismounted and walked beside him.

"This is where it happened," he said stiffly. "This is where my people died."

He stopped and knelt on the ground, running his hands through the grass. His stomach tightened when he felt rocks beneath the turf and recalled the day he and the others had placed the stones over the graves of their loved ones.

The stones were still there, the grass having made its way up between them.

"Here, beneath the ground and rocks, is where many are buried," he said, his voice catching. "There was no time to take them to our true burial grounds. Each was buried where he or she had fallen. The lodges of my people have been gone for some time now. All traces of what once was a thriving village are gone."

He stood and turned to Shoshana. "Those who

are buried here today had no chance to flee the pony soldiers," he said. "My *ina* and *ahte* are buried somewhere on this land, one next to the other. Mother died first, Father a short time later. I made certain they were together before I fled to the mountain heights."

He took Shoshana's hands in his. "It is my plan to soon take my people far, far away from all of this," he said. "I will take them to a land where they will be safe forever."

"Where will you go?" Shoshana asked, her eyes widening in wonder. "Your stronghold seems safe enough, and everyone seems to be so happy."

"No one is safe on land claimed by the United States Government," Storm said angrily. "Although the pony soldiers have not touched my people's home in the mountain, they will some day, because they own the mountain as they own all this land that once belonged solely to the red man."

He paused, looked around himself, then gazed at her again. "Where will I lead my people?" he said softly. "To Canada. We must leave before the arrival of the next cold winter."

"Canada . . ." Shoshana said, surprised that they were fleeing the United States altogether. Yet why not? America had not been good to the Apache. She had heard that Canada welcomed the red man with open arms.

"Come with me to Canada," Storm blurted out,

his eyes searching hers. "Remember that the man who claims you as his daughter is not your father. Remember that he was a leader of those who massacred your people."

"My feelings for George are a mixture of many emotions—gratitude for sparing my life, hatred for having had a role in the massacres, and pity that he has no understanding of the horrors he perpetrated in his past," Shoshana said, her voice breaking.

They walked onward slowly, hand in hand.

"After I realized that I was Apache, it was hard to live in the white world," she murmured. "Even before that, the white children saw my skin color. They knew I was an Indian. Many treated me as though I carried the plague!"

She stopped and gazed up into his eyes. "But I came through it all right, and I am even a better person for it," she said softly. "As for now? I must return to the fort one last time, and then I will never be a part of the white world again. I want to be with you. I want to be with Mother. I want to live as an Apache. We are already far from your stronghold and not all that far from the fort. It would be a good time for me to go there and do what must be done."

Storm took both of her hands in his. He frowned at her. "I cannot allow that," he said, his voice drawn. "Shoshana, I cannot allow you to return to the fort, especially to George Whaley."

"What?" Shoshana gasped, searching his eyes and

finding cold determination in them instead of the kindness she'd come to expect.

She yanked her hands free. "Did you say what I thought you said?" she asked. She took a slow step away from him. "Did you say you won't allow me to go to the fort?"

"I cannot allow it," he repeated, stepping toward her. "There are two reasons for my decision. The first is because I love you and I do not want to chance losing you by allowing you to return to George Whaley. The second reason is because I do not want George Whaley to know what has become of you. I want him to struggle, sweat, and hurt as he searches for his beloved daughter but never finds her. Just as our Apache people have been hurt through the years by inhumane treatment from the white-eyes, George Whaley in particular."

"You are serious about this, aren't you?" Shoshana asked, stunned to realize that he was. "You won't allow me to go there, will you?"

"If you stop and think about this, you will understand my reasoning," Storm said thickly. "I want George Whaley to feel empty inside when he realizes that he will never see you again. I have wanted vengeance for so long against that man for what he did to my people and so many other Apache. But dying is too easy for him. Living the rest of his life filled with regret and loneliness is what he deserves."

"I understand how you feel and how this need for

vengeance must have lain heavily on your heart through the years, but things are different now," Shoshana tried to reason. "You and I have met. We are in love. That is all that should matter."

"It does matter, but I still cannot allow you to go back to that fort," Storm said flatly.

"Because you are afraid they will not let me return to you?" Shoshana asked, trying to understand his reasoning.

"No, that is not my only reason," Storm said flatly. "I have already told you the whole reason. How can you not understand it?"

"How can you not understand how I feel when you tell me what I can and cannot do?" Shoshana said, her eyes searching his. "It isn't right, Storm. I never want to feel imprisoned by you. Never! I will not be anyone else's captive."

"You should not look at it that way," Storm said, sighing heavily.

"If you refuse to let me come and go as I please, I am no less a captive than when I was chained in Mountain Jack's cabin," Shoshana said. "If you love me, you will not do this to me. How can I love a man who would? I cannot." She swallowed hard. "Do you choose vengeance . . . over . . . me?"

He didn't respond quickly enough.

Shoshana turned and ran to her horse. Quickly mounting, she rode away at a hard gallop, tears blinding her as her heart broke.

Storm leapt on his own horse and rode after her, soon catching up with her.

"Yes, come and make sure you keep an eye on your captive!" she shouted, her heart aching over how things had suddenly changed between them.

He grabbed her horse's reins, stopped the animal, then forced it to turn alongside his own, back in the direction of the stronghold.

Shoshana felt drained of emotion. How could this be happening! She had thought she'd found a man she could love, but he had turned into someone she did not know at all!

How could he treat her like this?

They rode silently up the steep mountain pass, each tormented by the strain that had developed between them. They both feared it might never go away.

Shoshana drew rein abruptly as Storm, with an exclamation of dismay, stopped suddenly ahead of her. Lying on the ground a little distance away was his sister, Dancing Willow. She appeared to be unconscious.

Storm dismounted and ran to her. He lifted his sister's head onto his lap and tried to awaken her, but her eyes remained closed, and her breathing was strangely shallow.

Wanting to revive her, Storm lifted her into his arms and carried her to a stream. He bathed her face with water, yet still she did not awaken.

Dancing Willow smiled to herself. She was feigning unconsciousness in the hope that Shoshana would flee. Dancing Willow had sneaked up on Storm and Shoshana and had overheard what they were talking about. She knew how angry Shoshana was and that she would flee at her first opportunity.

Well, Dancing Willow had made a plan that would give Shoshana all the opportunity she needed. While Storm was seeing to his sister's welfare, her rival could ride away. Surely Dancing Willow's brother would see to his sister first and Shoshana second, giving Shoshana the chance to return to the fort. Dancing Willow wanted Shoshana to disappear from their lives forever.

Suddenly realizing that he had left Shoshana alone, Storm looked quickly over his shoulder. She had disappeared. While he was seeing to his sister, she had sneaked away. She was probably well on her way down the mountainside by now.

Then he gazed down at his sister. He was torn. His sister was apparently ill. Perhaps she had been thrown by her horse, which was nowhere to be seen.

But if he didn't go for Shoshana, she might become injured or lost before she arrived at the fort. Two evils might befall Shoshana before she reached the fort.

Mountain Jack!

The elusive panther!

"The panther," Storm whispered, looking quickly down at his sister. He couldn't leave his sister alone and unconscious, not with the panther on the prowl.

Storm had no choice but to let Shoshana go while he took Dancing Willow back to safety at their stronghold. He carried her to his horse, his heart bleeding at having surely lost Shoshana forever.

With his sister on his lap, he rode up the mountain. When he reached their stronghold, he carried Dancing Willow to the shaman's lodge.

Storm stood aside as White Moon performed a ritual over Dancing Willow. Finally her eyes slowly opened.

As her gaze met Storm's, he stepped back in dismay. He saw that he had been duped. The look in her eyes told him as much.

"Sister, you have shamed yourself in the eyes of not only your chieftain brother, but also our shaman," Storm said tightly as he glared into her eyes. "I know you well. I can see in your eyes what you have done, so do not even try to deny it."

He leaned down into her face. "Did you ever think that by allowing Shoshana to return to the fort, you have endangered our people? She might be angry enough at what I had planned for her to bring white-eyes to our stronghold," he hissed. "She is the only outsider who has been allowed to know where we make our home! I allowed it, sister, but only because it was my intent for her never to leave except with us when we departed for Canada land."

He didn't give his sister a chance to defend what she had done, or tell him she was sorry for her mistake. He ran from the tepee, leapt onto his horse, and rode away, down the mountain pass.

If he did not find Shoshana before she reached the fort, then he would have to ride into the fort and ask for her. He would risk everything now to have Shoshana.

He was wrong to have told her she was his captive. Those words might have turned her into his enemy.

Only time would tell. If she hated him now, *he* might be the one taken captive.

Chapter Twenty-one

Beauty is but vain doubtful gain,
A shining glass that fadeth suddenly.
                    —William Shakespeare

Worn out and weary, and afraid he would never see
Shoshana again, George sat slumped over in the
saddle as he and the soldiers rode back in the direction of Fort Chance.

His eyes rose quickly when a soldier shouted in
alarm. When George saw why, he felt sick inside.

A horse with an empty saddle and a bloody left
flank was limping from the shadows of the aspen
forest.

As the animal approached, it became obvious
how the wound had been inflicted. There was a
huge claw scratch, raw, red, and bloody on its flank.

194

"God almighty, I wonder whose horse it was," Colonel Hawkins said as he grabbed the reins. His gaze went to the blankets covering something behind the saddle.

"Mountain Jack's horse?" George gulped out. "God, it might be Mountain Jack's. If so, where . . . where . . . is Shoshana?"

Everyone circled around the horse as Colonel Hawkins began unwrapping the blankets. The colonel's face drained of color at what he saw. "Pelts— but, Lord, there are also many scalps here," he said. "This had to have been Mountain Jack's horse."

"Lord," George groaned, hanging his head.

"The wound on the horse seems to be the work of either a panther or a bear," Colonel Hawkins said as he examined the wound. "It must have happened when the animal attacked the rider. It surely killed its victim, then took the body to its den."

George swallowed hard as he tried to compose himself. "Is . . . there . . . a sign of another horse anywhere?" he asked, his eyes searching around him. He stared into the aspens. "If Mountain Jack had Shoshana with him, who is to say what might've happened to her?"

The colonel, along with the others, followed the trail of blood on the ground. It seemed the ambushed man had been dragged away by the animal, disappearing into the trees for a moment, then out again into open space.

Colonel Hawkins's eyes locked with George's. "I see no signs of anyone else having been here, George," he said tightly. "I have no idea what to think, except I imagine the scalp hunter has got his due. As for Shoshana? George, I . . . just . . . don't know."

"Send several soldiers to search further," George said, tears filling his eyes. "Maybe there is a chance. . . . There is one thing that gives me some hope."

"What's that?" Colonel Hawkins asked as four soldiers rode back into the aspens.

"Since there is no sign whatsoever of Shoshana being with the scalp hunter at the moment of the attack, just maybe she managed to escape his clutches earlier," George mumbled. "Perhaps she was found by someone else. Perhaps even now she is being held by the Apache chief."

He gave the colonel a hard stare. "I say turn around," he said thickly. "Our destination should be the stronghold, not the fort."

"George, you're not being rational about this," Colonel Hawkins said. He sidled his steed closer to George's. "Your grief is keeping you from thinking clearly about things."

"I'm as rational as you, and I say let's go and search for Chief Storm's stronghold and not stop until we find it," George growled out. "I say you've been too lenient on him. Why? Do you two have a secret pact, or what?"

"Listen to yourself," the colonel said, his face an angry red. "Pact? Do you truly think I'd do that? George, you're tired. I see it in your eyes. I hear it in your voice. You're drained. We must return to the fort for now. You can get some badly needed rest, and then we'll meet again and make plans. But as for now? We're headed for home. Those I've sent to investigate will be enough for now."

George felt a sudden tightening in his chest. He raised a hand and grabbed at his heart, his breathing coming suddenly in short, sharp rasps.

"George, are you all right?" the colonel asked, his eyes widening. "Is it your heart?"

"Seems so," George gasped out, pale, his eyes showing his fear. "I guess I have no choice but to return to the fort. But, by God, as soon as I'm rested up, I'll go myself to find the stronghold. To hell with you."

He inhaled a deep breath, the pain cutting like a knife in his chest as he snapped the reins against the horse's muscled body and rode away from the others.

Colonel Hawkins took off after him. As he pulled up on his right side, he saw a strange gray pallor on George's face, and noticed perspiration on his brow.

"George, stop! Slow down," he shouted. "You'll

not be worth anything to Shoshana dead. Think of Shoshana."

"You go to hell," George shouted back at him and rode away as fast as his wooden leg would allow.

The colonel refused to give up. He reached George's side again. "Okay, George," he shouted. "I give you my word that after we all rest for one night, we'll set out again and we will search for the stronghold. But I must warn you, if you think the travel we've done so far is backbreaking, what lies ahead is twice as bad." He gazed down at George's wooden leg, then up at his face. "I'm not sure you can make it up the steeper passes of the mountain."

George glared back at him. "For Shoshana, I'll do anything," he shouted. "Anything! I'll prove to you that even though I have only one good leg, I can still keep up with the best of your able-bodied men!"

Somewhere behind them the screech of a panther split the still air, causing all of the horses to shudder and whinny.

George looked over his shoulder in the direction of the panther's scream.

He went cold with fear as he wondered anew where Shoshana might be.

He gazed back at the horse that was being led behind one of the soldiers. George shuddered at the thought of what had happened to the man who rode that horse. "You bastard, you deserved this sort of death, but not my Shoshana," he whispered to himself.

He looked ahead again, away from the horse. "Not . . . my . . . Shoshana . . ."

Chapter Twenty-two

Come, on wings of joy we'll fly
To where my Bower hangs on high.
                              —William Blake

Shoshana's heart was pounding, but not so much
from fear of being alone as from the realization of
what leaving Storm meant. It meant losing not only
the only man she would ever love, but also her
mother!

It tore at her heart to think that she had just found
her mother and now had been forced to leave her.

Perhaps she had been wrong to flee from Storm.
With him she had finally found what she wanted
out of life, yet she just couldn't accept the fact that
Storm had forced something upon her that was
wrong.

She should be able to come and go as she pleased. No man should be able to hand out orders to a woman in such a way, especially to a woman he had confessed to loving.

"Captive!" she whispered, tears filling her eyes. It was just not right for any man to deny a woman her freedom, no matter where that freedom might take her.

Her thoughts went to George Whaley. She could understand why Storm was so adamant about achieving vengeance against Whaley.

She understood this need, for deep down she had always had the same need but had not, until now, admitted it to herself. She had grown up loving this man as a father. She had never been able to really accept the enormity of what he had done.

But now she felt the need to punish him herself. She was just not sure what form her revenge should take.

A sudden noise at her left caused Shoshana's horse to shy. She heard a rustling in the brush, and then the threatening scream of a panther.

"No! Not again!" Shoshana cried as she hung on to the reins while the horse reared and bolted.

The horse settled down somewhat, but seemed frozen now instead of running away to safety.

Shoshana got a glimpse of a panther through the thick brush, and then she saw something else.

There were three kittens with the panther. It

seemed the mother was standing protectively between Shoshana and the kittens, and she could just make out their den behind them.

Shoshana started to flick her reins in an attempt to get her horse to move, but it remained frozen on the rocky path, its head low.

"Come on, boy," Shoshana urged desperately.

And then Shoshana's heart skipped a beat when she heard something else. It was a horse approaching.

Just as she turned to see if it was Storm, he came up a few feet behind her, and the panther gave another loud scream.

Storm gazed at Shoshana, then at the panther, then yanked his rifle from the gunboot.

He was in luck. He had found not only the woman he loved, but also the deadly panther. He took aim.

"No!" Shoshana shouted. "There are three kittens there. Don't you see them?"

The panther was now pacing protectively back and forth before the kittens, its green eyes moving from Shoshana to Storm.

"Storm," Shoshana said. "This is a mother. She is only protecting her young."

Storm glanced over at Shoshana, so glad that he had found her, and found her safe. Then he looked at the panther again. It had not yet crouched to attack. It still paced, its eyes ever watching.

He had a strong feeling that this panther was not

the one doing the killing. He slowly lowered his rifle as the panther took one of the kittens in its mouth and bounded away, while the two others followed until all were out of sight.

Storm slid his rifle into his gunboot, then rode up to Shoshana.

His eyes took in her loveliness and the stubborn look in her dark eyes.

He understood now what he had done that had angered her; she had the right to be angry. He never should have given her any ultimatum, especially one that threatened the loss of freedom.

Yes, he had been wrong, and he would make it up to her. He knew now that he could not live without her.

"I was wrong," he blurted out. "*Nuest-chee-shee*, come. Come back with me to my village. You will not be there as a captive. You will be there as my future bride. Your mother—she was so happy to have found you again. I saw the happiness you felt at finding her. Come back with me, Shoshana. I . . . was . . . wrong."

"Storm, I want nothing more than to be with you and my mother," Shoshana murmured, her whole being eager to have his arms around her. "But I have something I must do. I will not ask you to *allow* me to do it. I *am* going to. I'm going to the fort."

"But why?" Storm asked.

"I will go to the fort and let George Whaley be-

203

lieve that I have come back to live with him. But the very next morning he will find me gone. He will know why I have left because I will leave him a note explaining that I no longer want anything to do with him," she murmured. "I would prefer to tell him to his face, but I know that would be too dangerous. If he knew what my plans were . . . to come back to you . . . he would probably put me behind bars. As it is, I shall wait until all are asleep at the fort and then leave."

She reached over and gently touched his face. "Storm, please come with me," she said softly. "Wait for me in the forest at the edge of the fort. I will leave the fort when it gets dark. I will come to you. We can return to your stronghold together. Then we can truly begin the rest of our lives."

"I still see danger in your plan," Storm said. "How will you know that everyone is asleep? And will there not be sentries posted to guard the fort through the night?"

"Yes, there are sentries, but as I have noticed many times since my arrival at Fort Chance, the sentries who are supposed to keep the fort safe almost always fall asleep on the job," Shoshana said, lowering her hand. "That is when I shall slip past them. But I won't be able to leave on my horse. That would make too much noise. I will come on foot to you in the forest."

She gave him a soft, sweet smile. "Don't you see?"

she said. "You and I will gain vengeance at the same time when George Whaley reads the note and knows that he has been duped, and duped by the daughter he adored."

"We must be far up the mountain when he awakens and finds you gone," Storm cautioned.

"Are you saying that you agree to my plan?" Shoshana asked, her eyes wide.

"*Ho*, I do," he said tightly. "But there are still many dangers in your plan. I have protected my people for many years in our stronghold. I have kept its location secret for so long. Should the pony soldiers track you and discover its location, I will be forced to hand over the chieftainship to someone more trustworthy than I. For in a sense, I will have betrayed my people's trust if the soldiers should find the stronghold because of what we do."

Shoshana's smile faded. She inhaled a nervous breath. "Knowing that, I'm not sure if I should go to the fort after all," she said, her voice drawn. "I don't want to be responsible for bringing trouble to your . . . our . . . people. Nor do I want the title of chief to be taken from you because of something I did."

"Something *we* did," he corrected. "For, my *ish-tia-nay*, we are going to follow your plan. I will escort you as close to the fort as it is safe to go. Then, as you suggested, I will wait in the forest for you. Shoshana, you must be cautious every moment that you are at the fort among *pindah-lickoyee*. Some might become suspicious of you. You do know the lack of trust the *pindah-lickoyee* have for Apache, and you, my *ish-tia-nay*, are a full-blood Apache."

"If you truly think that I should do this, I will," she murmured. "And I promise that I will be very careful. I would die before bringing harm to you or our people."

"Do not say such a thing," Storm said. He reached over and twined an arm around her waist and drew her closer to him. He gazed intently into her eyes. "My Shoshana, my Shoshana. How I love you. I was so afraid after you left that I would never see or hold you again. I came after you not because I still felt the need to hold you captive, but because I love you and could not live without you."

"Nor could I without you," Shoshana murmured.

Her insides melted when he leaned closer and kissed her.

He straightened up again and brought his hands back to his reins. "We have lingered too long here," he said tightly. "We are fortunate that that panther was not the one that haunts my mountain. Let us go now. And be watchful, my *ish-tia-nay*, be ever watchful. You know how quickly a panther can appear and attack."

Shoshana shuddered at the thought, for she also recalled the way Mountain Jack had appeared out of nowhere.

He and others like him were always out there, threatening havoc. Danger lurked everywhere, it seemed, in Arizona. Missouri had been so tame in comparison.

But Missouri was no longer her home. She was where she belonged. She was with Storm and her mother.

They set out toward the fort together, able to ride side by side now because the pass was not so narrow here.

"And how is your sister?" Shoshana asked, drawing Storm's eyes quickly to her. "Why was she unconscious? Had she fallen from her horse?"

"She was not ill at all," Storm said, his voice tight with anger. "It was all pretense. She had sneaked up near us when we were talking and heard what we said. She heard me call you my captive. She saw how it angered you. She pretended to be ill in order to give you a chance to escape. She knew that was what you wanted, and it was what she wanted, as well."

"It was all false?" Shoshana said, stunned to know that Storm's sister could hate her so much. "She did this in order to make certain I would no longer be a part of your life . . . or hers? Why, Storm?" she quickly added. "Why does she dislike me so much?"

"It is not dislike that caused her dishonesty, but instead . . . jealousy," Storm said, hating to admit such a thing about his sister. "She believes you mean too much to me. She knew that if I did hold you captive, you would eventually forget your anger toward me, as my white mother forgot her anger at my father, who also held her captive. She feared that like my white mother and my Apache father, we would marry. Dancing Willow has been the most important woman in my life since my mother's death. She enjoys doting on her younger brother."

"Why hasn't she married?" Shoshana asked softly. "If she had a man, she would not worry so much about you."

"She has never found a man who interested her enough to marry him," Storm said. "As a Seer, she enjoys a position of much respect among our people. I see such contentment in her eyes when she makes someone else happy. She is a good person. But in this one thing, she must change. She must accept that I have found the woman I wish to make my wife. And she will accept it. She will have no other choice. Soon she will understand, and there will be peace among we three."

Shoshana's eyes wavered, for she now recalled the coldness and resentment she'd seen in Dancing Willow's eyes. If Dancing Willow could go as far as to pretend to be ill in order to take Storm's attention from Shoshana, what else might she do?

"She will accept you," Storm said, smiling at Shoshana. "You will see. She is good at heart. She would never do anyone harm."

"Yet she pretended to be ill to gain something for herself," Shoshana said tightly.

Storm's smile faded, for he knew that Shoshana did have cause to be wary of Dancing Willow.

"Storm, you are suddenly quiet," Shoshana said. "What are you thinking?"

"That I love you so much," was all he would say. He could not voice his doubts about his own sister.

They rode off the mountain onto open prairie land that stretched to the trees fringing the Piñaleno River. The cottonwoods were beautiful. Beneath them grew bushes that produced many kinds and colors of wild berries.

They rode onward, and Shoshana sighed with pleasure when she saw a large field of wild sunflowers. She saw a number of fat wild turkeys eating the sunflower seeds, as well as many other birds swooping down to challenge them for their late-afternoon meal.

"It is all so beautiful," she murmured, yet deep inside she was beginning to dread the task that awaited her.

If she couldn't pull this off, she knew she might cause Storm's people a lot of grief.

Even if she *did* succeed, the same could be true. If George Whaley got angry enough, would he not demand that the cavalry search for her? Would they know to look for her in Storm's village?

That was one thing she certainly wouldn't reveal in her note to George . . . that she would be marrying a powerful Apache chief. It would be too dangerous.

No. He would never know where she had gone, or with whom.

Chapter Twenty-three

As I long for your love,
My heart stands still inside me.
—Love Songs of the New Kingdom

Shoshana arrived at the fort just before dusk. As she passed by the sentries, she saw that they hesitated to greet her even though they knew very well who she was. There was something odd in their eyes . . . in their behavior toward her.

Riding on past them, she got the same cold treatment from the soldiers coming and going from one adobe hut to another. She was puzzled by this reception. Surely George Whaley had told them that she was missing, and had probably even been searching for her.

In the sunset's orange glow, she rode onward,

211

stiffening when she wasn't greeted in any way by anyone.

Then it came to her in a flash why she was being shunned. She glanced down at what she wore. Yes, it was the way she was dressed. She was dressed in doe-skin. She was dressed as an Apache, not a white woman.

Proud that she was Indian, and was now finally dressed as one, she lifted her chin and rode on past the soldiers.

She stopped at her father's quarters. She dismounted and hurried inside, then paused and gazed slowly around. The room was strangely quiet. There were no lamps lit, even though darkness was quickly falling. There was no fire in the fireplace to ward off the chill that came with night.

"He's not here," Shoshana whispered to herself.

Then it came to her that surely he was with soldiers, out searching for her.

Perhaps it would be just as well to avoid seeing him again. With George gone, she would write the note that would conclude her relationship with the man she'd once called father. Tonight, after everyone at the fort was asleep, she would leave once and for all.

But first, she would go to the trunk in the storage room and take from it some mementos of her adoptive mother, for she had loved her with all her heart and still missed her so much.

If anyone was responsible for how Shoshana was today . . . a happy, well-centered person . . . it was Dorothea Whaley, not her husband.

Until George had retired from the military, Shoshana had rarely seen him. It was his wife who had given Shoshana her undivided attention, building within her the confidence that had been taken from her by the attack on her village.

It had been her adoptive mother whose arms had given comfort to Shoshana when nothing or no one else could.

"Yes, I want to take something of Mother's to keep with me always," she whispered.

She lit a kerosene lamp and started down the corridor that would take her to the room where the trunks and travel cases were stored.

As she started to walk past George Whaley's bedroom, the lamplight shone in, and she realized he wasn't gone after all. He was there on his bed, his back to her as he lay on his left side.

She tiptoed to the door and held the lamp out before her so as to get a better look at George. Her pulse raced at the thought of what she was going to do. She was going to awaken him and pretend she was happy to be reunited with him.

She would get his hopes up, only to dash them in the morning when he found her gone and discovered the note explaining why she was no longer there . . . and that he was nothing to her. Nothing!

She could even now envision his reaction. His eyes would grow wide with disbelief. He would clutch at his heart, a habit that he had started a year or so ago.

She wondered if knowing how much she detested him would cause George Whaley to have a heart attack.

That made her frown. She didn't want to be responsible for anyone's demise, not even a man who had the blood of so many Indians on his hands.

She held the lamp up higher and gazed more closely at George. An eerie feeling came over her when she noticed how still he lay. He was much, much too still. She didn't see his body moving at all, not even the rise and fall of his chest.

She leaned over so that she could see his eyes.

She gasped and took a quick step away from him when she realized that he was dead!

His eyes were open and directed straight ahead, locked in a death stare. The fingers of his right hand were clutched to his shirt above his heart. He had apparently died of a heart attack.

"It can't be," she whispered. "He's dead!"

Then she saw what his other hand held—the red bandanna he had given her to wear before she left the fort. It seemed an eternity ago, so much had happened in the intervening time.

She only now realized that she had left it in Mountain Jack's cabin. That meant George must have been there. He knew that she had been with Mountain Jack!

He had probably surmised that she was dead.

Tears came to her eyes, for even though she had wanted to hate George Whaley for who he had been in his younger years, she could not forget the good times they had known together.

He *had* loved her.

He had tried to give her the world to make up for what he had taken from her. She had never wanted for anything . . . except the knowledge of who her true people were.

Now that George Whaley was dead, neither she nor Storm was going to achieve vengeance. If George was dead, how could they? He would never know that she left him because she wanted to. He would never know that she was reunited with her true mother and people of her own tribe.

"Shoshana?"

A familiar voice drew her quickly around.

Colonel Hawkins stepped into the room. "Shoshana, I knocked on the door, but when you didn't come I became alarmed," he said. "I was told you had arrived at the fort. I had to come and tell you how glad I am that you are safe. We had all thought you were . . ." His gaze swept slowly over her. "The way you are dressed . . ." he began, a troubled note in his voice.

Then, noticing the way she was looking at

George, seeming not to even hear him, Colonel Hawkins glanced quickly at the other man.

When he leaned over and saw George's eyes and their transfixed stare, he gasped. "Lord, oh, Lord," he said. "He's dead."

"I found him that way," Shoshana said, setting the lamp on a table beside the bed. "I feel responsible. Had I not left . . ."

Colonel Hawkins went to her. He took her hands. "Do not blame yourself," he said softly. "From what I have noticed, your father has been having trouble with his heart. It was only a matter of time. Do not blame yourself for what was going to happen anyway."

Shoshana slid her hands free. She hurried from the room.

Carrying the lamp, Colonel Hawkins came after her. He followed her into her room and set the lamp on a table. "Shoshana, I'm so sorry," he said softly. "And don't you worry about a thing. I'll take care of all the arrangements. I imagine we should bury him in our small cemetery. And, Shoshana, he will get a full military funeral."

"I knew you would see to that," Shoshana said, recalling the many funerals she'd attended back in Missouri and at the other military forts. "Thank you."

"Is there anything I can do for you?" Colonel

Hawkins asked, his eyes filled with sympathy. "Are you going to be all right?"

"I'll be fine," Shoshana said, nodding.

"I'll send someone soon for the body," Colonel Hawkins said. "Then you get some rest. And do you want food? Are you hungry?"

"I'm fine," she said, swallowing hard, for she was taking this death much worse than she would have imagined.

"I'll tell the soldiers not to disturb you in any way," Colonel Hawkins said.

"Thank you," Shoshana murmured. "I appreciate all that you are doing for me."

"I wish I could do more," he said, then walked from the house, leaving Shoshana alone with her thoughts, and her guilt.

"What must I do?" she whispered to herself, pacing. She had not expected to feel so torn. Should she stay and attend the funeral?

But, no. Storm was waiting for her. And she truly didn't want to be a part of the funeral.

She walked to a window and gazed up at the sky. It was finally dark. And there wasn't any trace of a moon. Escaping would be easy, for that was what she had decided to do. She would leave this place as soon as she could.

She would leave a note, but not the one she had originally planned. She would explain to the colonel how she felt about things and that she needed time alone; she would ask him not to send anyone to look for her.

She would explain that she had her future mapped out, and beg him to respect her privacy.

But she wouldn't give any details. He would just have to accept that she was gone.

She hoped he wouldn't come looking for her. She doubted that he would. She was nothing to him. He might even be glad that she was gone.

Returning to her original task, Shoshana carried the lamp into the room where the trunks and bags were stored. After placing the lamp on the floor, she sat down before a distinctive-looking trunk. She knew it was the one that held Dorothea's things, but now she recognized it as similar to ones she'd seen in Apache lodges. It was made of rawhide. In the Apache trunks, ceremonial garments and other articles were stored when they were not in use. She suspected that George had stolen this from an Apache home before . . . before . . . burning it.

Slowly she lifted the lid. Everything inside was neatly organized. She saw some of her mother's pretty dresses and jewelry, a pile of her lovely lace hankies, a Bible, and other personal items.

The first thing she took from the trunk was a dress of her mother's which she decided to take. She would never forget how beautiful and petite her mother had been. The dress was made of a beautiful soft, silky gauze. It was an almost translucent material.

She also took a lovely embroidered hankie that had been her mother's, and a few other small, personal items.

When she saw a piece of maroon velvet folded neatly at the bottom, she raised her eyebrows curiously. The velvet was wrapped around something.

"What could it be?" Shoshana whispered, lifting the velvet piece onto her lap.

Slowly she unfolded a corner, then felt the blood rush from her face when she got her first glimpse of . . . of . . .

No!

Oh, surely it wasn't what she thought it was!

But after unfolding the velvet wrapping, she felt sick to her stomach to discover a scalp.

The hair was not an Indian's.

It was golden!

George Whaley had surely killed a white woman and taken her scalp. But why would he, unless . . . unless he found that woman living with Indians?

Then her heart seemed to drop to her toes. She recalled how Storm had described his mother as a golden-haired princess, so beautiful.

Could this be her scalp?

Shoshana was sickened by the thought that this man she had once loved had been vicious and heartless enough to take a white woman's scalp, and had even kept it as a sort of spoils of war . . . as a trophy!

Was that how he had seen Shoshana?

As a trophy of sorts?

Was that why he had taken her? Had his first intention been to take her back to the fort to show her off, and then . . . then . . . kill her?

Sobbing, she folded the hair back inside the velvet wrap. She took it with her and stood over George's dead body, which had yet to be removed. "Why?" she sobbed. "Why? How? How could you have killed and scalped a white woman? Why did you keep the scalp? Was it something you were proud of?"

The fact was that he *had* done this terrible deed. It was something she would never understand or be able to forget.

"Shoshana?"

Colonel Hawkins's voice drew her quickly around.

She glanced down at the velvet wrapping, panicking that the colonel might find her with it. What if he had seen it and knew that the wrapping held a scalp within its folds?

Colonel Hawkins came into the room with four other soldiers.

Her heart pounded as she awaited his reaction to what she was holding, but when he didn't seem a bit interested in it, she assumed that he had never been shown George Whaley's "prize."

She watched as George's body was removed; then when the colonel came to her and gave her a tender gaze, she smiled up at him, still holding the velvet wrapping in her arms.

"Thank you," she murmured. "Thank you for everything."

"I'll see you in the morning," the colonel said, turning to leave. He stopped as he noticed what she held. "I see that you've found something of your mother's to keep. That's good, Shoshana. That's good."

He placed a gentle hand on her shoulder. "I'll send word ahead that we need a stagecoach brought here for your return to Missouri," he said. "That is where you want to go, isn't it?"

She was taken aback by the question.

She had not thought ahead to what would be expected of her. "Yes," she quickly said. "Yes, I would like to be taken to Missouri. I have a lot of friends there."

"I knew you did," the colonel said. He placed a soft kiss on her cheek. "Try to get some rest, Shoshana. I'll see you tomorrow."

He started to leave, but again stopped and turned to gaze at her. "Shoshana, I think you'd like to know that many things point to Mountain Jack's death," he said. "We found his horse . . . and the scalps he was carrying with him. The horse was badly injured. We believe it was a panther attack. Apparently, Mountain Jack was dragged away by the panther."

"Lord," Shoshana gulped out.

"Just thought you'd like to know that he won't bother you ever again, or take any more scalps," he said. "You see, we know you were taken prisoner by the man. We found your bandanna there."

Shoshana gazed down at what she still held . . . the scalp . . . then looked quickly up at him again. "Yes, I was taken captive by that man. And . . . and . . . thank you for telling me that he is dead," she murmured.

"I have to ask, Shoshana," Colonel Hawkins said, an eyebrow lifting. "Did Mountain Jack harm you in any way?"

"No, he didn't harm me," she murmured.

"How did you get away?" Colonel Hawkins asked.

Shoshana was beginning to feel trapped. She was not a skilled liar. But neither would she want to tell of Storm's role in all of this.

"He was careless," she murmured. "After he left to deliver the scalps and pelts to the man who bought them from him, I was able to unlock the chain that held me prisoner."

"The dress?" Colonel Hawkins asked, gazing at it. "He gave it to you to wear?"

"I found it among his things," Shoshana said softly, her lies deepening. "My clothes were quite soiled. I was eager to exchange them for something cleaner."

"You were gone for so long," Colonel Hawkins said questioningly.

"I had trouble finding my way down the mountain," she said. "I was lucky I finally arrived here, out of harm's way."

"Well, there isn't anything to worry about now," Colonel Hawkins said. "You're safe. That's all that matters."

Shoshana smiled and nodded as she watched him leave.

Then she hurriedly gathered together her mementos and placed them, along with the velvet wrapping and its golden hair, in a small travel bag.

Then she sat on the couch in the living room before a fire that she had just lit and waited for everyone at the fort to retire for the night, and for the sentries to carelessly fall asleep.

Finally she was able to flee into the night. She hurried through the darkness, making sure no one saw her. She was glad when she reached the outer fringe of the aspen forest where Storm still waited for her.

She set the bag down on the ground and flung herself into his arms. "Oh, Storm, it's so awful," she cried, clinging.

"What is so awful?" he asked, holding her close. "Leaving him? Do you regret leaving him, after all?"

She stepped away from him. "No, it's not that," she murmured. She reached for the bag and opened it. Slowly she removed the velvet bundle. "No. *This* is what I find so awful," she said, her voice breaking.

She unfolded the velvet wrapping.

She watched Storm's reaction as the moon slid from behind the clouds, sending its bright light down onto the golden hair.

"Where . . . did . . . you get this?" he gasped out.

She explained about everything that had happened since her arrival back at the fort, about finding George Whaley dead, and then finding the scalp.

"This is my mother's hair," Storm said, tears filling his eyes. "I would know it anywhere."

"I'm sorry," Shoshana murmured. "I did not know the fiend I was living with until recently."

"And now he is dead," Storm said thickly.

"Yes, dead," Shoshana murmured.

"I must take this and place my mother's hair at our people's burial grounds," Storm said, placing the scalp within the velvet again, and folding the corners so that the scalp was hidden from his sight. "Although I no longer know exactly where her grave is, if I place the scalp among the graves of our people, her spirit will find it there and be able to rest again in total peace."

After Shoshana's belongings were secured at the side of Storm's horse, he came to her and wrapped his arms around her. He kissed her sweetly, then lifted her onto the saddle.

He mounted behind her and they rode off together, now as one, their shadows merging in the moonlight, their hearts beating like the same drum. The far-off singing of a coyote could be heard in high staccato notes.

Shoshana tried to think of some happier topic than these last hours.

She smiled as she thought of her and Storm's upcoming marriage.

She would wear her adopted mother's favorite dress. Dorothea Whaley had been all sweetness and loveliness.

Although Shoshana wanted to look like an Apache for her wedding, she wanted to remember her mother Dorothea and her sweetness in her own special way . . . by wearing her dress.

In her mind, she knew she would never understand why George Whaley had kept the scalp, or even why he had taken a five-year-old child that day, and then kept her.

Had he been so proud of playing the role of a murdering cavalry leader that he could never totally let go of it?

In the end, his actions had condemned him in Shoshana's eyes forever and erased whatever good feelings she had ever felt for him. Her ambivalence was over.

Now she was at peace with herself about everything.

She had her future with Storm and her true mother to cherish.

They rode onward into the night. She leaned back against him, his arm holding her in place.

"I love you so much," she murmured. "You make me feel whole . . . you make me feel Apache!"

She knew she had told him that before, but she could not resist telling him again, for she was so glad to have found him.

Chapter Twenty-four

What is love? It is the morning and
the evening star.

—Sinclair Lewis

The deed done, his mother's beautiful hair now buried among his Apache ancestors, Storm and Shoshana rode on awhile, then made camp for the rest of the night.

He awakened early in the morning before Shoshana and found sweet, fat berries for their breakfast, which would be eaten with the pemmican he always carried in the parfleche bag that hung at the side of his steed.

Although Shoshana had told him Mountain Jack was no longer a threat, Storm left her again only long enough to gather dry wood to add to the glowing coals of their campfire.

Then he sat, watching her sleep. On her lovely face he saw peace and happiness, for she knew that soon they would become man and wife, never to part from one another again.

Also, she was looking forward to being with her mother. But Storm was concerned about that. He knew that Fawn had not been well for some time now and that her days on this earth were numbered.

He had prayed to *Maheo* that Shoshana would be given some more time with her before Fawn took her last breath.

He watched Shoshana stirring, her eyelashes fluttering as her eyes slowly opened. When she found him sitting there watching her, she reached a hand out to him.

"Good morning," she murmured, stifling a lazy yawn behind her other hand.

He took her hand, turned it so that he could kiss its palm, then knelt down over her and gathered her into his arms. "It is good to awaken with you at my side," he said huskily. "Never shall my blankets, or yours, be cold again. As soon as arrangements can be made, we will marry."

He brushed soft kisses along her brow. "Does that make you happy?" he whispered against her lips.

"Oh, so very much," Shoshana whispered back, her arms twining around his neck.

Although the night had been cool and windy, they had slept nude beneath their blankets. They had made love before falling into an exhausted sleep.

She hungered for the same this morning, more than she wished for anything else at this moment.

While he had still been asleep, she had awakened and crept from their blankets to wash herself so that she would be fresh for him when he awoke. Then, tired from her ordeal, she had fallen asleep again.

They had much to celebrate, although their happiness was tinged with some sadness. His sadness was for his mother, whose death had been recalled so vividly by the sight of her scalp. The pain of losing her had begun anew, as fresh as it had been those years ago when he was a boy, soon to walk in the moccasins of a man.

The prior evening his mother had filled his heart and soul as he held her golden hair before placing it in the ground.

Shoshana would never forget the gentleness with which Storm had laid the hair in the small grave he had dug for it.

She would never forget the words of love he spoke to his mother as he slowly filled the grave with dirt, saying that he regretted not being able to place her hair with her body in the ground, but that he knew her spirit dwelled there among the spirits of all the other Apache dead.

Tears sprang to Shoshana's eyes when she recalled how he had said that his mother and father could now walk hand in hand amid the stars with smiles on their faces, for the man who'd taken his mother's hair no longer had it in his possession.

Shoshana's thoughts of these things were stilled when Storm swept aside the blanket that covered her. Then he blanketed her with his body as his hands moved over her soft flesh and his lips came down on hers in a passionately hot kiss.

When he filled her with his heat, she lifted her legs and brought them around his hips, giving him easier access to her.

As they kissed and he held her in a torrid embrace, their bodies moved rhythmically together.

His hands slipped between them. As one hand found a breast, cupping it, the other swept downward and began caressing her where her heart seemed to be centered. She was throbbing almost in unison with her heartbeat.

As their bodies strained and rocked together, strange new sensations were born inside Shoshana, so sweet and wonderful, she realized now that this man she loved would always find new ways to show his love for her.

Delicious shivers of desire raced across her flesh as his lips moved downward and his tongue swept around one of her rose-tipped nipples. His hands now moved to her buttocks, splaying his fingers across her soft flesh and holding her more tightly against him as his manhood moved even more insistently within her.

Storm was in awe of this woman and what she could do to him. His passion for her was like a burning flame. He felt a tremor beginning deep within him and knew that the moment of rapture was near.

He wanted to be certain that she reached that same peak.

He paused and gazed deeply into her midnight-dark eyes. "I have never known such happiness as when I am with you," he said softly. He reached one hand to her face and slowly traced her features with his fingers. "My woman, it is magic that you have brought into my life. I love you, Shoshana. Oh, how I love you."

"Before you, I had no idea such love existed," Shoshana murmured back to him. "It *is* so magical, Storm. Every moment I am with you is better than any fantasy someone could think up. Oh, Storm, just to think that I fled from you—"

He placed a gentle finger against her lips to still her words. They were together now, and what he or she had done to get them to this point was not important. That they were together, and would be forever, was all that mattered.

"Hush, my woman, and just enjoy these precious moments, for soon we will be facing reality again and I will have difficult decisions to make for my people." He gave her a lingering kiss, his arms around her, anchoring her fiercely against him as again he thrust into her.

Shoshana felt a blaze of urgency building within her. It stole her breath away. She clung to him as she felt the passion building.

Then they both gasped as the world began to spin around them in silver flames, their bodies coming together as one as they again found that secret place of rapture that only those truly in love could ever know.

Breathing hard, Storm rolled away from her. He closed his eyes and waited for his heartbeat to slow. He was keenly aware of her lips moving over his body, causing the passion to begin anew within him.

But, knowing what lay before them—the journey up the narrow passes, which would be especially difficult with only one horse for the two of them—Storm opened his eyes and smiled at Shoshana. He placed his hands at her shoulders and gently eased her away from him.

"If you continue, my energies will be spent, and I need much strength to get us through the next hours as we travel up the mountain to our stronghold," Storm said huskily.

"'*Our* stronghold,'" Shoshana said, sitting up, her eyes filled with contentment. "Ah, how I love the sound of that. It is so good to know that I am a part of your life now and will be for always."

"Yes, for always," Storm said, sitting up and reaching for her. "One last kiss and then we must bathe quickly, eat, and be on our way."

"I wish we could stay here with the magic we have created beside this lovely stream," Shoshana said. Then, sighing, she rose from the blankets and gazed wonderingly at the slowly meandering stream. "I bathed there before you awakened. It was so cold!"

"You were there while I slept?" Storm said, his eyes widening. "I normally do not sleep that soundly."

"It is because so much has happened to tire you," Shoshana said, taking his hand as he rose to his feet. "Soon everything will be as you wish it to be."

"I would not say it will be as I wish it to be when it comes to moving my people to Canada, but I see it as the only way for my people to survive," he said sorrowfully. "The United States Government has done a lot to trick all men with red skins. The Apache no less than the others."

They waded into the stream, splashed water on each other's bodies, then hurriedly left the water and wrapped themselves in warm blankets as they sat down before the fire.

"I've heard how the government has tricked so many tribes," Shoshana said, drawing her blanket up to her chin. "How have the Apache been tricked, Storm?"

"In many ways, but I will tell you mainly of one incident," Storm said tightly. "My father was chosen to go into council with many white-eyes from Washington. The Apache tribe, as a whole, unanimously sent him to ask for peace. My father told the white-eyes that the Apache chiefs had chosen to offer all their mountains, waters, woods, and plains in exchange for peace. Those Americans said they saw that the Apache truly wanted peace. They sent my father back to our Apache people with assurances that the Americans wanted none of their woods, waters, or mountains, but that they desired peace, as well."

"And then they broke the promise," Shoshana said sadly.

"*Ho*, the *pindah-lickoyee* broke their promise," Storm said, nodding. "And so it is that most Apache are now on reservations. My band has been spared, but mainly because we live where no white man wants to live, and where no white man has ever found us. Were they to discover our stronghold, I believe it would be the end of our band of Apache. They would come and slaughter us."

"And this is why Canada looks so good to you," Shoshana said, nodding her thanks as he gave her a small wooden dish of berries and sliced pemmican.

"This is why we have no choice but to go there," Storm said. "And soon."

"I will be happy no matter where I am as long as I

am with you," Shoshana said, enjoying the food and reveling in these special moments with the man she loved.

They ate their fill, then dressed and broke camp and headed once again for the stronghold. As they rode upward on the pass, Shoshana saw flowers that she had not seen before.

"Those lilies are so beautiful," she murmured as she clung to Storm's waist, this time riding behind him on his steed.

"After a long winter, glacier lilies bring the first color back to the high country," Storm said, smiling at her over his shoulder. "Their bright yellow blossoms flourish in the bare earth and melting snow."

He gazed at the lovely flowers. "The cheerful little lilies follow that elegant black and white boundary up there, drinking thirstily from the steady drip of the vanishing snow," he said. "They chase the departing snow like a brilliant yellow fire, one wave after another, up and over the ridges. The Apache children of our stronghold, who gather flowers, are taught gratitude and respect for them. The girls are reminded that glacier lilies are the season's first food for the grizzlies."

"They look good enough to eat," Shoshana said, laughing softly and trying not to think about grizzlies. She still could not forget her fear of the panther that still prowled this mountain; the idea of bears was even more frightening.

"They *can* be eaten," Storm said, again smiling at her over his shoulder. "But more than a handful will give you a stomach ache. It is best to eat only a few, no matter how tempting their sweet crispness."

They rode onward, Shoshana taking in everything with delight. She felt as though she had entered paradise.

"Look up and to your right," Storm said, knowing how much she was enjoying the beauty of his mountain. "I call what you see 'sun fields,' because they are filled with the purple and gold fairy slipper. This wild orchid can also be found close to my stronghold. The girls are instructed to take only one of these flowers each year, though they can pick any other flower to their heart's content."

"I see so many varieties of flowers and plants; this place takes my breath away," Shoshana said as they rode steadily upward.

"Yes. There is the sweet-scented royal-blue lupine, fire-red paintbrush plant, the cerise fireweed, and then there are the oxeye daisies," he said.

Suddenly the lovely sweet mountain air was disturbed by a noise that brought Storm's eyes around to meet the questioning look in Shoshana's.

"You heard it too?" Shoshana asked, snuggling closer to Storm.

"Yes, it sounds like someone crying for help, but with a voice not much louder than a tiny bird's cry," Storm said, drawing rein.

"Then it wasn't my imagination," Shoshana said, her eyes searching around them for any signs of life.

"Let us sit here for a moment and listen," Storm said, his eyes darting from bush to bush, then into the thick aspen forest at his right side.

Shoshana's heart beat loudly within her breast as she listened. And then she heard it again, this time more clearly.

She and Storm exchanged quick glances. "Yes, I too heard it," he said.

He dismounted, grabbed his rifle from the gunboot, and lifted her from the horse.

After tethering its reins to a low tree limb, they moved stealthily, hand in hand, toward the spot where they had heard the second cry for help.

"We must be wary of the panther," Storm said, his rifle held tightly at his left side, while Shoshana was at his right.

"Yes, the panther," Shoshana said. "Storm, I'm so afraid!"

"I am with you, so do not fear anything," Storm reassured her. "I will protect you from all harm."

"But the panther could be stalking us even now, above us, watching our every move," Shoshana said.

She glanced up at the ledges of the mountain. She was relieved when she didn't see anything but lovely flowers and green growth.

Suddenly they heard the cry again, and this time

so close, they knew that it was a man . . . a man in much pain.

"Please . . . help . . . me," Mountain Jack pleaded as his eyes met Storm's.

Shoshana's knees almost buckled beneath her when she saw Mountain Jack. Not out of fear because he was alive after all, but out of horror at just how badly injured he was. His hair and whiskers were filled with dried blood.

She gulped and turned her eyes away. One of his arms had obviously been chewed on, while his bare chest revealed many deep, bloody claw marks.

His clothes were half torn off him, and what was still there was stained with blood.

But the worst of his injuries was to his legs. Shoshana did not want to even think of the pain he must be enduring with so many teeth wounds in his leg.

She did not see how he could still be alive after losing so much blood. But surely men as vile as Mountain Jack, without heart or conscience, did not die all that easily.

Storm gaped openly at Mountain Jack, deep revulsion filling his senses at the sight of his enemy. The knowledge that this man took scalps from any red man he could manage to corner made Storm look past his terrible injuries and see the killer he was.

"Please . . . please . . . get me away from here," Mountain Jack pleaded, tears streaming from his eyes. "The panther might return at any moment. It . . . it . . . is keeping me as though I am some sort of toy. It injured me enough to make it impossible for me to escape. Please, oh, please have mercy."

Storm's jaw tightened. He swung his rifle up and aimed it at Mountain Jack. "When did you ever show mercy to any of my people?" he growled out.

Shoshana scarcely breathed as she waited to see what Storm was going to do. She understood his need for vengeance.

She sought her own, for she would never forget sweet Major Klein, and how heartlessly the scalp hunter had taken his scalp. Nor would she ever forget how he had taken her hostage, chaining her up and threatening her life.

This man was pure evil.

"Please don't kill me," Mountain Jack begged, reaching a bloody hand out toward Storm. "I'm sorry for what I did. Chief Storm, you are a man of peace, a man of good heart. Look past your need of vengeance and show me mercy!"

Storm's eyes narrowed. His finger found the trigger of his rifle.

Chapter Twenty-five

Out of your whole life,
give but a moment.

—Robert Browning

The report of the rifle caused Shoshana to flinch and close her eyes.

She trembled as she turned her back to what must be a terrible sight.

Even though she detested and loathed Mountain Jack with every fiber of her being, and knew he deserved to die, she just wasn't used to seeing death up this close.

Young Major Klein's death was the first she had witnessed. This time, Mountain Jack deserved to die. Yet she did not want to look upon the face of death again so soon.

"Thank you, oh, Lord, thank you, Chief Storm . . ."

Stunned by the sound of that voice, Shoshana opened her eyes wide in wonder. The evil scalp hunter was still alive.

She spun around and gazed at Storm, who still held the smoking firearm, then looked down at Mountain Jack, who had a strange twisted smile of relief on his face.

"I decided that it was not what I wanted to do after all," Storm said, lowering the rifle to his side. "Why should I be the one to give this man a quick, merciful death, when he took so many lives in unmerciful ways? It is best that he be made to suffer the wounds the panther has inflicted on him. To kill him would have taken his pain away. It would have been too merciful . . . too quick."

"But you fired the rifle . . ." Shoshana said, gazing down at it, then looking slowly up at him again.

"I felt that it was best to fire it, in case the panther was close by. The sound will frighten it," Storm said, looking sternly down at the man groveling at his feet. "We need time to get this man away from here."

"Where will you take him?" Shoshana asked, gazing down at Mountain Jack.

"To Fort Chance," Storm said without hesitation.

"Fort Chance?" Shoshana gasped out. "Truly? You are going to Fort Chance?"

241

"*Ho*, and I want you to go with me," Storm said, reaching a gentle hand to her shoulder. "It is best that we hand over this hunted man to those who will know what to do with him. He is a wanted man, hunted by both my people and the white-eyes. I would rather his final fate be decided by whites, not the Apache. If I give the *pindah-lickoyee* this opportunity, I believe they will realize, once and for all, how I long to have a permanent peace with them."

"But you were going to achieve that by going to Canada," Shoshana murmured. "Are you considering not going there now? Do you think those who are in charge in Washington will truly be swayed by this act of friendship? Will it be enough to make them respect your people?"

"I will still take my people to Canada land, but I feel that handing over the scalp hunter to them will assure that our people's journey there will not be marred by possible attacks from the white eyes," he explained.

"But if you take him to the fort, I must go with you, and you know I left a note that might not have been taken kindly by the colonel. Also, they might follow you to your stronghold," Shoshana murmured. "I'm not sure about any of this, Storm."

He took her hands in his. "I feel that it is best to allow them to see the truth between you and me, that we will soon marry," he said softly. "If not, the colonel would always wonder where you were, and possibly decide to try to find you, even though you said in your note that you didn't want to be found."

"I still don't," Shoshana said, her voice full of emotion. "I want to just look forward, not backward. I'm afraid that if I return to the fort now, while George Whaley is still being prepared for burial, they will expect me to stay long enough for the funeral. How can I explain my feelings about him? Perhaps I should have shown them the scalp that I found in George Whaley's trunk. Then they would understand."

"It is not important that they understand anything but that you and I are going to be married and that you will live out the rest of your life as an Apache," Storm said firmly. "I truly believe you should go and let them see that you are all right and let them know what your future holds. Afterward, they can go on with their own lives, no longer concerned about you."

"You do believe I should?" Shoshana asked, her eyes searching his.

"It is best that we clear the way for many things today by taking this man to the fort," Storm said, glancing down at Mountain Jack, who regarded them with a look of horror.

"I'd rather you'd have shot me," Mountain Jack said, his voice breaking. "Shoot me now, Storm. Put me out of my misery. I can't bear to come face to face with Colonel Hawkins. That man hates me with a passion. He'll surely torture me slowly before he hangs me, for he *is* a hanging man. He hangs any man he hates and can get away with hanging."

"Your fate is what you have made for yourself," Storm said, his jaw tight. "You will go to the fort. We will leave you there. Whatever happens then is nothing to me, or Shoshana."

"Ma'am, tell him he's wrong," Mountain Jack begged. "Surely you're grateful to me for not hurting you. You know I could've."

"I know that if Storm had not saved me, I would probably be dead now," Shoshana said. "I have no pity for you. As Storm said, your fate is what you have made it."

Storm slid his rifle into the gunboot on his horse, then began gathering limbs that had fallen from the aspens. "We must lash together a travois and get out of this area before the panther returns," he said, already laying the limbs out. "Come and help me, Shoshana. I'll show you how. This is the only way we can get Mountain Jack to the fort."

They worked together until the travois was large enough to carry Mountain Jack. They soon had him tied onto it and covered with a blanket.

Shoshana clung to Storm's waist as they made their way down the mountainside, and then rode across a straight stretch of land.

This time Shoshana didn't admire the flowers, or anything else. Her mind was on what lay ahead, and what she would say to Colonel Hawkins when he saw her with Storm.

She gazed down at her dress. It was the dress her mother had given her, the doeskin beautifully embellished with pretty beads of all colors. She felt Apache today and knew that she looked it. Even the soft, beaded moccasins on her feet were like those her Apache sisters wore.

She reached a hand up to her hair and ran her fingers through its thickness. She wished she had taken time to braid her hair before going to the fort. In that way, she would have looked totally Apache.

Today she would show everyone who she truly was, and how she wished to live the rest of her life. She was proud of her Apache heritage, and could hardly wait to begin life as it would soon be with Storm.

As the fort came in sight, Shoshana's insides tightened. And when she realized they had been spied by the sentries, she felt a frisson of fear over what Storm had decided to do. After so many years of staying hidden in the mountains, avoiding these soldiers at all costs, he would now come face to face with them.

She hoped that his generous offer of handing over the scalp hunter to them would be taken in the way it was meant—as a friendly gesture that would prove he was a man of peace.

"Halt!" ordered one of the soldiers who had ridden out to meet them. He drew rein beside Storm, his hand on his holstered pistol as he gave Shoshana a surprised stare, then looked past her and looked in wonder at Mountain Jack.

"He is now yours," Storm said stiffly. "We found him. A panther had taken him to its den."

Another soldier rode up. His gaze met Shoshana's. "What are you doing with Chief Storm?" he asked, his gaze slowly raking over her, taking in her Indian attire.

"I would rather explain things to Colonel Hawkins," Shoshana said, even now seeing the colonel riding toward them.

When he drew rein a few feet away and gazed questioningly at Shoshana, then at Mountain Jack, and then at Storm, she felt her insides tightening. She went over what she had said in her note, how she had made it clear that she wanted nothing more to do with the white community, especially soldiers.

She knew that the words must have insulted the colonel, and felt that he looked at her now with antagonism.

"Shoshana, why are you with Chief Storm?" Colonel Hawkins blurted out.

"In my note I failed to tell you that Storm saved me after Mountain Jack took me hostage in his cabin," Shoshana said, her eyes meeting the colonel's. "Storm took me to his stronghold. There I was reunited with my true mother, who I believed dead ever since Colonel George Whaley rode into my village and spared no one . . . but . . . me. I want nothing more now than to live the rest of my life with my people, the Apache. I plan to marry Chief Storm soon."

"Marry?" Colonel Hawkins said, his eyes widening. "But, Shoshana, you have known nothing but how it is to live with white people. Can you truly live as an Apache?"

"As I said, I want nothing more than that for myself," she murmured.

"Storm took a chance by coming today to bring the scalp hunter to you," she said anxiously. "He knew that you could follow him and finally learn where his stronghold is. He trusted that you wouldn't."

"That trust is appreciated," Colonel Hawkins said, smiling at Storm. He glanced down at Mountain Jack, then looked at Storm again. "I appreciate this, Chief Storm. Know this: You will not be followed."

Then he gazed at Shoshana again. "Your father's . . . I mean George Whaley's . . . funeral is in a short time," he said thickly. "Would you want to stay long enough to attend?"

"Sir, in the past few days I have come to terms with George Whaley, who he was, and what he truly was to me. I have concluded that I was wrong ever to show any love for him," she murmured. "As a child, he took everything precious from me. Only because the terrible day was erased from my mind was I able to show this man any love. After I remembered what happened that day, and how much I lost because of him, my love turned to loathing."

"Then you go on your way, my dear," Colonel Hawkins said softly. He reached a hand out to Storm. "Chief Storm, thank you for what you did here today. We've been searching long and hard for this despicable man. I know you could've taken him to your stronghold and dealt with him in your own way. I'm glad you brought him here to meet his punishment."

"All I want is for my people to live in peace without being threatened by white-eyes," Storm replied. "Do I have your word that you will not follow me and Shoshana?"

"You have my word, and I will make certain none of the men under my command will go against that promise," he said. He smiled at Shoshana again. "My dear, you deserve happiness. I do hope you find it with Storm and his people."

He cleared his throat. "I am so glad that you have been reunited with your mother," he said. "Your true mother. Be happy, Shoshana. And know that I will never forget you."

"Thank you," she murmured.

Storm clasped the colonel's hand and shook it, nodded, then waited for the travois to be detached from his steed. When it was done, he did not bother to take even one more look at the scalp hunter. He wheeled his horse around and rode toward his mountain, with Shoshana clinging to him, her cheek on his muscled back.

Suddenly a voice rang out from behind them. "I'll get you for this, you damn Apache!" Mountain Jack screeched. "I'll . . . get . . . *you*, Shoshana!"

Shoshana's skin crawled at those words, but she knew that there was nothing more to fear from that man. She ignored his threat, as Storm ignored it.

"Now we can concentrate on our marriage and on the rest of our lives together. We can concentrate on making plans to go to Canada," she murmured. "All of the ugliness has been left behind us."

Storm gave her a smile over his shoulder, but could not help having doubts about what had been promised him. Too many white-eyes had spoken with a forked tongue to the Apache. How could he believe that the lies would stop just because he had handed over an evil man to these soldiers?

"Yes, behind us," he said, but only to help put Shoshana's mind at rest.

He glanced over his shoulder to be certain Colonel Hawkins had not sent soldiers to follow him and Shoshana.

He could not get home quickly enough.

Chapter Twenty-six

Yes! This is love,
the steadfast and the true,
the immortal glory
which hath never set.

—Charles Swain

It seemed hardly possible to Shoshana that this day was really happening. She was getting ready for her wedding!

Everything ugly was finally behind her.

"Daughter, you have a visitor outside," Fawn said as she stood back and admired Shoshana in the dress she had chosen to wear on her special day.

Although Fawn would have preferred that her daughter dress in the way all Apache women were attired on the day of their marriage, in a doeskin dress, she did understand why Shoshana wanted to wear the gossamer gown.

"Shoshana?"

Dancing Willow's voice came from outside Storm's tepee.

Fawn turned slowly as Shoshana, too, gazed toward the closed entrance flap.

"Yes?" Shoshana said, not taking even one step toward the entranceway.

She had stiffened at the sound of Storm's sister's voice, for how could she ever forget what Dancing Willow had done? She had pretended to be ill so that Storm would pay attention to her instead of keeping his mind on Shoshana. Dancing Willow had wanted Shoshana gone. She had not wanted her brother to bring her back to their stronghold.

Dancing Willow had wanted Shoshana out of their lives forever!

Now everything that Storm's sister did was silently questioned by Shoshana. She did not believe the Seer could change her feelings so quickly.

"I have brought you something special for your wedding," Dancing Willow said, still speaking through the closed entrance flap. "Shoshana, may I bring it inside the lodge for you? I want to prove how sorry I am for what I did. But I can only do this if you will allow it."

Shoshana and her mother gave each other questioning gazes; then Fawn reached a gentle hand to Shoshana's arm and nodded. "She is making an effort, my daughter," she murmured. "I think you should at least see what she has for you. You know that if you and Storm's sister could put your differences behind you, it would make Storm very happy. He loves you both."

"Yes, I know," Shoshana said, slowly running her hands down the softness of the dress that she had seen her adoptive mother wear only once. On that day, only a short time before she had died suddenly of a heart attack, she had been radiantly happy.

Shoshana had seen how beautiful and content Dorothea had been that day. She had been dancing with her husband at a ball in Saint Louis while an orchestra played lovely waltz music for the huge room of dancers.

"Then go, daughter, and hold aside the flap for Dancing Willow," Fawn softly encouraged, breaking through Shoshana's thoughts of her other mother. "Prove to her that you are a woman of good, generous heart."

Shoshana sighed, gazed into her mother's faded brown eyes again, then went to the entrance flap and held it aside. "Come in," she murmured. "It is so nice of you to care."

As Dancing Willow entered, Shoshana was very aware of the beautiful doeskin dress that Dancing

Willow held stretched across her arms. Shoshana had admired her mother's handiwork in the beads she had sewn onto her dresses. But this dress Dancing Willow held was even more breathtaking.

Despite its loveliness, Shoshana did not believe the dress was an overture of friendship.

Dancing Willow had openly resented Shoshana's choice of the dress she was going to be married in. She had glared openly at Shoshana as she said it would not be right for her to wear the dress of a white woman at an Apache wedding.

"I can tell that you think the dress is beautiful. I finished sewing it only this morning," Dancing Willow said guardedly. "Shoshana, I was making it for myself, but decided that by putting extra beads on it to make it even more beautiful, I could transform it into the perfect dress for my brother's woman to be married in."

"I thank you for your kindness and generous offer, Dancing Willow," Shoshana said, seeing a look of triumph in the woman's eyes. "But, as I have told you, I have already decided which dress to wear. As you see, I already have it on," Shoshana said, reaching toward the frail, lovely gauzy skirt of the dress and holding it out away from herself. "There is also embroidery work on this dress. It was done by my adoptive mother. Do you not think it is beautiful? I know how you admire embroidery work."

253

Suddenly Dancing Willow's eyes flared with anger. She flung the dress she had brought to the floor.

That violent action caused Fawn to gasp and blanch and back away from Dancing Willow.

Dancing Willow stepped up to Shoshana and spoke into her face. "You will shame my people if you wear a white woman's dress when you marry their chief," she hissed. "And the dress you will wed in is not just any dress. It is the dress of the wife of the very man who killed so many Apache ... who ..."

Dancing Willow swallowed hard, for she could not say what she was thinking. It was hard to speak of how that man had taken the scalp and life of her stepmother, and had also taken her own father's life.

"It is insulting," Dancing Willow said instead, her chin held high.

"To you, everything about me is insulting," Shoshana replied. "You would rather I had stayed angry at Storm when he said I was his captive. But our love is too strong for anything to keep us apart."

She took a step away from Dancing Willow. "I will wear my adoptive mother's dress today, and there is nothing you can say or do that will change my mind," she said tightly. "I know what George Whaley was guilty of doing to your people. But his wife had nothing to do with it. She had no role in any of the bad things her husband did. She had no control over him. She was a quiet woman, who bent to the will of her husband. I had a very happy life with this woman. She was the one who was responsible for my childhood happiness. She was precious to me. I am remembering her in this way."

Dancing Willow said nothing for a moment, then untied a small buckskin bag from the belt of her dress. "I am sorry I have made your day unpleasant," she said, her voice soft and filled with . . . false . . . apology. "Shoshana, I have brought you something else. At least please take it, even if you do not take my dress."

As she held the bag out, Shoshana hesitated to take it. She just couldn't feel comfortable about anything Dancing Willow did. It was not credible that she could be so hateful one minute, then sweet and understanding the next.

Yet there she was . . . offering a gift.

Shoshana wanted to refuse it, but she knew she must accept. If she made overtures of peace with Storm's sister, she knew it would make him happy.

For him only she held out her hand and accepted the small bag Dancing Willow placed on her palm. Shoshana saw a gleam in Dancing Willow's eyes that made her realize the Seer was up to no good.

"Please open it, Shoshana," Dancing Willow murmured. "It is my way of apologizing for causing you distress on your wedding day."

"You are so kind," Shoshana murmured, though she did not mean what she said at all. She was truly ill at ease about this bag. But she had no choice but to open it.

She slowly untied the leather strings that held the bag tightly closed.

"It is something you can wear on your wedding dress," Dancing Willow said as again Shoshana paused before fully opening the bag. "It will bring you good luck in your marriage. I truly do apologize for not having been friendly to you, Shoshana. This gift is to make up for my actions. I have just found it so hard to trust anyone who is white . . . or should I say . . . who lived with whites."

"But, Dancing Willow, how can you feel that way when your very own brother, your people's *chief*, is in part white?" Shoshana said, searching Dancing Willow's eyes.

"My brother's heart is all Apache," Dancing Willow said, her jaw tense. Then it relaxed again. She smiled at Shoshana. "Go ahead. See what I have brought for you to wear on your dress. It is lovely, Shoshana. Lovely!"

Shoshana gave her mother a questioning gaze.

Her mother nodded. With Fawn's encouragement, Shoshana smiled and opened the bag.

A huge black spider leapt out onto her dress. She was afraid to move or scream.

Fawn stood there, frozen in fear.

Storm stepped into the tepee just in time to see what was happening. He moved hurriedly around

Dancing Willow, who was standing there smiling and gloating.

"Do not be afraid," he said as he held his hand out to the spider and let it crawl onto his palm. "Do you see, Shoshana? It is not poisonous. It was meant to frighten, to discourage, not to kill."

He turned and glared at Dancing Willow. "You shame your brother . . . you shame yourself . . . when you do things like this, especially to the woman your brother is going to marry," he said dryly. "Dancing Willow, if you do anything else to the woman I love, you will no longer be my sister."

Dancing Willow paled. She gasped. Then she hurriedly apologized.

"I will never ever do anything like this again," she said, her voice breaking. "Truly, I will not."

Storm gave her a lingering gaze, then took the spider outside and placed it on the ground. When he went back inside, he drew Dancing Willow into his arms.

"I understand why you are doing these things," he said thickly. "Big sister, I promise never to put you far second in my life again. I am here for you always."

"I truly apologize for what I did," Dancing Willow said, clinging to Storm. "And thank you for forgiving me . . . for understanding that I have been feeling so neglected. I was wrong to behave so childishly. I never shall again."

She stepped away from Storm and went to

Shoshana. "I do apologize and I vow to you that I will never do anything against you again," she murmured. She slowly reached her hands for Shoshana's, hesitating, then took her hands in her own. "Let me prove it to you. Let me finish preparing you for your marriage. I will prepare your hair." She looked over at Storm. "May I?"

Seeing that his sister was seriously sorry about what she had done, and knowing that it would take something special for Shoshana to forgive her, Storm smiled at his sister. "Yes, it is good that you wish to prepare my woman's hair for her wedding," he said softly. "But only if Shoshana feels comfortable about you doing it." Perhaps this intimate ritual would break down the barrier of misunderstanding and mistrust between his sister and the woman he loved.

Dancing Willow gazed into Shoshana's eyes. "May I?" she murmured. "May I prepare your hair?"

Shoshana looked over at Storm. She knew how badly he wanted her and Dancing Willow to be friends. She turned to Dancing Willow. "Yes, please do," she murmured.

She glanced at her mother, who was smiling. She was being very generous to Dancing Willow, for Fawn had wanted the special task of preparing her daughter's hair for the wedding. But apparently she also saw the importance of Dancing Willow performing the task.

Storm smiled and left the women to make their preparations, as he was going to make his own. He had to ready his face for the first kiss from his bride. He would pluck his whiskers, one at a time, with tweezers made of bent strips of tin.

He would wash his hair and braid strips of white rabbit fur in one lone braid, worn to the side of his head.

He would dress in his best buckskin, and smile as he awaited the moment that he and Shoshana would become husband and wife.

"Do you know that our people's hairbrush is made from the tail of a porcupine attached to a decorative handle?" Dancing Willow said, nodding a thank-you to Fawn as she handed the brush to her.

"Yes, I am already familiar with that," Shoshana said, trying not to be so stiff as Dancing Willow fussed over her. She couldn't get the huge spider off her mind. How disgusting it was.

Shoshana hoped that she was doing the right thing now to trust Dancing Willow.

Dancing Willow brushed Shoshana's hair until it was glistening, then parted her hair with a slender, pointed stick.

"Fawn, I know you want to do the rest for your daughter," Dancing Willow said as she stepped aside and made room for Fawn. "Please go ahead. It will mean much not only to you, but also to your daughter."

"Thank you," Fawn said, stepping behind Shoshana to braid her hair. As she completed each braid, she tied the ends with strings of painted buckskin. The hair strings were works of art. They were wrapped with brightly colored porcupine quills and tipped with ball tassels of porcupine quills and the fluff of eagle feathers.

Shoshana looked quickly at the closed entrance flap when she heard drums and rattles being played outside as everyone gathered for the ceremony.

Tears came to her eyes to know that finally everything had come together for her and Storm. In a matter of moments she would be his wife!

It all seemed like a dream, one that she hoped never to awaken from because it was so magically wonderful.

She was glad that all of their concerns about the scalp hunter were behind them. Surely by now he had met his fate. She was certain Colonel Hawkins had given him a quick trial and gladly placed the noose around the evil man's neck.

Chapter Twenty-seven

Come live with me and be my love,
And we will all the pleasure prove!
—Christopher Marlowe

The marriage was not to be celebrated in the village, but beside a lovely waterfall that splashed into the river below.

Drums played in unison with rattles as everyone stood back and awaited Shoshana's arrival.

The smell of food filled the air, awaiting the moment when the ceremony was over and everyone would share a feast, dancing and singing.

A limited amount of planting was done at the stronghold, mainly of maize, pumpkins, squashes, and beans. They never ate creatures that lived in water.

Their staple food was mescal, the roots of which were collected in quantity and baked in a large hole dug in the ground.

The mescal roots had been deposited there late last night, covered with green leaves and grass, which were overlaid with earth. A steady fire had been kept burning on top for the whole night.

After the ceremony, the mescal would be unearthed, then pared and eaten with great zest. It had a sweetish taste, not unlike beets but not as tender.

For some occasions, an intoxicating beverage was made from the mescal. The roasted root was macerated and allowed to stand several days in water, where it fermented rapidly. The liquid was then boiled down until it produced a liquor.

But today no intoxicating drink was needed to make everyone heady and happy. All eyes were focused in the direction where Shoshana was expected to appear. The waterfall would make a lovely backdrop behind her.

Storm awaited her arrival as he stood with his sister on one side of him and his shaman on his other.

Fawn was too weak to stand any longer. Instead, she sat on plush pelts with others who were too old or weak to stand. She was at the front, so that she would have the best view of her daughter.

Shoshana was taking a husband today, and not just any husband. Storm was the ultimate prize for any woman.

As for Storm, he would find new responsibilities in marriage. He would take up the task of beginning a family. No longer would he while away the hours with the other bachelors in the warriors' lodge.

He would now have a wife to look after, and he would take the responsibility very seriously. His hunting would no longer be just for himself, but for his wife, and soon children, as well.

Suddenly the drums and rattles ceased playing and all eyes watched as Shoshana came into view, riding a fine gray horse, a gift from Storm to his bride.

When her shawl dropped from her shoulders, and rested around her waist, her tawny form was seen through the transparent silky gauze of the dress she so loved.

Her back straight, her braids falling far down her back, her face radiant with a smile, she gazed at Storm, who awaited her arrival.

Suddenly the shadow of a huge bird fell across her path, making her gasp and gaze up to find a golden eagle in the sky.

It was, it seemed, the same eagle that she had seen that day just prior to discovering her mother. Its golden eyes gazed down at her now as it continued to soar above her.

Her eyes met the eagle's momentarily. It seemed to her that the eagle was speaking to her through its eyes, and telling her that its deed was done. It had led her to her mother, and now it gave its blessing on her marriage.

"Thank you," she whispered up at the huge bird, then watched it soar away from her, soon disappearing high above in the clouds.

Feeling blessed now in so many ways, and realizing that this day had been her destiny, even when she was a tiny egg in her mother's womb, Shoshana gazed again at Storm and smiled, then rode onward to him.

When she reached him, she drew tight rein. He came to her and reached his arms up for her.

Overwhelmed by her passionate love for this man, Shoshana gave him a smile that sent a silent message of forever into his heart. She leaned into his arms and let him take her from the steed.

"Come, my woman," Storm said thickly as he placed her gently on her bare feet. "This is the moment we were born for, you and I."

"Yes, I know," she murmured, clasping his hand, and following him up to the shaman.

She glanced momentarily at Dancing Willow. She saw nothing threatening in her eyes, yet neither was there the friendship she would like to see.

Then she gazed over her shoulder at her mother and gave her a smile. The tears in her mother's old eyes were understandable. It seemed that her mother had made herself live until she knew that her daughter's future was mapped out for her . . . a future that included a man such as Chief Storm.

She gave her mother a nod to say that everything her mother had wanted for her was coming true, that she could relax now and enjoy these special moments that would stay within Shoshana's heart like a sweet melody for the rest of her life.

She then turned and gazed into White Moon's eyes as he took one of Storm's hands and then one of her own. Her heart pounded inside her chest as the shaman spoke the words that would make her and Storm husband and wife.

"*Maheo* has brought you two together, to know the love you feel for each other, and to give you a future together which will include many children," White Moon said, slowly nodding as his eyes moved back and forth between them. "*Maheo* blesses you today. So does this shaman bless you. Live in peace and happiness for the rest of your days in the knowledge that your marriage was written in the stars . . . was meant to be. From here on, you are husband and wife." He smiled at Storm. "Now do you have something to say to your bride?"

Storm smiled broadly, nodded, then took both of Shoshana's hands in his as he turned and faced her. "My wife, my lovely Shoshana, I promise that nevermore will you suffer any injustice or sadness," he vowed. "I am here to see that your life does not lack for happiness and blessings from above. As your husband, I promise you these things, Shoshana. I love you. I shall always love you."

Tears filled Shoshana's eyes . . . tears of happiness. She smiled at Storm. "My darling husband, I promise never to disappoint you, to keep your home filled with happiness and joy . . . and . . ." She paused, blushed, then finished what she had wanted to say. "And I also promise you many children, especially a son who will be born in your image. I will be at your side, Storm, to love you and to share my happiness with you. If you ever need more from me than these things, ask, and they, too, will be yours."

She slid her hands free of his and flung herself into his arms. "My Storm, my husband," she whispered against his lips before he gave her a tender kiss.

Then they parted and smiled at White Moon, and at the people who stood so quiet, watching and listening.

"Your chief now has a wife!" Storm shouted, taking one of Shoshana's hands and lifting it for everyone to see.

There were loud cheers, words of congratulations, and then the women broke into song as Storm swept Shoshana into his arms and took her to her steed, then mounted the horse a young brave brought to him.

He gave his people a broad smile, and Shoshana

smiled down at her mother. Then they rode away, side by side, until they arrived at a place Shoshana had been told would be readied for her and Storm on their wedding day.

She had been told only today that Storm had slipped away in the middle of the night to prepare a retreat for their honeymoon. He had erected a beautiful snowy white tepee. Its entrance flap was open. There were slow spirals of smoke rising from the smoke hole.

"Here we shall stay two days and two nights," Storm said, dismounting and then helping Shoshana from her steed.

He tied their reins together and tethered the horses to a low limb, then turned to Shoshana.

"Come and see where we will spend these private moments alone," he said, again sweeping her into his arms and carrying her to the tepee.

When he took her inside, she gasped in delight at what he had done. Colorful, beautifully scented wildflowers were strewn everywhere, over and beside plush pelts, and food was cooking in a copper pot over the fire, sending off aromas that made Shoshana's stomach growl.

"You are hungry?" Storm asked, his eyes gleaming into hers.

"Yes, but not for food," Shoshana said, her own eyes twinkling. "I believe you know what hungers need to be fed."

"I believe yours match my own," he said, gently sliding her down to her feet amid the flowers. He framed her face between his hands. "My wife. I can now call you my wife. And you can call me husband."

"My husband," Shoshana murmured, everything within her feeling deliciously warmed by his embrace and by the electricity that flowed between them.

"And I believe a husband should undress his bride, do you not think so?" Storm asked, already sliding the dress over her head.

When she was totally nude, he bent low and kissed the nipple of one breast, and then the other, then sucked a nipple between his lips and gently nibbled on it with his teeth as his hands wandered lower and found her wet and ready between her thighs.

"You need to be undressed, too," Shoshana murmured, though she hated to remove his beautifully beaded buckskin outfit, for she had never seen him as handsome as today.

"Then undress me," Storm said huskily, holding his arms out on each side.

Soon he was undressed as well.

He twined his arms around her waist and led her down to the plush pelts that he had prepared for them beside the fire. As he covered her with his body, flesh against flesh, his mouth went to hers with a hot and passionate kiss.

Shoshana twined her arms around Storm's neck and strained her body up against his. The need she felt within her was so strong, she could hardly bear to wait for him to thrust himself inside her. And when he did, she shuddered with the intensity of the feelings that swam through her.

His mouth seared hers, leaving her breathless and shaking. Their bodies moved together rhythmically.

Wondrous, sweet feelings overwhelmed Shoshana.

It was a drugged passion that she felt as his body moved more vigorously against hers. A husky groan of pleasure came from deep within him.

She emitted her own cry of passion and her senses began spinning as her hips strained upward, meeting his every thrust, surrendering herself to the pleasure that he was giving her.

Storm moaned throatily as the fire spread within him, his loins aching for fulfillment. He pressed endlessly deeper, then felt the wondrous drugged pleasure that he sought as her body answered his in a quiet explosion of their love.

Breathless, her head still spinning with the rapture of the moment, Shoshana clung to Storm as he lay atop her.

And then he rose, swept his arms around her, and carried her outside where the sun was lowering in the sky behind the mountain peak. Still carrying Shoshana, he took her to where she could see the waterfall more closely.

The setting sun blazed orange on the treetops, reflecting its last glow in the water as it splashed over the rocks. It made a rainbow of colors, then fell down below into the river.

"The sun wields the greatest power of all," Storm said, glancing up just in time to see the last of the sun as it crept behind the peaks above them. "Just think what life would be if Father Sun withheld his light from us . . . or how damaging would be the rays of the sun if he let his rays shine day and night without cessation."

They watched the moon replace the sun, then went inside the tepee and made love again, this time more slowly, more tenderly, as the stars twinkled through the smoke hole above them.

Suddenly all of Shoshana's past was just a memory that she could let go. She was happy to be making a new life now with Storm, one which she could look back on and smile.

He had given her the Apache life that had been denied her those long years ago. He had given himself to her as her husband!

"I shall always love you," she whispered against his lips as he paused before taking them both over the edge into paradise again.

"As I will you," he whispered back. The howl of a distant wolf suddenly split the night air outside the lodge.

And then . . . there was the screech of a panther.

Shoshana and Storm both heard it but pretended they hadn't. They clung to one another and continued making love.

Chapter Twenty-eight

Dreams of the summer night!
Tell her, her lover keeps watch!
  —Henry Wadsworth Longfellow

Several days had passed. Birds were settling in their nests for the night in the cottonwoods beside a slow, meandering stream.

A slow fire blazed in a camp that only a short while ago had been set up after a full day of capturing wild horses.

Storm's people had felt the need for more horses before they left for Canada. They needed more for the grueling journey, and in case there were no wild horses in Canada to keep replenishing their already powerful herd.

As Shoshana had watched, Storm had captured

many beautiful horses. There were mares and stallions of all colors and all sizes. They were all handsome and well muscled. There were buckskins, sorrels, pintos, bays, and chestnuts.

Storm had especially rounded up a snow-white stallion just for his wife . . . his Shoshana.

All the captured horses were now penned in a nearby canyon, contentedly grazing.

Although Shoshana was not happy about it, her sister-in-law had accompanied Shoshana and the warriors on the horse roundup. Storm had told her earlier that Dancing Willow loved the chase and would be riding with them as she always did.

It still hadn't made Shoshana happy, for she knew that Dancing Willow continued to resent her and probably always would. It was hard to be civil to the Seer knowing that every time the woman looked at her, she did so with quiet jealousy in the dark depths of her eyes.

At this very moment, Shoshana had to pretend to be pleasant to Dancing Willow as they bathed together in a deep pool of water fed by the shallower stream. They were far enough from the camp so that they had total privacy for their bath.

Had Shoshana not felt so grimy and dirty from the long day on her horse, and were she not anxious to be with Storm tonight amid their blankets far from the others, she would have just let herself stink instead of bathing with Dancing Willow alone.

273

She felt she needed to keep an eye on every move that Dancing Willow made. After the spider incident, how could she trust Storm's sister?

Although Dancing Willow had apologized, Shoshana knew deep in her heart that it was an apology laced with a lie!

"The water is not too cold, is it?" Dancing Willow asked as she splashed herself. "After a day on a horse, does it not feel good to have the water soothe your aches and pains?"

Shoshana wanted to strike back at Dancing Willow and say she was surprised that the Seer would admit to having aches and pains from riding. She would have expected Dancing Willow never to confess to anything that might make her look less strong in Shoshana's eyes.

But again Shoshana felt deceit in Dancing Willow's sudden friendliness. The other woman had hardly spoken to her all day.

Shoshana glanced where she had left her rifle at the edge of the pool. Storm had told her to take it with her because the panther was still a threat in the area.

But Shoshana felt she needed it more for protection from Dancing Willow. If the Seer wanted Shoshana done away with, was this not the perfect place and time, when they were totally alone?

"Shoshana, you do not hear me?" Dancing Willow said, drawing Shoshana around to gaze at her.

"You are so quiet. Why? Is it the panther that makes you so afraid? For you are afraid. I see it in your eyes. I sense it in everything about you."

"Yes, it's the panther," Shoshana said, not really lying. She did worry about that large, sleek cat.

"To escape your fear, think of something else," Dancing Willow said, running her fingers through her long black hair, then wringing water from it as she started walking toward shore. She gave Shoshana a look over her shoulder. "Come. Let us dress and get back to the camp, for I see that nothing I say takes the fear from your eyes."

Angry at herself for allowing this woman to see her fear, Shoshana left the water and was glad when she was dried and dressed again in full buckskin attire, which included leggings that her husband had given to her for the long day on horseback.

"The horses that were captured today are beautiful, are they not?" Dancing Willow said, slowly sneaking away from Shoshana while her sister-in-law's back was to her. Dancing Willow had seen a movement in the grass at the edge of the water.

She smiled devilishly as she realized what it was. A snake!

A snake had come at an opportune time for Dancing Willow. It was going to be very useful to her. She would not give up until she had intilled cold, stark fear within Shoshana's heart. She wanted

Shoshana to long for the sort of life she had known when living as a white woman.

"It was fun," Shoshana said, her back still to Dancing Willow as she braided her hair. "It was exciting to see several bands of wild horses and how they galloped off with such great speed at our approach. I especially enjoyed that one time the herd headed by that superb black stallion came directly toward us, not halting until it was thirty yards from us. It was so exciting how that black stallion threw up its head, snorted, and regarded us with intense curiosity, then made a quick turn and led its herd away."

Shoshana was suddenly aware of how quiet Dancing Willow had become. She started to turn to see what Dancing Willow was doing, but didn't get all the way around before she heard a screech from somewhere above her in the trees and knew that the panther was near. Her heart pounding, her knees weak, Shoshana slowly bent down and picked up her rifle.

Just as she turned to search for the panther, she saw a huge snake slithering toward her. At the same time she spotted the panther right above Dancing Willow on a low limb, ready to pounce.

"Lord," she gasped, not knowing what to do. Should she save herself from the snake, or Dancing Willow from the panther?

She prayed that the snake wasn't a poisonous

one, for she knew what she had to do. She had to save Dancing Willow from the horrible death awaiting her from the panther.

She trembled as she took steady aim and fired her rifle. At the same moment she heard another gun blast.

The snake leapt as a bullet pierced its body at the same time the panther fell from the tree, dead.

Storm came running to Shoshana.

He dropped his rifle and grabbed her in his arms, while glaring at his sister over Shoshana's shoulder. Dancing Willow stood there, trembling, with a very uneasy look of guilt in her eyes.

Dancing Willow stepped up to Shoshana just as Storm dropped his arms from around her. He turned to face his sister, his eyes accusing her, but he did not say anything just yet. His sister seemed to want to say something to Shoshana.

"Shoshana, I cannot believe that you chose to kill the panther instead . . . instead . . . of the snake," she said, her voice trembling. "Especially knowing that the snake could bite you and send its deadly venom into your bloodstream."

"I couldn't let the panther kill you," Shoshana murmured, glancing down at first the snake, and then the panther, which lay only a few feet away.

She was so glad that the young boy long ago had allowed her to use his father's rifle to practice her marksmanship. Yes, she was proud of the skill that had saved Storm's sister today.

She turned back to Dancing Willow. "I'm so glad I was able to stop the panther from harming you," she murmured.

"I will never forget this," Dancing Willow said. "I . . . I . . . am forever in your debt, and please, oh, please forgive me for what I did."

Shoshana's eyes widened in wonder. "Forgive you for what?" she asked, stunned that Dancing Willow suddenly lowered her eyes, seemingly finding it hard to answer Shoshana's question.

"I will tell you why my sister is filled with guilt," Storm said thickly. "Shoshana, I came to warn you both that the panther had been sighted. As I approached I saw my sister chasing the snake toward you. At the same time, I saw the panther. I could not believe that my sister could still hold such hate in her heart for you, Shoshana. It is good that Dancing Willow knew that the snake was not a deadly one . . . or I would disown my sister forever."

Stunned almost speechless, Shoshana gazed at Dancing Willow, whose head was still lowered in disgrace. Despite this show of humility Shoshana still believed she was insincere, for only moments ago hadn't Dancing Willow talked about the snake's venom? Although she knew that the snake was not deadly, she still wanted Shoshana to believe it was, while in the next breath, Dancing Willow pretended that she was sorry for what she had done.

Because Storm was so stunned over his sister's behavior, he had not noticed what his sister had said. But Shoshana would continue to be wary of Dancing Willow's every move, especially when they were alone.

It stunned Shoshana that Dancing Willow could be so vindictive, could hate her so much, when all that Shoshana had ever done was marry Dancing Willow's brother.

When Dancing Willow came to Shoshana and embraced her, Shoshana stiffened. She knew that Dancing Willow was embracing her for only one reason . . . to make her brother believe that she was genuinely remorseful for what she had done.

Dancing Willow then stepped away from Shoshana. "I am truly, truly sorry," she murmured. "I will never do anything against you again, Shoshana. I do thank you, ever so much, for saving my life." She lowered her eyes, then slowly raised them. "Can you forgive me?"

Shoshana looked over Dancing Willow's shoulder at Storm and saw the weariness in his eyes . . . the disappointment he felt in his sister. Storm had the weight of the world on his shoulders. They were strong, but they could hold only so much.

She hated doing it, but she twined her arms around Dancing Willow and gave her a gentle hug. "Yes, I forgive you," she murmured. "Let's put the past behind us and live for a wonderful tomorrow. Canada. Soon we will leave for Canada."

Storm came and embraced them both. He whispered "Thank you" in Shoshana's ear.

She smiled and nodded, then said, "Thank you for killing the snake."

Storm stepped away from them, a smile on his face where a frown had been only moments ago. "From here on I will expect only good between you two," he said, then took each by a hand and led them away from the dead panther and snake.

He gazed at the panther across his shoulder, then looked ahead, at the glow of the fire against the darkening sky. "I will send someone back to take the panther's skin. It belongs to the mother who lost her two children that day when the creature attacked and killed them."

Shoshana was so glad to hear Storm sound content that finally the panther's killing days were over.

She went with Storm to the campsite, where all who had heard the gunfire were standing and waiting to hear the reason for it. Apparently, they had not gone to see for themselves, because they knew the women were bathing and did not want to come up on them unclothed.

Storm explained what had happened, leaving out the part about what his sister had done.

Several men left to bring back the beautiful panther pelt, while the others gathered around the fire and sat and laughed and talked.

"It is time now to catch beaver for our meal,"

Storm said, rising with his rifle in hand. He smiled down at Shoshana. "*Nuest-chee-shee*. Come and join us. See how plentiful the beaver are in this area and how we shoot them in the moonlight. Their tails roasted in ashes make a delectable dish."

All of this was interesting, but Shoshana had something else on her mind. She had news she wanted to share with Storm tonight after the others went to their blankets for the night.

She had purposely waited until now, while they were beneath the stars after an exciting day, to tell him that she was with child!

A sudden realization made her look quickly at Dancing Willow, who sat on the opposite side of the fire from Shoshana and Storm. If Dancing Willow had caused Shoshana to miscarry, it would be Dancing Willow who would have to look over her shoulder for the rest of her life ... to make certain Shoshana wasn't there to avenge the loss of a child.

Shoshana felt that God and *Maheo* were looking out for her and had kept her child safe in its mother's womb.

Chapter Twenty-nine

His heart in me keeps him and me in one.
　　　　　　　　　—Sir Philip Sidney

Storm had made a small shelter from saplings and brush so that he and Shoshana could have privacy for the night. The red embers of the fire glowed in a small pit just outside the entrance of the shelter. They cast a faint light upon Shoshana's golden face, her lustrously dark eyes, and long black hair.

The moon was high in the sky. A wolf howled its mournful song somewhere in the distance.

Storm and Shoshana were some distance from the others, who slept even now around the safety of the campfire.

The horses that had been captured whinnied now

and then from where they were corralled in a nearby canyon.

"It's so wonderful to be here with you," Shoshana said, snuggling close to Storm inside the small dwelling. "The entire day was exciting. Thank you for including me. I do love horses so much."

She snuggled even closer to him. "Thank you especially for the white stallion that you captured just for me," she murmured as she sat up and gazed down at him. "Now I have two horses that were gifts from my husband. I shall take turns riding them both."

"My wife, what do I see in your eyes?" Storm asked, reaching to gently touch her cheek. "Why are you sitting instead of lying beside me? Do you not want to make love? Are you too tired from the long day on the horse?"

"No, I'm not tired. Why do I look at you like this?" she said, taking his hand from her cheek and lovingly holding it. "Because I love you so much. I am so happy that you are mine and are such a wonderful husband."

Storm slipped his hand free of hers and placed it at the hem of the robe she had donned.

Shoshana trembled and sucked in a wild breath when his hand reached the juncture of her thighs and he began stroking her there. She closed her eyes, sighed, then reached down and gently took his hand away.

"Not yet, my love. I have something even more magical than this moment to share with you," she murmured.

Storm sat up. He placed his hands at her waist and lifted her onto his lap so that she was facing him. "What could be better than this?" he asked huskily, the fire's glow reflecting in his gleaming eyes. "My wife, my lover, I cannot think of anything else at this moment that would please me more than holding you naked in my arms—"

She placed a gentle finger to his lips, silencing what he was about to say. She wanted what he was suggesting as much as he, but she could not hold inside herself any longer the news about being with child. She had missed her monthly flow by several days, and she was the sort who had always been regular.

She guessed that she must have gotten pregnant the very first time she and Storm had made love.

It thrilled her heart to know that she was carrying his child.

Now she was going to let him in on the secret. She had only waited this long because she wanted to be certain that she was indeed carrying his child. She did not want to tell him news that might, in the end, be wrong.

But now she was sure. There was no doubt!

"Storm, you are going to be a father," she blurted out.

She saw the reaction in his eyes. His expression was one of wondrous happiness. She had known he would feel that way about her news.

He had told her how he had sworn never to marry, that he had not wanted to feel the same hurt his father had known when he lost each of his wives.

But once he'd met Shoshana, that vow had been impossible to keep. And now, not only was he married, but he was also going to be a father.

She was so happy to be the reason for these changes in his life. She knew these new roles were fulfilling a part of him that he had too long denied himself.

"You . . . are . . . with child?" he said, his eyes searching hers. "We are going to have a baby? I am going to be a father?"

His thoughts went back to his own father and the closeness they had shared. Storm had always wanted to be his father's double in everything.

As a small child, he had often walked in his shadow, wanting even then to be as large, as powerful as he, and to be as loved by their Piñaleno River Band of Apache. He wanted now to be as loving a father as his had been.

"Yes, my love, I . . . we . . . are with child," Shoshana said.

She moved into his embrace. She treasured this precious moment, one that would remain in her heart forever.

"You are going to be such a wonderful father," she murmured. "Our child will adore you as much as I do."

He drew her lips to his and gave her a soft, gentle kiss. Then he drew away from her slightly and gazed down at her belly.

He placed a hand there, then smiled up at her. "I have often watched the women in our village as their bellies grew large," he said tenderly. "I always saw such radiance about those women, as though carrying a child gave them more grace, more—"

A noise at the back of their temporary lodge caused Storm's words to trail off.

Shoshana could feel him tense up as he looked quickly over his shoulder, then gazed with concern into Shoshana's eyes. "You heard it, too?" he asked, gently lifting her from his lap and placing her beside him.

"Yes, it sounded like someone . . . or . . . something moving around in the brush behind us," Shoshana said, fear clutching her heart. "Oh, Storm, what if I killed a panther other than the one that stalks humans? What if—"

They heard the sound of breaking twigs again, and knew that they definitely were no longer alone.

"Who goes there?" Storm asked, hoping it might be one of his warriors who had come to tell him something.

When there was no reply, Shoshana and Storm questioned each other with their eyes.

"Perhaps it was no more than a beaver, or something of the sort, that has now passed by," Shoshana murmured.

"*Ho*, perhaps . . ." Storm said, unconvinced.

He reached for his rifle. He crawled toward the entranceway, then stopped as all hell seemed to break loose. Something was breaking through the back of their makeshift lodge, the limbs cracking and breaking as they were forced apart.

"Oh, no, what if it is the panther?" Shoshana cried as Storm grabbed her by a hand and half dragged her from the small dwelling just as it collapsed.

Shoshana's heart skipped a beat and her insides recoiled with a fear never known to her before when she beheld Mountain Jack standing amid the debris. He held a shotgun leveled at them.

"Drop the rifle," Mountain Jack growled, standing shakily as he glared from Shoshana to Storm. "Shoshana, I gotcha again, and this time you won't get away from Mountain Jack."

Mountain Jack snickered as Storm carefully placed the rifle at his feet. "Kick the firearm away from you," he said, his eyes narrowing angrily. "I'm gonna enjoy sendin' you both to hell tonight. I'll show you how little mercy I'll pay you. You were wrong, Chief Storm, for not shooting me when you

287

had the chance. You saved my life, and in return I shall take yours."

Storm and Shoshana stood stiffly together.

Shoshana couldn't believe this was happening. She hadn't thought that Mountain Jack, with all of his injuries, could have gotten this far from the fort.

She felt sick inside as she gazed at the wounds that the panther had inflicted on him. They were still bloody and gory, especially those on his legs.

Tonight he wore buckskin pants that had been cut away up past his knees, surely because it hurt too much to have the garment rub against his terrible wounds.

One arm seemed to dangle from his shoulder where it had come close to being torn from the socket by the panther.

But he had enough movement left in it to help him hold the shotgun aimed at his two captives!

"How did you get away from the fort?" Shoshana blurted out. "How could you get this far? How did you know we were here?"

"Now, ain't you jest full of questions," Mountain Jack said. He laughed throatily. He glanced over at Storm. "And how about you? Why are you so quiet?"

Storm just glared at him, his mind working out how he could stop this man's madness once and for all.

He now knew how wrong it had been to hand this man over to the white people. It was obvious they did not know how to deal with such criminals as Mountain Jack.

Storm was waiting for just the right moment to lunge at the man, for it was obvious it would not take much to down him. Mountain Jack's wobbly, injured legs were barely holding him up.

"How did I get free?" Mountain Jack said, snickering low. "How did I get here? First let me say that I wasn't even looking for you. You were the furthest thing from my mind. I just wanted to get as far as I could from the fort."

He paused, licked his lips, then continued. "I ain't never seen such lazy soldiers as I witnessed at Fort Chance," he said. "And dumb. I guess they thought I was too injured to even think of escaping, much less succeed. They left me in the hands of the fort doctor. They didn't even put me behind bars."

He laughed again. "I fooled 'em all," he said. "I pretended to be dying. You wouldn't believe the amount of groanin' I did. It's funny to think about. All who came and looked at me thought I was at death's door. Well, seems I play a mighty good game. After everyone was asleep, even the useless sentries, I just walked out as free as a fiddle. I even stole me a firearm and knife. Even now they have no idea I'm gone. Not until daybreak, and by then, I hope to be even farther away than I am now. But first things first. I have you two to take care of, since I just happened upon your camp."

"You don't look like you are able to ride a horse," Shoshana said. "Did you?"

"Yep, and it's tethered only a short distance away," Mountain Jack said. "A while ago, it whinnied as I was tying my reins to a limb. I thought that gave me away. But no one came to investigate. I guess everyone just thought it was one of those horses you have penned up in that corral."

Shoshana remembered hearing the whinnying now. She had, in fact, concluded it was one of the horses they'd captured.

"Now, you two just walk quiet-like away from this camp, and then you'll finally get your comeuppance for what you did to me," he said tightly. "Yep, you rescued me from the panther's den, but then handed me over to those who I thought would have hanged me by now. Seems I'm as elusive as ever, especially to that hangman's noose."

Just as Mountain Jack started to back away from the debris that had not long ago been Shoshana and Storm's dwelling, a noise startled him.

He turned just long enough for Storm to grab his rifle. He used the weapon to knock the firearm from Mountain Jack's hand.

As his shotgun struck the ground, the impact caused it to fire. Mountain Jack was shot full in the chest.

"No, no . . ." Mountain Jack said, crumpling to his knees. He rested there for a moment, staring from Shoshana to Storm, then fell over face forward, dead.

Shoshana looked quickly around as the others, awakened by the gun's blast, came running, weapons in hand. Their eyes were wide with fear, especially Dancing Willow's.

Storm noticed a beaver scurrying away, oblivious to what it had caused by having made so much noise as it scurried through the brush.

Storm smiled at Shoshana, then drew her into his embrace. He felt how hard she was trembling. "That evil man is finally, truly dead," he said, stroking her back. "My wife, he will never trouble us again."

"I can't believe he was able to threaten us again," Shoshana murmured, clinging to him. "I thought Colonel Hawkins would make certain of that."

"Mountain Jack was skilled at deception. He was able to fool everyone into believing he was dying," Storm said from across Shoshana's shoulder. He spoke loudly enough for everyone to hear as they gathered around, their eyes on the dead man. "He escaped and found his way here, although I am certain we were the last people he wanted to come across. He was a fool not to travel onward when he saw our camp, but the need for revenge kept him here."

He looked toward the spot where the beaver had disappeared. "It was a beaver that got the best of Mountain Jack tonight," he said, laughing low.

Shoshana gazed up at Storm. "A beaver?" she said, eyes wide.

"It was a beaver that startled Mountain Jack into turning around," Storm said. "I imagine he thought it was the panther coming to finish what it had started. He didn't know that the panther was dead."

"In a sense, the panther did finalize its kill," Shoshana said, shivering at the thought. "It was fear of that panther that killed Mountain Jack."

Storm turned and gazed at the scalp hunter's body again, then looked over at Shoshana. "But enough about Mountain Jack," he said. "Although it is night, I would like to start for home. I do not think this is the place a woman carrying my child should be."

"Yes, take me home," Shoshana said, sighing.

"Did we hear right?" Dancing Willow asked as she stepped up to Storm and Shoshana. She gazed with a strange expression at Shoshana. "Are . . . you . . . with . . . child?"

"*Ho*, my *ish-tia-nay* is with child!" Storm said proudly, causing his men to smile.

He tried to ignore the bitterness he saw in his sister's eyes, for he now knew that nothing would ever make her accept Shoshana. He just hoped that she would never carry her jealousy too far again. If she did, he knew what he would have to do.

Banish her!

He placed a gentle hand on Shoshana's belly.

"And I will do everything within my power to protect our child . . . to protect my *wife*," he said thickly. He spoke three names. "You three ride with us tonight. The rest stay. Tend to this man's body, and protect our horses. Start for home tomorrow with the new horses at first daylight."

Everyone agreed, but Dancing Willow stamped away. Shoshana ignored her.

She was so glad to be on her horse alongside Storm as they made their way toward home. She was still trembling from what had happened.

But she knew that the terror of the attack had not harmed her child. She was determined not to allow anything to get in the way of her having Storm's son, especially not Dancing Willow!

Yes, she thought to herself, smiling. This child she was carrying *was* a son.

She thought of her mother. She hoped that Fawn would live long enough to hold her grandson in her arms. In some way she felt it would make up for the years Fawn had been separated from her daughter.

"I'm so anxious to be home," Shoshana said. "Except for our journey to Canada, I don't plan to go on any more outings like this. I am ready to be a wife who tends to wifely things."

"And then motherly things," Storm said, smiling at her. "My wife, you make this husband very happy and proud."

"That is my mission," Shoshana said, smiling

softly. "I have never felt more feminine than I do now."

"You could never be anything less," Storm chuckled.

They rode onward in silence, and soon morning began to break along the horizon.

"We are soon home," Storm said, nodding.

"*Ho*, soon . . ." Shoshana murmured, yet something made her suddenly uneasy.

She could not put her finger on what it was. She just had a strange sense of dread. . . .

Chapter Thirty

Can I see a falling tear,
And not feel my sorrow's share?
——William Blake

Riding up the familiar pass, Shoshana recognized that she was close to the stronghold. She was sorely tired, and after she went to her mother and hugged her, she would sleep the rest of the day.

She had her baby to protect.

She sat up straight again in her saddle when she caught a movement at her right side, where something had slithered into a loose pile of rocks. It was chunky and striped and very fast.

"That is a marbled salamander," Storm said, noticing it. "With fall so near, most salamander females will be seeking out sheltered nooks. As summer gives way to fall, these salamanders breed. The salamander we just saw is not seeking safety in the rocks. It will travel on down the mountain and when it finds a low-lying swale in the forest, it will lay clusters of up to one hundred eggs in dry leaf litter, or under a rotting log, then wait for the water to come."

"What water?" Shoshana asked, always amazed at Storm's knowledge of nature.

"Rain water," Storm said. "As fall rains fill these low depressions, rising water inundates the eggs. They hatch and within days are on the prowl, seeking out tiny aquatic animals. Months later, when spotted salamanders, wood frogs, and other spring-bred amphibians arrive at the pools, the marbled salamanders are months old and far ahead of the competition."

"How do you know these things?" Shoshana asked, eyes wide.

"My grandfather and my father taught me many things I am certain white fathers do not know to tell their children," Storm said softly.

"Please be the teacher to our children that your grandfather and father were to you," Shoshana said, then gazed quickly ahead when she heard a horse approaching down the narrow pass.

She soon saw that it was one of Storm's warriors who had stayed behind at the village to keep watch on the band. Storm did not completely trust Colonel Hawkins to leave his people alone.

Would Mountain Jack's escape bring the soldiers up the mountain in search of the evil man? After Mountain Jack died, Shoshana had thought it might be best to take his body back to Fort Chance in order to prove that he was dead. Then the soldiers would have no need to search for him.

But Storm and Shoshana had chanced going there once. A second time might prove deadly.

They had decided to leave the body for the soldiers to find when they came looking for him.

"Who is that coming toward us?" Shoshana asked, drawing rein just as Storm stopped to await the warrior's approach.

"This warrior is called Two Wings," Storm said, nodding a welcome to the warrior.

"What takes you away from the stronghold?" Storm asked the warrior, whose eyes went to Shoshana and lingered there.

"From our lookout I saw you coming up the pass," Two Wings said. "I chose not to wait for the signal of your arrival."

"And why did you decide that?" Storm asked. "What do you have to say that could not have waited until we arrived?"

"I have sad news," Two Wings said thickly, his eyes sliding over to Storm, then back to Shoshana.

Shoshana's heart skipped a beat. The face of her mother flashed before her eyes.

"Tell us, then," Storm said, drawing the warrior's eyes back to him.

"It is No Name, whom we now know as Fawn," Two Wings said, his voice drawn. "She passed on to the other side peacefully in her sleep, a smile on her face."

"No!" Shoshana choked out, tears spilling from her eyes.

She was heartbroken over the news, yet she had been half expecting it.

But it seemed so unfair that she had only recently been reunited with her mother, only to lose her again. But this time she was truly gone. There would be no chance meetings again, not until Shoshana joined her in the sky.

Storm saw how the news had devastated Shoshana. He reached over and wrapped his arms around her, lifting her over to his horse and onto his lap.

He held her close as she sobbed and buried her face against his chest.

"It is unfair," he said to her, as though he had read her thoughts. "But I urge you to look at what happened in another way. Fawn has not been well for some time now, yet she lived long enough to be reunited with you, Shoshana, her daughter. And did you not hear what Two Wings said? Your mother died with a smile on her face—a smile of happiness over having gotten to see and be with her daughter before she took her last breaths of life."

"Yes, I know," Shoshana sobbed out. "I know how wonderful it was that we spent time together again after having been separated for so long, but—"

"My wife, your reunion was, in itself, a miracle," Storm said softly. "That Fawn survived when so many others died on that terrible day, that she had the will to survive until she held her daughter one last time, is a miracle. She went happily, Shoshana, peacefully in her sleep. She is in the sky even now, gazing down at you with a smile."

"Yes, it was a blessing that we were together again, if only for a short while," Shoshana said, wiping tears from her eyes as she gazed up at Storm. "I will bury my mother without feeling resentment or regret, without feeling cheated."

To herself, Shoshana was thinking how glad she was that she had revealed to her mother that she was pregnant before she died. Her mother at least knew that, although she would never get the chance to hold the child in her arms.

But yes, her mother would be watching from the heavens. She would see, and Shoshana would feel her mother's presence everywhere she went.

"I am all right now," Shoshana murmured. She inhaled a deep, quavering breath. "I am ready to go to my mother and help prepare her for burial. I know that your customs vary from those I have learned in the white community. Will you please teach me what is right for the burial of my mother?"

"I will teach you as I help you," Storm said, then placed her back in her own saddle.

With Two Wings riding ahead of them, Storm and Shoshana traveled onward in silence. When they reached the stronghold, Shoshana went to her mother's lodge and dismounted.

A young brave came and took her horse away. Then Shoshana went inside where their shaman, White Moon, was kneeling beside her mother's bed of rich pelts and blankets.

A soft fire burned in the firepit. There was a smell of sage in the air, intermingled with other scents that Shoshana did not recognize.

When White Moon saw Shoshana standing there, he rose slowly to his feet.

He went to Shoshana and gently embraced her. "She went softly into the night," he murmured. "She is now where there is no pain or heartache. She is with those who have gone on before her."

He gave her one last hug, then left the tepee.

Tears streaming from her eyes, Shoshana knelt down beside her mother. She noted how peaceful she looked, and that she did have a soft smile on her lips.

Her hair had been unbraided and brushed. She

wore her loveliest doeskin dress, which displayed her own fancy beadwork.

Vermilion had been placed on her face, and her hands lay with twined fingers across her bosom.

"*Ina*, oh, Mother, I missed you so much through the years, and now I am forced to live with missing you again," Shoshana sobbed, gently stroking her mother's hand, which was cold to the touch. "But these past days were wonderful, *Ina*. Memories were made for me to cling to until the day I join you in the sky."

She wiped tears from her eyes with her free hand and smiled down at her mother, whose eyes were peacefully closed. "I am so glad that I shared the news with you about the coming child," she said softly. "I can feel in my heart and in my soul that I am with child. I need not count out the days until I see that another monthly flow has failed to come. This babe's heart will beat within me just as mine beat in your body those long years ago. *Ina*, I shall cherish being a mother. And I will always keep you alive inside my children's hearts and minds. I will tell them all about you so that they will actually be able to see you as if they had known you."

Storm came into the lodge and knelt down beside Shoshana. "Are you all right?" he asked, sliding a comforting arm around her shoulders. "Is this too hard for you to bear?"

"It's hard, but I shall make it all right," Shoshana murmured. "*Ina* is still with me, you know." She placed a hand over her heart. "In here, Storm. She will live on here until the day I die."

"*Ho*, that is as it should be," he said. "I urge you to rest before starting the task of preparing your mother for burial. I shall send for White Moon again. He can sit with her."

"*To-dah*, I shall do it," a voice said from behind them.

Shoshana and Storm turned. They were both surprised to see Dancing Willow standing in the entranceway. "Sister, it is you?" Storm said, rising. "How did you get here so quickly? Did you not wait to travel with the rest?"

"I dreamed, my brother, a dream that awakened me abruptly. After that I came on ahead of the others," Dancing Willow said, entering and kneeling down beside Storm.

She looked past Storm at Shoshana. "Shoshana, I dreamed of your mother's passing," she murmured. "I knew that you would arrive home and find her gone. I came to be with you . . . to help you, for I am truly sorry about your mother. I am sorry for what you must be going through. I, too, lost a mother. I know the sorrow that fills the heart at such a loss."

Shoshana was uncertain how to feel about what Dancing Willow was saying. Her sister-in-law had taken a risk, coming ahead of the others despite the dangers of traveling alone. There was more than one panther on this mountain.

Shoshana was touched by the effort she'd made to return to the stronghold. She rose and went to Dancing Willow. She held out her arms for her.

Dancing Willow rose. They embraced.

Storm looked on, feeling good about what he was witnessing. It seemed that his sister had finally gotten past her jealousy. There was no false note in what she said today.

He believed that Dancing Willow was finally ready to be Shoshana's friend, and a sister that Storm could again admire, be proud of, and love.

"I am so sorry about all that I have done to make you uncomfortable as my brother's wife," Dancing Willow murmured. "I shall never again behave unkindly toward you."

"I believe you," Shoshana murmured, then stepped away from her. "You said that you dreamed of my mother's death. Dancing Willow, I ofttimes have had dreams, too, that came to pass. Sometimes I feel that it is a blessing, yet other times I don't. Do you feel blessed to have such dreams?"

"*Ho*, I do," Dancing Willow said, nodding. "Those of us who dream *are* blessed. It is a miracle to dream of what is yet to come."

Shoshana turned and gazed down at her mother. "I dreamed often about finding my mother before it finally happened," she said softly. "I shall . . .

never . . . forget those dreams, nor the eagle that was a part of them."

"You dream of eagles, too?" Dancing Willow asked, bringing Shoshana's eyes back to her.

"*Ho*, I have, often," Shoshana murmured.

"Does it have large, golden eyes that seem to talk to you, and does it have large, golden talons?" Dancing Willow asked, her eyes searching Shoshana's.

Shoshana was amazed by what Dancing Willow had just revealed to her. It did seem the same eagle visited each of their dreams.

Knowing this made Shoshana feel a sudden close bond to her husband's sister.

Storm came to them and hugged them both. "My big sister, my wife," he said softly. "It is good to see that you two are becoming friends."

He held them away from him and looked at them one at a time, then smiled. "I believe you are going to be even more than friends," he said, then took Shoshana's hand. "Come, my wife. We must get you in your bed of blankets so that you can rest. Tomorrow is another day, and one that will be especially trying for you."

"Do go ahead and rest," Dancing Willow said, coming once again to embrace Shoshana. "I shall sit vigil at your mother's side. I shall be here until you come to prepare her for burial. Then, too, I shall be here for you. I shall help you."

"Thank you, Dancing Willow," Shoshana said,

flinging herself into her sister-in-law's arms. "It is so good to know this wondrously generous side of you."

"Soon you will know all of my sides," Dancing Willow said, laughing softly. She stepped away from Shoshana. "Little brother, see to my sister, will you?" she said, smiling at him.

Shoshana felt the closeness of having been called Dancing Willow's "sister" like a warm embrace. She smiled a thank you to her over her shoulder as Storm whisked her away.

Shoshana took one last look at her mother before going outside with her husband.

"It will be so hard tomorrow," she said, tears again shining in her eyes.

"Saying a final good-bye is always hard," Storm said, taking her into their lodge. "But remember this, Shoshana: your mother died happy."

Shoshana moved into his arms. She clung to him as she began to cry again. She would get the tears shed today so that tomorrow she could be brave and strong in Storm's people's eyes as she went through a day that surely would tear at her heart.

She knew this to be true, for she had already buried one mother. It would be no easier burying the other. She would cling to her memories of both, all of which were precious.

Chapter Thirty-one

Farewell to one now silenced quiet,
Sent out of hearing, out of sight.
                                    —Alice Meynell

The procession to the burial place of Shoshana's mother was slow and solemn.

Once there, Shoshana found that Storm had come before her and had prepared the earth.

The burial grounds of this Apache band were not as vast as the one that Storm had taken Shoshana to, where he had placed his mother's hair among his ancestors. It was obvious that this burial place had only been established after Storm and his people had been forced from their other home along the Piñaleno River.

The grave markings were there, made from

stones. No names appeared, for it was the Apache custom that the name of the deceased would never again be spoken among the living.

Storm had explained to Shoshana that many, many years ago, it was even considered wrong to go near the burial site. But that was before the Apache felt a need to establish a place where they could go and visit their dead.

The superstitious fear of the older generation, that the spirit of the dead might return to haunt and harm them, was long ago forgotten.

Back then, when lives were governed by such beliefs, the nearer the relationship that bound one to the deceased, the more terrible this dread seemed to be. Even if a relative kept anything that had belonged to the departed, he would fear that the ghost of the dead would come back to claim it.

Shoshana was glad that her people did not follow the rules of those long-ago ancestors, so that she could visit her mother's grave often before the Piñaleno River Band moved on to Canada.

It was the custom of whites to place flowers on the graves of loved ones, and even to sit and speak to the dead whenever they wished.

Shoshana needed these special moments with her mother, for she had not had enough time with Fawn since she had found her.

Carrying Fawn's beautifully wrapped body, enclosed in the whitest doeskin, Storm and several other warriors walked solemnly, with Shoshana following behind them. Dancing Willow gave her comfort as she walked hand in hand with her.

The soft songs being sung seemed to beautifully harmonize with the bird song that filled the air this early morning.

And when a huge golden eagle swept suddenly from the sky, Shoshana's breath was momentarily stolen. Its huge shadow fell over the body of her mother.

Shoshana felt the mystery of this moment when the eagle swept lower, its huge golden talons open, drawing gasps from everyone. For a moment Shoshana felt that the bird was going to sweep up her mother's body and carry it away as she had seen it do so often in her dreams. Yet she was wrong. It hovered for a moment longer, turned its huge golden eyes to Shoshana, then flew away. It soared above them for a moment, then soon was lost in the shadows of the mountain peak.

Shoshana and Dancing Willow exchanged quick, knowing looks and smiled at one another. Then they continued walking until they finally came to the spot where the ground had been opened to welcome Fawn's body into it.

Once everyone had circled around in order to witness the burial, Shoshana approached the grave and looked into it. Her eyes widened in wonder.

Then she gazed at her husband, whose eyes met

hers as he stepped back to stand with Shoshana while the other warriors began lowering Fawn's body into the grave. All the while the singing continued, soft and sweet.

Shoshana knew that it would be disrespectful to speak at this time, but she longed to tell Storm just how much she appreciated his loving attention to her mother. He had placed in her grave many of the things that she had loved during her time with the Piñaleno River Band of Apache.

Her sewing equipment was there, as well as her second-favorite dress, for she wore her most favorite. He had included beautifully colored satin ribbons that he had traded for her through the years.

There were so many other things, yet not too many to crowd Fawn's resting place; just enough so that she would not feel alone once her daughter and the others who loved her had to return to the duties of the living.

Before leaving for the burial, Storm had explained to Shoshana that not so long ago there was a big difference in burial ceremonies of women and warriors. The demise of a warrior provoked a lavish demonstration of woe and general sense of serious loss, whereas the death of a squaw was almost unnoticed, except by her friends and female relatives.

Today the ceremony was to be quiet and serene, but everyone would join in, not only family.

And that was how Shoshana felt it should be, for

her mother had become beloved by everyone in this band of Apache, not only a few.

Now White Moon came from the crowd. He brought with him in a small wooden tray some sprigs of dried sagebrush which he had set aflame.

As he spoke to the deceased in low, loving tones, he brushed his hand through the smoke of the sagebrush, then waved it over Fawn's prone body. He then bent lower and waved his hand through the smoke again, sending it down into the grave.

Then he handed the tray of burning sagebrush to Shoshana, who performed the same ritual with the smoke. She passed it on to Storm.

Once that was done, White Moon stepped away, to be replaced by several young girls and boys who knelt around the grave and sang softly to Fawn. Once again the eagle appeared overhead, casting its shadow over them.

Everything seemed like a dream to Shoshana, so mystical she had to fight back the tears that burned at the corners of her eyes.

She had already cried a river. Yet there were more tears that needed to be shed.

But not now.

This was a time of rejoicing as her mother was being sent off to join those she had loved, oh, so long ago.

Shoshana could barely remember her true Apache father, since she had been so small when he had passed away. But she recalled enough about him that she could almost see him in the clouds, his hands reaching out for his wife, who would soon join him.

Shoshana hid a sob behind a hand, for she now truly felt her father's presence. She could even feel him putting his strong arms around her, as he had done so often when she had adored the tall, muscled Apache warrior whom she proudly called *Ahte*.

The word *father* brought another face into her mind's eye, one that caused bitterness in her heart.

That man had stolen many precious moments from Shoshana that could have been spent with her mother if he had not stolen Shoshana from her true home and people.

She brushed her thoughts aside as quickly as his face had appeared, for he did not belong there with her this day, nor ever again.

She was saying good-bye to her mother, and would begin the rest of her life where she belonged, and with a man who was a hundred times the man Colonel George Whaley had ever been.

The children's song was over. They rose and went to stand beside their mothers. Storm took Shoshana's hand and stood with her over the grave.

When he spoke gentle, loving words to her mother, the woman who had come into his people's lives so long ago, Shoshana could no longer hold back the tears.

She was touched deeply by the love her husband had had for her mother. His respect for her was evident in the words he was saying to her now.

When Storm glanced at Shoshana and nodded, she told her mother her own deep feelings, and said this was not a final good-bye. They would be reunited one day among the stars; they would laugh and sing again as they had done before their worlds had been torn asunder.

Dancing Willow then approached the grave, and as her people's Seer, said special words that touched Shoshana deep within her soul. She knew that things *had* changed between her and Storm's sister.

They were friends. More than that, they were family.

After all was said, everyone but the warriors whose duty it was to cover the body stepped away from the grave. Lovingly, and with much devotion and care, the warriors securely covered the dead with brush, dirt, and rocks.

Fawn's marker stone would be placed there before they started their journey to Canada.

Soft prayers were said once again after the warriors stepped back from the grave. Then a young girl, of the same age Shoshana had been when she was taken from her mother that day so long ago, stepped up to the grave, her arms filled with a variety of wildflowers.

She slowly sprinkled them on the grave until no fresh dirt, rocks, or brush could be seen.

There was only the loveliness of the flowers, their scent filling the air.

Shoshana stepped away from Storm and went to the small child. She swept her into her arms and hugged her. "Thank you," she whispered into her ear. "Thank you, child."

The little girl, with braids hanging almost to the ground, and with the sweetest smile and midnight-dark eyes, hugged Shoshana back, then stepped away and stood with her mother.

Shoshana returned to Storm's side.

White Moon distributed sprigs of green grass until everyone, even the children, held some in their hands.

Shoshana followed Storm's lead as he began brushing himself all over with the wisps of grass. The others now joined in this ritual. Everyone then filed past the grave, and at the head everyone placed this grass on the ground, until it formed the shape of a cross.

Again Shoshana stifled a sob behind her hand, took one long, last look at the grave, then joined Storm and everyone else as they walked in a slow procession back to the village. Upon arriving there, they all stood around the tepee which had been Fawn's.

White Moon lit a torch from the huge outdoor fire, then stepped up to the tepee and set it ablaze. As it burned, everything that had not been buried with Fawn would go up in flames.

They stood silently watching until only ashes remained on the ground where the tepee had stood. And then White Moon again set a huge clump of sagebrush aflame and spread it on the ground before the simmering ashes of the burned lodge.

One by one, everyone disinfected themselves by stepping through the smoke of the sagebrush. Shoshana held Storm's hand so that they could step through the smoke together.

"And now it is finished," White Moon said, reaching his hands heavenward. "Our loved one now joins the spirits of those she loved in the sky!"

Everyone disbanded and returned to their day's normal activities, except for the children. They had been instructed not to laugh as they played, for it would show disrespect to Shoshana, who was in mourning.

She was touched to see the love and consideration everyone showed her. She knew that she was where she belonged, where she should have been all along.

But she was there now, the wife of a beloved Apache chief. And she had had so many special moments with her mother before Fawn gave up her fight to live. Shoshana did feel truly blessed.

She walked with Storm back to their home, and once there, found much food sitting around the fire. The tantalizing aromas made Shoshana realize how hungry she was. She had not eaten since before she had learned of her mother's death.

But now that the burial was behind her, and she had done everything she could for her mother, she knew she had someone else to be concerned about.

Her child.

She was not eating for only one person now. She was eating for two, and knew that what she ate must be nourishing.

She gazed at the food, then looked over at Storm. "I remember the very first time I went to a funeral. It was for the wife of a cavalryman. After the funeral, everyone went to his home. I was surprised at how soon everyone lost their sad faces and, instead, laughed, joked, and ate," she murmured. "It seemed wrong, disrespectful of the dead."

She paused, then said, "Then . . . then . . . When Mother, my adoptive mother, died, and they did the same after burying her, I was enraged. I told everyone how I felt," she said softly. "George Whaley was so insulted by my behavior, he scolded me and sent me to my room and did not allow me to leave until the next day. I was not brought any food, nor was I even spoken to. The maids were told to leave me be, to let me think about the wrong I had committed, while all along I grew even more angry over how my mother's death seemed so quickly forgotten by everyone."

She sighed. "I shall never forget her, nor my true mother," she murmured.

She turned to Storm and smiled. "I was lucky, you know, to have two mothers who loved me so much, and to have two mothers to love," she said, her voice breaking with emotion. "So many speak nastily of stepmothers. I could never, ever say anything but good about mine."

"And now you will be an *ina* yourself," Storm said, gently pushing a fallen lock of hair back from her brow. "And what a beautiful mother you will be."

"Both of mine were beautiful," Shoshana said, sighing. "Both were so beautiful."

Her stomach growled, breaking through her nostalgia. She giggled as Storm placed a hand on her there. In his eyes was an amused twinkling.

"One day when you touch me there you will feel our child moving within its safe cocoon," Shoshana murmured, placing her hand over Storm's. "My adoptive mother could never have children, but her best friend had several. I was enchanted by how this woman's stomach grew so large during those times. She would allow me to feel the baby's movements inside her tummy. I was intrigued by how the babe could live inside such a small, cramped place."

"Sometimes two grow in that small place," Storm said, gently pulling his hand away. He reached for two wooden platters and set one before himself and the other before Shoshana. "Twins have been known to have been born on my father's side of our family. I have more than one set of twin cousins."

"You do?" Shoshana said, her eyes wide. "Do you think we might . . . have . . . twins?" She grinned. "Perhaps even triplets?"

"Everything is possible," Storm said, chuckling.

He ladled out an assortment of food for both himself and Shoshana, then poured two cups of a sweet drink that had also been brought with the food.

"Well, if it is possible that I might have two or three children inside my belly, don't you think I had better eat my fill of this delicious-looking food that has been brought to us?" Shoshana said, smiling mischievously at Storm.

It felt good to forget her grief for just a moment.

She ate ravenously as Storm watched with amusement in his dark eyes. He was hungry himself. It had been many hours since they had feasted on baked beaver tail.

That now seemed so long ago, when they had sat peacefully beneath the stars eating and laughing with friends.

"Do any of your twin cousins live here at your stronghold?" Shoshana asked, pausing before eating anything else.

"*To-dah*, I have not seen them since our different bands were separated when the pony soldiers began tearing asunder the lives of all Apache," Storm grumbled. "Who is to say, though, that perhaps I may find them in Canada land? Several of our different bands have gone there already."

"When are we leaving?" Shoshana asked.

"Before you get large with child and before the cold winter winds begin to blow," Storm said, nodding. "Soon, my wife. Soon."

She felt a wrenching sadness at the thought of leaving her mother behind, yet she had to remind herself that she was not actually leaving her mother. Only Fawn's shell lay in the ground. The important part of her, her spirit, soared even now somewhere in the heavens, looking down upon Shoshana.

"I look forward to arriving there so that we can start building our new life which soon will include our child," Shoshana said, sinking her teeth into a piece of corn on the cob, which had recently been harvested.

She knew, because it was harvest time, that they must make haste to leave. Not long after harvest came winter.

"Do you not mean that we will be starting our new life with our *children* . . . not a lone child?" Storm teased. "Twins are destined for us, my wife. You can count on twins."

She knew that he was speaking in jest, yet it was a possibility.

She was anxious to see what her dreams told her

tonight, whether she was carrying one, or two, children in her womb. Her dreams had revealed so much to her already in her life.

Her thoughts went to the eagle and how magically it had appeared today at her mother's burial. She would never forget that eagle and what it had brought into her life, and she had first met *it* in a dream.

Chapter Thirty-two

If ever wife was happy in a man,
Compare with me, ye women, if you can!
                        —Anne Bradstreet

Four years later—Canada

The grass, once crackling and brittle underfoot, had been transformed into huge carpets of green. Shoshana stood at the door of her log cabin, gazing out at everything beyond the village of tepees, cabins, and wickiups.

Canada was a beautiful place. As now, Shoshana admired the long stretch of land for as far as she could see, and the patches of color along the ground, where spring wildflowers had just opened their faces to the warmth of the sun.

Far in the distance she could see mountain peaks that still showed a covering of snow, which would soon melt, swelling the creeks and rivers below with delicious, sweet water.

Shoshana was, ah, so content at their new home. It was indeed a wilderness, and far from humanity except for their band of Apache, and another band that had recently established themselves downriver.

They needed no white man's supplies, for they made do with what they took from the earth and sky.

She looked around, and smiled when she gazed at freshly upturned earth where soon corn would be planted, as well as pumpkins, squash, beans, and many other vegetables that would be added to the meat that the warriors kept their families supplied with.

She had helped prepare the earth for seeds in this communal garden, but knew that Storm would soon curtail all of her strenuous activities, for with the last child, she had experienced some frightening moments. She had almost given birth too early, which would have made it impossible for the baby to live.

She and Storm had decided that after this third child was brought into the world, they would be cautious so that Shoshana would not get pregnant again.

Along with feeling that their unborn baby's life had been threatened during those many frightening moments when pains, and some blood, had interrupted her last pregnancy, there were moments when White Moon had feared for Shoshana's life.

She placed her hand on her stomach now, resting it there against her doeskin dress.

She would do nothing to endanger this child's life.

Nothing!

And she had no enemies such as Mountain Jack to fear, which might have threatened her and the child.

Thus far, no white man had come to interfere in the life of the Piñaleno River Band of Apache.

But she knew that could not last forever, for she knew how white men planned and schemed against all people with red skin.

Ho, yes, in time, she knew to expect the same sort of interference that she had seen happen in America.

But she would not dwell on that.

This was now.

Everything was wonderful!

While Storm was in council today, and their two children were with their Aunt Dancing Willow to spend the night with her, who still had not found a man for herself, Shoshana dropped the buckskin entrance flap and went and sat beside the fire and resumed beading herself a new pair of moccasins.

The ankle-high moccasins to which she was

adding beads today were more lightweight, for spring and summer wear, very unlike the coarser, heavier, knee-high moccasins she wore during the blustery cold months of winter.

"Yes, the winters are very cold here," she whispered to herself, wincing when she pricked her finger, then resumed sewing the colorful beads onto the doeskin, in the shape of spring flowers.

After they had arrived in Canada land, the erection of lodges was the first priority, because hints of winter had already begun to breathe across the land.

Since she was with child, Storm had not allowed Shoshana to help him build their home, but she had watched as he lovingly built their wickiup, as he thrust the long, slender poles into the ground about two feet apart, bent them inward until they met, and then bound them together at the top, leaving a little hole to let their lodge fire's smoke out.

They had planned to live in the wickiup that first winter, and a log cabin the second winter and thereafter.

Shoshana had watched Storm skillfully weave branches into the framework and then cover it with bark and deerskins.

After the structure had been completed, she had watched him scoop dirt out in the floor at the far back of the lodge, from eighteen inches to two feet deep, to serve as their bedroom. He had secured it for warmth with flooring made of heavy bark, and then rich pelts that they had brought from Arizona.

The dirt that had been dug out had then been packed around the inside base of the wickiup, to give solidity to the house, and afford protection against driving storms.

A firepit had been dug in the center of the floor, where Shoshana had then lovingly prepared meals for her husband.

She found this way of life vastly different from how she had lived when she had been a part of the white man's world.

But although the home she had lived in at Missouri had been what some called a mansion, she preferred her cabin, for it was her home.

She was glad that Storm had built a cabin, and much larger than most, for after she had borne one child, another had come only nine months later.

Now she was pregnant with a third, but only barely. Her stomach had not begun to swell yet.

But she was anxious for it to grow, for she would never forget the pride she had seen in her husband's eyes those two times she had carried their children in her womb.

Yes, she had to do everything that was required to go full term with this child, and she, oh, so hoped it would be a daughter, to finally give her two sons, Two Moons and Panther Eyes, a sister.

Except for two things, both sons, age two and

three, were the exact image of their father. Panther Eyes, the younger, had much lighter skin, and his hair was light brown, which seemed to reflect that part of Storm that had been white, taken after his white mother's side of the family.

But in all other respects, this son had his father's noble-featured face, flashing dark eyes, and a frame that proved that one day he would be as muscled as his father.

As Shoshana waited for Storm to return home, she again thought about the past winter, how the ground had been transformed into huge carpets of white, and how, during the first fierce blizzard, the snow had piled up in the coulees and built strange mounds around any obstruction of brush or rock that stood in its path.

Inside their lodges, the people had relaxed and waited for spring. She had soon discovered that winter and blizzards were as much a part of the Apache people's life as the pleasant days of summer.

At times like this, a man could visit with friends, tell stories, and reminisce about the past.

A woman could finish some intricate quillwork on a pair of moccasins, repair her husband's leather shirt, or teach their children songs of their people's past.

When the Apache people of the village ran short of firewood, the younger girls hunted and collected buffalo chips, which burned hot and quick—*too* quickly, but if their mother hung a bit of fat, suspended above the fire so that it slowly dripped on the dung, it made it last longer and created a better heat.

At night, when the fire burned low and then went out, everyone wrapped themselves snugly in their buffalo robes and stayed there until the morning fire cast its tongues of heat into every part of the lodge.

Shoshana had been amazed that first time, when even though on the coldest mornings, her husband, along with the other men, insisted on stripping to their breechclouts to go outside to rub snow on their bodies.

Trim, fat, and hardened by life in the outdoors, they had adjusted to the cold so they could more easily withstand the rigors of the hunt.

"My wife is so deep in thought she does not even realize that her husband has returned home for those special moments we spoke of before he went into council with his warriors?" Storm said, drawing Shoshana's eyes quickly up at him as he stood over her, his eyes twinkling.

Seeing him there, knowing what he meant when he spoke of "special moments," Shoshana placed her sewing aside and rose to her feet and twined her arms around his neck.

"I was thinking of how cold it has been this past winter," she murmured. She giggled softly. "I was getting to the part in my thoughts that would have snuggled us together in our blankets after the children were asleep in their own."

"I should have waited longer before coming to you, so that thinking about our private moments in our blankets, when the children were not aware of what we were doing, could heat up your insides like the flame on the wick of our lamps, so that you would be better prepared for our lovemaking today," Storm said huskily, his arms sweeping around Shoshana's tiny waist.

He was still amazed to see how tiny she was after bearing two children, whereas so many women remained thick in the middle.

"Do you truly believe that I need thoughts to 'prepare' me?" Shoshana teased. "My love, all I need is you, your hands, your mouth, your lips—"

"All are yours," Storm said, softly interrupting her.

"Now?" Shoshana teased again, her eyes dancing into his.

"Yes, now, except first I wish to show you something very special," he said. He reached a hand out for her. "Come. I want you to share the magic of the moment."

Anxious to see what he was talking about, she moved eagerly to her feet and took his hand.

She went outside with him and walked to a slight hill beyond the village, where they had a good look at the river in the distance.

"They are still here," Storm said, sliding an arm around her waist. "Now do you see why I call it magic?"

She gasped with delight as she looked and saw what Storm was so in awe of. Now, in early spring, along the river, migratory sandhill cranes poured in, attracted by the shallow rivers' abundant roosting sites and meadows.

Looking like legions of gray ghosts from a distance, the birds covered the meadows and water from one end to the other.

Now more were flying low over the river, their voices rising and falling as they approached, then passed overhead and disappeared.

Storm whisked Shoshana up into his arms, carrying her back home and to their bedroom.

Standing beside their bed of blankets and rich pelts, Storm undressed Shoshana. Then she stood before him nude and unclothed him.

And when the fire cast its golden light on their copper skins, Storm again swept Shoshana into his arms, then lay her on their bed, and soon stretched out atop her, their bodies already straining hungrily against each other's.

"My love, will it always be this way?" Shoshana murmured breathlessly as Storm brushed kisses from one breast to another. "Will our love always be this strong, this magical?"

"I will make it so," he said, leaning up to gaze into her eyes. "I will always give you such loving."

His fingers caressed her breasts and then made a slow, sensuous descent downward until he found her swollen, throbbing womanhood and began caressing her there.

She twined her arms around his neck. She smiled sweetly up at him, then inhaled a quavering breath of ecstasy and trembled when he parted her thighs and gently thrust himself inside her damp valley and began the rhythmic strokes that she knew would soon carry her to paradise.

He bent his head and touched her lips in a gentle, lingering kiss, his strokes within her speeding up, her hips responding in her own rhythmic movement.

She was responding to every nuance of his love-making, a blaze of desire firing her insides into an almost roaring inferno.

Her whole body quivered as he continued his rhythmic thrusts.

She had a lethargic feeling of floating.

Passion glazed in her eyes as her husband paused for a moment and gazed down at her. "How fiercely I always want you," he said huskily. "I never have enough of you."

"Nor I you," Shoshana breathed out, her pulse racing as again he began his thrusts, his mouth closing hard upon hers in a hot, even more demanding kiss than before.

Storm could feel the pulsing crest of his passion, the fires of his passion spreading through him. Their bodies tangled as he molded her even more closely to the contours of his lean, muscled body.

And then both of their bodies exploded in spasms, taking them once again to that place of wonder where no one else could enter.

Afterwards, as they lay on their bed, Shoshana reached for Storm's hand and placed it on her stomach. "I feel so blessed," she murmured. "Another child, Storm. We are going to have another child!"

She turned to him and smiled softly at him. "Do you remember those years ago when we were thinking we might have twins, and you even mentioned possibly triplets?" she asked softly. "Are you disappointed that we are having children one at a time?"

"Nothing you do could ever disappoint me," Storm said, slowly running his hands across her belly. "You have given me the world, Shoshana. How could I ever complain about anything?"

"I just want to have a daughter," she murmured, snuggling closely to him. "Do you think we'll have a daughter this time?"

"Wish hard enough for it, and it will be yours," Storm said, smiling at her. "I shall also wish for the same."

"Dancing Willow says she has already dreamed

about this child and she did see it as a girl baby," Shoshana said, sighing pleasurably at the thought. "But, truly, my love, I shall be happy with whatever *Maheo* blesses us with. All children are miracles."

"As it was a miracle that we found one another when all things would point against it ever happening," Storm said, running his fingers through her waist-length black hair. "Had I come to Canada earlier, we would not have met, but something held me back. That something was you. You were beckoning to me, Shoshana. You were saying, 'Storm, Storm, I am near, please wait . . . please wait.'"

"Yes, I truly believe so," Shoshana said, nodding. "And here we are, man and wife, mother and father, and happier than I had ever thought could be humanly possible."

"I have news for you that I purposely waited to tell you because I could hardly wait to make love with you," Storm said, sitting up. He smiled down at her as she turned on her back to gaze up at him.

"What is it?"

"You know how glad I was that another band of Apache had eluded the United States government and fled to Canada land, and settled not far downriver from us," he said.

"Yes, I know how happy you were that more Apache had escaped a reservation sort of life," she murmured.

"My wife, one of the warriors there came to join

331

our council today and spoke to me of something beside the hunt," he said, his eyes twinkling.

"What could he speak of that would bring such a twinkle into your eyes?" Shoshana asked as she sat up next to him.

"This man, who is one winter older than Dancing Willow, has come to ask to court my sister," Storm said, beaming. "I went to Dancing Willow with the news. I have never seen her smile so brightly."

"She truly is interested in him, as well?" Shoshana asked, her eyes wide in wonder. "Did she remember him when you spoke his name to her?"

"Ah, yes, she remembered," he said, chuckling. "He has been here several times now for council, and has joined one hunt with me and my warriors this early spring. Each time he has managed to somehow walk into the path of my sister. She has also seemed to manage it that they would meet. It began, I believe, the first time they saw one another."

"And so you gave him permission to court her?" Shoshana asked, happy for Dancing Willow, for she had mellowed since arriving in Canada land. Shoshana thought it might have been her nephews that had caused the change.

She enjoyed them so much, Shoshana had begun to see that Dancing Willow felt that she had missed something in not having children.

"She is my big sister. No one needs permission from me for what Dancing Willow does. She can answer for herself, especially about a man," Storm said, chuckling.

"I am so happy for her," Shoshana said, moving into Storm's arms. "Is it not wonderful, Storm, how things are for us all in Canada land? There is such an air of peace in our village."

"Yes, I see it and feel it, too," Storm said. He sighed. "I strive to see that it remains that way. But there is only so much that I can do. Now it depends on the Canadian government and how they choose to see the red man—as friend? Or enemy?"

Shoshana clung to him and refused to think anything negative at this time, for her life was so different from what it had been when she had been forced to live the life of white people.

She was, oh, so content to be with her true people, to have a husband such as Storm.

Before departing from the stronghold, she had realized the importance of leaving everything behind that had to do with that other life.

She had left all mementos of her past at the stronghold.

Even the dress that she had been married in. It did not belong in her world now, and she now realized that she should not have even worn it on her wedding day.

But everything of this life was new to her, and she had still clung to the love she had had for her adopted mother.

That was the only reason she had worn the dress . . . in honor of her.

She remembered leaving it with her other things, buried beneath rocks. She had thought that perhaps she should have burned them in case whites might find the stronghold and somehow trace her personal possessions back to her.

But she knew that she would be long gone by then and safe in Canada where the United States had no jurisdiction.

Once the border was crossed, Shoshana and those she loved of this Apache band were finally free.

And ah, how she delighted in their children, and no, she would never look back at what had been, nor would she look ahead at what might happen that could be bad for the Piñaleno River Band of Apache.

For now, it was a wonderful place to be . . . with her husband, her children, her Apache people!

She could not ask for more than this!

Not in her lifetime!

"It took four years, but finally we found Chief Storm's stronghold," Colonel Hawkins said tightly. "But damn it, we're four years too late."

He looked around him where the remains of tepees and wickiups had been, all but the poles thrust in the ground having fallen away.

It was as though he was looking at skeletal remains, and it did make him angry that he had allowed Storm to get away.

The ruling had come down shortly after he'd had that one meeting with Chief Storm, when Storm had handed the scalawag scalp hunter over to him, that all Apache must be sent to reservations.

None were to be spared.

Not even those who had never caused the cavalry any problems.

As Washington had stated it, no red man could be trusted, that if they chose to rebel, many white lives could be taken in Arizona, especially of the settlers who trusted the government to protect them.

"I don't know why it was so important to catch this one Apache chief," Lieutenant Jake Turner said as he sidled his horse closer to Colonel Hawkins.

"It's just the principle of the thing," Hawkins grumbled. "If I'm told to round up all Apache, why would I let even one escape?"

"But he never caused anyone any problems," Lieutenant Turner said flatly. "And you know that Chief Storm's wife was Colonel Whaley's adopted daughter. He'd not have wanted you to do anything that might cause her harm."

"Yes, and I'm sure Colonel Whaley turned over in his grave when Shoshana married that savage chief," Colonel Hawkins said, riding slowly onward, weaving his horse around things that lay on the ground. "I just know this was Chief Storm's stronghold. And damn if he didn't have it hidden away in such an ungodly place. No wonder it was never found before today."

"I thought after you found Mountain Jack's body shortly after he escaped, and you surmised that he was killed by the Apache chief, that that was enough for you to forget chasing after Chief Storm," the lieutenant said. "He did you a favor, so why not return the favor and let him live in peace?"

Colonel Hawkins ignored him; then his eyes widened and he drew rein when he looked down at something familiar on the ground.

He dismounted, picked it up, and looked at it closely.

"Well, I'll be damned," he said. "See this? It belonged to Colonel Whaley's wife. Shoshana apparently took it with her when she fled in the night away from the fort."

"That dress?" the lieutenant said, his eyebrows forking.

"Yes. And were it not for a stone having fallen down over it, it would've blown away and I'd have never found it," Colonel Hawkins said, gazing intently at the gauzy dress. "Mighty pretty it was on that woman, too."

"You saw Shoshana in the dress?" the lieutenant asked.

"No, her mother," Colonel Hawkins said. "You see, I went to Missouri to meet with Colonel Whaley way before his wife died. I asked him then to come to Arizona and help search for the damnable scalp hunter. That one night, when I came downstairs at their mansion to dine with them, and I saw this beautiful, petite woman in this dress, I could have sworn I'd never seen anyone as beautiful. It was for certain I'd never forget the dress. I'd never seen any like it before or since."

"And so you know this is that dress, huh?" the lieutenant said, idly scratching his brow.

"There's no doubt," Colonel Hawkins said, then looked north. "Damn it all to hell, those savages went to Canada. They fled America and went to Canada, for there could be nowhere left in America for them to hide."

"Are you going after him?"

"Nope. I have no jurisdiction there," Colonel Hawkins said, shrugging. He wheeled his horse around. "Come on. Let's head back. We've been gone from the fort way too long."

"Yeah, it'll be good to get back to civilization," the lieutenant said, sighing with relief.

Colonel Hawkins tossed the dress over his shoulder to the ground. He did not see how it suddenly seemed to take wing and begin fluttering through the air in the steady breeze, northward.

337

* * *

"A daughter," Shoshana sighed as she placed the tiny newborn child to her breast.

Storm knelt beside the bed. He ran a hand softly over the child's copper head, as the baby's two brothers stood watching. "You have a sister," he said, gazing from son to son. He smiled at Dancing Willow, who stood behind the children, then gave his wife a smile. "We are a complete family now. I have never been as proud of anyone as I am proud of you, wife."

"I am prouder of you for having given me our daughter," Shoshana said, smiling sweetly at her husband. "Thank you, Storm. I so love you."

Outside, where the wind was a soft, cool breeze, a huge golden eagle swept and soared over the cabin, its golden eyes ever watching.

Dear Reader:

I hope you enjoyed reading *Savage Courage*. The next book in my Savage Series, which I am writing exclusively for Leisure Books, is *Savage Vision*, about the Caddo Indians of Texas. The book is filled with much passion, intrigue, and adventure.

Those of you who are collecting my Indian romance novels, and want to hear more about the series and my entire backlist of books, can send for my latest newsletter, bookmark, and fan club information, by writing to Cassie Edwards at the following address:

Cassie Edwards
6709 Country Club Road
Mattoon, IL 61938

For an assured, quick response, please include a stamped self-addressed legal-sized envelope with your letter. And you can visit my website at www.cassieedwards.com.

Thank you for supporting my Indian series. I love researching and writing about our beloved Native Americans, our country's first people.

Always,
Cassie Edwards

Turn the page
for a special sneak
preview of

WALKS
IN
SHADOW

by

Joyce Henderson

On sale now!

Prologue

Walks in Shadow stood amid the oaks, shrouded in the inky darkness for which he'd been named. Overhead, tree limbs bent and groaned. Their leaves rattled in the slicing rain of a blue norther. Dawn, dreary and icy, would creep over the land before long.

Focused on the squares of light in the ranch house windows fifty yards away, he didn't bother to brush away the strands of shoulder-length hair whipping against his lips and bronze-skinned cheeks. Water cascaded from the brim of the white man's Stetson he wore. He looked down at the oilskin-wrapped boy-child in his arms.

Little Spring slept peacefully. His small body and

breath warmed Walks in Shadow's buckskin-clad chest. In, out—relaxed, trusting. The fifteen-month-old boy had been played with, protected, and loved by the man who held him. Trust for his adopted uncle was all the little Comanche had ever known.

That was about to change.

Walks in Shadow clenched his jaw and shook his head. Water droplets sailed from the hat's brim.

I do not want to do this. I cannot.

I must. A promise is a promise.

He glanced up when a distant, indistinct sound carried above the wind's wail. A figure stepped out on the porch and spoke to another inside the house. Thunder cracked, drowning out the voice as he closed the door and turned toward a shed. A bucket swung in his hand as he dashed through the downpour, head angled against the buffeting rain.

The figure was garbed in trousers, a hip-length coat and a wide-brimmed hat. Bubbling Water had not mentioned a boy. Only a woman, a kind man, and a girl.

Walks in Shadow's eyes dimmed as he remembered how enraged he had been when his adopted sister disappeared. A tested warrior, having seen twenty-three winters himself at the time, he had joined three others to scour the countryside for her. That had been over two years before, but he could still feel the rage, the gut-wrenching fear when she had not been found.

Twelve suns later, Bubbling Water walked into camp wearing white women's clothes. The tale she told still made his stomach clench. While gathering herbs, she had been abducted by a white man, raped and left to die. The man who owned this ranch where Walks in Shadow now stood had found her and cared for her until she recovered.

The names of its inhabitants were imprinted on Walks in Shadow's heart. Hiram Timberlake, his daughter, Samantha, and the older woman, Mattie Crawford. Another name circled in his mind, too.

Clarence.

The man had uttered his own name to Bubbling Water when she scratched him in a vain attempt to escape.

"Ya goddamn bitch! What Clarence wants, he takes!"

He had.

Now holding the results of that rape in his arms, Walks in Shadow trembled with the same rage he had felt when Bubbling Water haltingly told of the evil committed against her. Clarence would die, Walks in Shadow vowed. One day he would find the man.

Only fourteen at the time, Bubbling Water had given birth, then within a few months she was taken to the Spirit world, defenseless against the white man's measles. Walks in Shadow shifted the sleeping child in his arms and watched the youth disappear into the shed.

"You are white, my brother." Bubbling Water's voice rose from the past to carry on the wind. "Disease and starvation are all that remain for the Comanche. Promise you will take Little Spring and return to the white world."

"I am Comanche by everything but birth!" Walks in Shadow had argued. A name from the past was all he remembered of the world whence he had been taken many years past. Holden. His life as a white child before age three was only fleeting images.

Conditioned to think like an Indian, he felt hate burning in his breast when he thought of the white scourge overrunning the Comanche. On the other hand, Bubbling Water had said Hiram Timberlake was kind, his family gentle and caring.

A thunderclap boomed and rumbled across the sky, jolting him from his musings. He looked down at the dark head peeking from beneath the oilskin, then slid his gaze to the windows and the shed.

Now or never.

His night vision keen, he circled behind the shed and angled toward the house. He lightly stepped onto the porch and laid his sleeping burden next to the wall. The porch roof shielded Little Spring from direct rain. For an instant he longed to pick up the child and run.

He could not.

He must leave Little Spring with these white people until he was sure he could live among white men himself. Only then could he protect the child. Only then could he secretly teach Little Spring about his Comanche heritage. His shoulders tensed with resolve.

Pulling aside the oilskin wrapping, he looked into Little Spring's sleeping face. His heart like a stone in his chest, Walks in Shadow caressed the babe's cheek one last time. "I will be back one day, little man." He re-covered the child's face and stole away as soundlessly as he had come.

Walks in Shadow had just regained the safety of the gloom beneath the oaks when the door opened and a man's silhouette filled the space.

He could not watch anymore. Tears stung his eyes as he vanished into the trees.

One day I will be back, Little Spring. That is a promise.

Chapter One

Samantha Timberlake wanted him from the first time she saw him. The yearning was so intense, so primal, it took her breath. She was twenty-five years old, and though she loved her father, Aunt Mattie and little Guy fiercely, she'd never experienced a desire so strong—until that moment.

He'd stood on a hill, wild, proud, fierce, as beautiful as Texas was brutal. Then he disappeared from view. The search lasted three weeks before she and a couple of ranch hands had found and captured him. She'd wanted him and now she had him. But at what price?

Dust flew as he twisted and fought against Oscar's rope. Oscar Dupree was strong, even if he stood only

346

five-five, shorter than Samantha by two full inches. His compact, wiry frame attested to a life of hard work. For once, he'd donned gloves over hands that appeared old beyond his forty years. Crookedly healed broken fingers, wire cuts, and old flesh-eating rope burns marred the skin. A ten-year veteran on Timberoaks, Oscar was the best broncobuster around, but he might lose the battle with this wild, beautiful black stallion.

The stallion's breath rasped. Deceptively spindly looking forelegs shot skyward as the animal leaped up, then came down stiff-legged, humpbacked, his head diving toward the ground. He bucked across the enclosure, dragging Oscar as if he weighed no more than a barnyard cat.

"Whoa!" Oscar yelled to no avail.

Guy, the six-year-old boy who was like a brother, whooped and laughed. He straddled the top of the corral fence an arm's length from where Samantha stood. "Ain't gonna win, Oscar!"

"You aren't going to," she automatically corrected, though her chocolate-brown eyes remained fixed on the writhing stallion.

"Yeah," Guy agreed.

From the corner of her eye, Guy's snaggle-toothed grin told her he hadn't listened to a word she'd said. For that matter, he didn't care about proper grammar, and probably never would. Like hers, his world centered on horses, and he was caught up in the war raging between tenacious man and obstinate horse.

Several ranch hands stood on the far side of the corral, arms crossed atop the fence, as enthralled by the tableau as Samantha and Guy were. This was simply the way a horse was broken to saddle. But the stallion might break a leg in the process. More than one leg if he continued the violent pitching. She scowled. Worse, if Oscar ultimately won the battle, the stallion's spirit might be crushed.

Samantha didn't want that. Part of the horse's allure was the untamed spirit she sensed in the animal. She wanted him gentled, not broken. There had to be a better way.

"Oscar, stop!" She scraped her booted foot off the bottom rung of the fence and strode toward the gate. "Oscar!" she called again. The buster couldn't hear her above the men's shouts of encouragement and the horse's frantic snorts and grunts.

Samantha opened the gate and stepped inside. The stallion bolted directly toward her. His surprise move jerked the rope from Oscar's hand.

"Samma!" Guy cried.

She raised a reassuring hand in his direction. "It's all right." That was debatable, but she'd left herself no room to maneuver. She stood her ground, back against the gate. "Stop," she whispered from a suddenly dry mouth as the stallion bore down on her.

Even if the horse were inclined to obey—which he undoubtedly wasn't—her faint command was lost amid concerned male shouts.

She stood mesmerized, watching the stallion plunge toward her. Then, as if he'd been grabbed from behind by the scruff of his sleek neck, he arched that neck, stiffened his forelegs, and slid to a halt not three feet in front of her.

Dust billowed up, coating her trousers and white shirt, surrounding her, choking her, but she could see the stallion's dark, challenging eyes. Head held high, sides heaving with each breath, the magnificent animal stared with disdain—and fear—down the length of his nose. The stallion probably tipped the scales at eleven hundred pounds, but the fence and the people scared him to death.

"Come out of there right now!"

Samantha recognized that authoritative voice. Her father's. Hiram Timberlake might be ill, but his spirit was still intact, strong as a bull's.

She licked dry lips. "Maybe I should—"

"Out!" her father snapped.

Samantha continued to face the horse as she opened the gate and stepped back through, pulling it closed. Her shoulders slumped with relief when the latch clicked. The stallion threw his head up at the tiny sound, whirled, and galloped back to the center of the corral.

Her father dragged her around to face him. His green eyes pierced hers, and she heard the concern in his gruff voice that others might not.

"Whatever possessed you to go into that corral, daughter?"

Shaking, she took a breath. "Oscar didn't hear me when I told him to stop. Pa, I don't want the stallion if it means he'll be—"

"Don't you go near that horse again until he's gentled. You got that?" He stood with his elbow cocked, thumb hooked on the gun belt he wore.

She reached out and touched his upper arm. "That's my point, Pa. I want him gentled, not broken." She shook her head when her father's eyes narrowed. "You don't understand—"

"What you want may not be possible. What you get may be a disappointment."

"I'd rather let him go."

"Yer kiddin'."

Guy's drawl snapped her head around.

"No, I'm not kidding."

"Holy moly, Samma—"

"Watch your mouth," her father growled.

Guy paid no mind. He had a head of steam already primed and chugging away. "You look-ted and look-ted. Now you wanna let 'im go? Geez—"

Still able to muster enough strength for his purpose, Hiram grasped a fistful of Guy's shirtfront and yanked him off the fence. "You, young man, can hie

350

yourself off to the house. Your mouth is about to run away with you and take the Lord's name in vain. I'll not have it." Hiram pointed in the direction he wanted Guy to go.

"Pa, I di'n't—"

"Not yet. But your smart mouth is going to get you a strop mark or two on your backside. I'd be mighty sorry to have to administer those marks, boy. Mattie has fresh bread cooling. Go ask her for a big slice slathered with her peach jam."

Guy's pale blue eyes lit, and Samantha suppressed a grin. Aunt Mattie's jams and jellies could bring men to blows if one hogged up the last of a jar without offering to share.

Guy took off at a run toward the house. His too-long black hair swung below his collar.

Her father's lips lifted in a half smile as he turned back to face her. The chance of his taking his razor strop to her sturdy brother's backside was so remote that she wanted to laugh.

"Oscar, take that rope off the stallion."

"Whatever you say, Hiram."

"Samantha," her father said, "I don't know of another way or a better man to tame that stallion than Oscar. You know how he works. You know how horses are broken."

She gazed into his gaunt face. Her heart constricted at the thought that he might not live much longer. How could she let him go?

How could she be so arrogant as to think she had a choice in the matter?

"In His good time and by His grace, I live," her father had admonished. "I'll die when He says it's my time, Samantha."

When the time came, she'd have to be strong like her father. She willed away the worrisome thoughts.

Holden Walker glanced up. Between the leaves and far, far away, the evening star glittered in the vast purpling sky. Before long, total darkness would be upon the land. Countless stars would splash across the heavens, joining the one that heralded the night. He tethered his dapple-gray cow pony to a spindly bush among the shadowy stand of oaks. He knelt to remove his spurs, then stood and stuffed them into his saddlebag.

A whippoorwill's call carried on the wind. Another answered, hidden in the spreading limbs directly over his head. Brush rustled in the breeze. A squirrel scolded.

Holden smiled, listening to the familiar sounds of approaching night as he adjusted the gun belt circling his narrow hips, then wove his way among the oaks. Though he wore white man's boots, he moved as quietly as a wolf, always had. His affinity for the night and ability to roam undetected had prompted the People to name him Walks in Shadow. Now, other than an occasional visit with Two Horns and

Swift Arrow, that life was behind him—by five long years.

A clearing stretched before him as he reached the edge of the trees' canopy. He paused and leaned a muscled shoulder against an oak's gnarled trunk. Not much had changed since he had stood in this spot once before. The house and barn had since been whitewashed, perhaps.

No. Another structure now stood north of the barn. Maybe a bunkhouse. Square windows flanked either side of the door in the plank walls. Lantern light shone from the windows in the new building and those downstairs in the ranch house.

He searched the area. His piercing gaze missed nothing. Other than a hound that lay on the porch scratching fleas, not a soul stirred. Supper time, perhaps.

While learning to live in the white man's world, he had worked on several ranges such as this, but often escaped to the prairie. Sometimes he went off during the night when a Comanche moon lit the sky. On those occasions he spread a blanket and communed with the Spirits. Though he should have cut all ties, twice a year he rode out to find his former band. Speaking with the People he still thought of as his own gave him the strength to live in the white man's world, to learn their ways.

His longest stay in a town had been in Waco, where he met Lillibeth. She had not only appeased his sexual needs, but she had also taught him to read and write. Now he was back, his promise kept.

Seeing Little Spring would have to wait until tomorrow. The boy was probably headed for bed before long. Holden sent up a prayer to the Great Spirit that Bubbling Water had not misjudged this family, that Hiram Timberlake had reared the boy.

Retreating through the trees to his tethered horse, he pulled a bedroll from behind his saddle and prepared to settle down for the night, with the sky as roof and the ground his bed. It was summertime in Texas, and with the coming of night, the searing heat had diminished.

With just a pinch of luck, maybe Timberlake would give him a job. Timberoaks was a horse ranch, and Holden was a master at handling horses. Gentling mustangs, herding and tending the remuda had been his job on cattle drives. While working in Waco, he had trained more than one horse so a greenhorn could ride without breaking his fool neck. That was how Walks in Shadow had become Holden Walker, horse trainer.

Until he was sure he could again live in the white world, Holden had resisted the temptation to check on Little Spring. Consequently, the boy would not remember his adopted uncle. Besides, Walks in Shadow had left Little Spring here under Timberlake's care. The man would not take kindly to a stranger who claimed to be kin carting off the child.

What could he say, anyway? *You have harbored a half-Comanche for five years, Mr. Timberlake. Now I want him back.* Holden grimaced. Oh, yes, that would sit well with a Texan! Perhaps he would never be able to reveal his former relationship with Little Spring. If that were the case, could he move on and leave the boy again? Doubtful.

Holden removed his black hat and gun belt and laid the weapon within easy reach. Settling his long frame on the blanket, he stared up through foliage with unseeing eyes, unsure if the boy was still on this ranch. Tomorrow he would know, and then he would take whatever came one day at a time.

That evening Samantha's thoughts were on her empty stomach. Her mouth watered at the scrumptious smell wafting through the kitchen. Surreptitiously, she lifted the corner of a flour-sack cloth. Before she could filch a slice of the warm bread, a wooden spoon whapped her knuckles.

"Ow!" She snatched her hand back and stuck stinging fingers in her mouth.

"Keep your grubby hands off the food, young lady," Matilda Crawford ordered.

"But it smells so good, Aunt Mattie. And I'm hungry."

"Then get washed up for supper. It'll be ready in a jiffy. While you're at it, change your clothes."

Samantha turned so Mattie couldn't see her face

and mouthed verbatim her aunt's next words. "You may wish you had been born a boy, but you're a girl. A girl comes to my table looking like one. Put on a clean shirtwaist and skirt."

Samantha rolled her eyes at the last order. It was her aunt's fondest hope that she would settle down and marry. Sooner rather than later. Though her father hadn't pressured her, he felt the same way.

Shoot, had she been born a boy, they wouldn't think twice about when she married. And, most importantly, there would be no question in her father's mind that she could run the ranch as well as he.

Since she was a girl, Aunt Mattie and every man on the place protected her from the heavier work: shoeing, occasional branding, and night riding or fence mending. She grimaced, then consoled herself with the thought that at least she had learned from her pa how to get the best price for Timberoaks's stock.

One day—she prayed that day would be far in the future—Timberoaks would come to her. When it did, she needed to know all there was to know about the horse business. As a woman, she'd have to work doubly hard to earn respect from men who considered females weak in the head about such matters.

Samantha climbed the stairs and walked down the short hallway to her bedroom at the back of the house. She went directly to the mirrored armoire and pulled open one door. She eyed the few feminine garments she owned.

Glancing sideways, she peered at her image in the looking glass mounted on the inside of the door panel. Dirt smudged her cheek. Beneath the brown Stetson, her hair was dust-laden, windblown and tangled. She crinkled her nose; the smattering of freckles all but disappeared.

"You *are* filthy," she muttered.

Pulling off her hat, she gave it a toss. The headgear sailed unerringly and plunked against the wall, squarely hooked by half of an old horseshoe.

After shucking her dirty outer garments, she made quick work of a spit bath, then donned a shirtwaist. Reluctantly, she fastened the buttons clear to the base of her throat. That was another thing that galled her about her aunt's insistence that she look and act like a girl. Comporting herself properly when necessary was not a problem, but women's clothing, fashioned for total cover-up, was so blessed hot.

She smoothed the long skirt over generous hips and took a modicum of satisfaction that she'd won a crucial concession from Aunt Mattie. Samantha had vowed never to wear a corset. That contraption harkened back to medieval torture and ranked right up there with chastity belts.

Grinning as she pulled a brush through her thick

hair, she spoke to her reflection. "Aunt Mattie would be shocked if she knew you even thought of such a thing."

She arrived back in the kitchen in the midst of a conversation. Her heart sank at Aunt Mattie's stern words to Guy. "Yes, you will, young man. Reverend Fuller only gets around this way a couple of times a year. Listening to his sermon and taking his words to heart won't hurt you one bit."

Samantha might have argued that point. Reverend Fuller preached "fire and brimstone." She doubted even one person had ever been brought to salvation through the grim preacher's harsh words.

"He's coming here?" she asked as she took a seat. The smell of fried chicken added to the lingering aroma of warm bread made her mouth water again.

"Not here," Aunt Mattie replied. "He's staying at the Butchers'."

Holy moly, far worse! Not only would she be forced to sit through a two-hour sermon but she'd have to do so in proximity to the two most odious men alive. Uriah Butcher was a tyrant, and his son, Clarence James, made her skin crawl. Older than her by ten years, C. J. believed her destined to be his wife.

Not if she had anything to say about it!

"Rev'end Fuller's a mean old man," Guy groused.

"He preaches the gospel, boy," Hiram interjected, then coughed.

Samantha's heart lurched when her father clapped a napkin against his mouth. His shoulders heaved as he rose and left the table, spasms racking his body. Aunt Mattie watched her brother-in-law, five years her junior, with troubled chocolate-brown eyes that matched Samantha's.

Samantha eyed his plate. He'd taken one bite of chicken and perhaps two of mashed potatoes and gravy. Six months before, Dr. Bennett, in Waco, had diagnosed her father's illness as consumption, but she wondered if starvation wouldn't take him first.

Samantha's gaze met her aunt's. Without uttering a sound, Mattie's compassionate expression spoke clearly. *Not long, not long for this world.*

"Is Pa gonna die?"

Guy's timid question slammed into Samantha's heart so hard that he might as well have hit her with a hammer. She sometimes forgot he was still a little boy. Rambunctious, for sure, but scared right now. Before she could respond, Aunt Mattie closed her hand over his.

Mattie never lied. She had never glossed over the truth for the sake of misplaced kindness. But thank God, this time she equivocated. "We all will die one day. We just don't know when the Lord will take us home."

"Pa *is* home!"

Mattie nodded. Her eyes glittered with unshed tears. "His earthly home, yes, Guy. But we all have a better place awaiting us on the other side of eternity."

Tears silvered his pale blue eyes, turning them gray. "I don't want him to die."

I don't either! Samantha wailed inwardly.

"Come, child." Aunt Mattie rose and drew him to his feet. "It's time to call it a day. Your pa will be with us a while yet."

Samantha stared at the uneaten supper on the plates and in the serving dishes. It had been over a week since her father had had such a coughing fit, and she'd hoped . . . She looked up at the ceiling, still able to hear him, though she knew he tried to suppress the sounds.

Rising, she began to clear the table. The hunger she'd felt moments ago had drowned in a heart awash with tears.

The next dawn, a faint tinge of orange lightened the gunmetal gray sky on the eastern horizon. Anxious to check the black, Samantha hurried through her morning ablutions.

As she descended the stairs, lantern light glimmered across the floor from her father's small office off the parlor. She stepped to the door. Undetected, she gazed at him bent over a ledger lying on the oak desk. The gray salted through his midnight hair gleamed silver in the lantern's light.

A faint hiss from the lamp mixed with the sound

of his quill scratching on paper. Although she hadn't made a noise, he must have felt her gaze on him, for he glanced up. His smile reached his green eyes. Dear God, how would she live without a daily dose of that cheerful expression?

"Morning," he said. "You're up early."

"Um, I wanted to check on the stallion."

"He's still out there." His grin widened. "Full of spit and fire, and not the least bit pleased at being penned."

He'd already taken a turn outside to see that everything was okay. One day that would be her job. A faint noise from the back of the house told her Aunt Mattie was also up, fixing breakfast.

Suddenly her father sobered. "I've been meaning to talk to you, Samantha." He motioned to the overstuffed wingback chair angled at the corner of the battered desk. "Come sit down for a few minutes. That stallion will hold for a bit."

Vaguely alarmed, Samantha didn't like the serious look in his eyes. Her boots thudded hollowly on the wooden floor until she stepped onto the circular rag rug her mother had made some thirty years before, when her parents had first come to Texas.

"Samantha, I have the feeling that before long I'm going to be treading ground in the 'Promised Land' we've heard so much about."

"Oh, Pa!" She sank onto the brown cushion and flung up a defensive hand, a futile gesture to ward off his pragmatism. His attempt at casualness failed—miserably.

"It's got to be faced," he went on relentlessly. "When I'm gone, this ranch will go to you, eventually."

Eventually? Her brow creased. "Is that supposed to make me feel better?" She couldn't help the sarcastic retort. "I don't want to listen to this." She didn't want to cry, either, but tears threatened.

"Sass won't change a thing, Samantha." He smiled lamely. "After I'm gone—"

"Must you harp on that?" She stood and took a backward step. "Please, Pa, not now."

She left her fears unsaid. If he'd stop talking about his death, maybe it wouldn't be so hard to listen to him. She'd learned some things about ranch operation, but there was far more her father needed to teach her if she was to run Timberoaks at a profit. Her gaze flicked to the ledger on the desk, which she knew nothing about.

He emitted a resigned sigh. "All right. But we must talk soon. You may not wish to face it, but time is short." Before he could continue, a fit of coughing shook him.

He drew out a handkerchief and covered his mouth until he breathed more easily. A telltale splotch of blood appeared on the cloth. He wiped his lips, crumpled the linen in his fist, then lowered his hand to his lap.

"Pa." Her voice quavered.

"I'm all right."

"But you're spitting—"

"It goes with this blasted ailment, Samantha. There's nothing to be done about it."

That was true. No one seemed to know how to stop the insidious march of consumption. Still . . . Heartsick with what she had seen, she wondered if her aunt knew his lungs now bled.

"Anyway," he said, as if there had been no interruption, "I need to explain some things so you don't think unkindly of me."

"What?" She shook her head, struggling to concentrate on his words. *Think . . . unkindly . . .* "Pa . . ."

He waved his hand in dismissal. "You'll understand soon enough. Now, if we aren't going to discuss ranch matters, you need to figure out what you want to do about that stallion. Oscar can break him, but that's what he'll do. Break him. It's the only way."

"You expect me to forget . . . You think I can—"

From one breath to the next, his mouth hardened. "You can and you will! Life goes on. Yours certainly will, Samantha. You can't avoid responsibility because you're upset or something strikes you as unfair. You were determined to have that horse, and now you've got him. Tell Oscar if you want him broke. If you've changed your mind, let him go."

* * *

Once again Holden stood half hidden-under the oaks, his dark clothes an effective camouflage. He scanned the clearing as daylight strengthened. A short-statured cowboy ambled out of what he assumed was the bunkhouse, a toothpick stuck in his mouth. At the same time, the front door of the main house opened.

As the figure stepped to the edge of the porch, the sun burst over the horizon and bathed the front of the house in golden light. A tall, willowy woman stood looking toward the corral. Holden's breath stalled.

She was the most striking woman he had ever seen. Hat in hand, she wore men's clothes—a surprise in itself. But it was her hair, lots of it, that claimed his admiration. Lit by the sun, gleaming tresses cascaded to the center of her back, golden around her shoulders. His gaze slowly tracked her length.

Ample breasts rounded beneath the white shirt, taunting a man to cup them, caress them. Below a tiny waist circled by a wide belt, denim hugged generous hips. And long legs. Lord of the white man, she had the shapeliest legs.

She stuck the hat between her knees and clamped them together. Heat boiled through Holden and settled heavily in his groin. He could actually feel silken thighs wrapped around his waist.

When she raised her arms, the shirt snugged

across her breasts, outlining them so effectively she might as well have been naked. He shifted and licked his lips. With both hands, she gathered that gorgeous hair at her nape, twisted it several times, and flipped it atop her head. She retrieved the hat and hid the glorious tresses inside the crown.

He felt oddly deprived, but only for a moment. When she stepped off the porch, her hips swayed provocatively. He wanted to rush forward, throw her down, and mount her like some green boy.

He forced himself to take slow breaths, coming out of a trancelike state. In the name of the lightning spirit, what was wrong with him? A woman was a woman was a woman. He had proven that to himself time and again. Not a one was worth getting hot in the trousers. Other than Lillibeth, most women he had ever come in contact with could be had with a look, a smile. Since his return to the white world, even a half-pleasant expression usually brought a woman to his bed.

He watched her easy stride as she approached the man who now stood next to the corral fence. When she halted beside him, Holden noticed she was taller than the wrangler. She hooked a boot heel on the bottom rung and rested crossed arms atop the fence. The movements stretched the shirt across her narrow back and cupped the denim around her derriere.

He envied the material caressing her bottom—which was lunacy. Still, he wanted to cup that derriere. He wanted to twirl her around, unbutton her shirt, and feast his eyes on her generous breasts. Damnation, the way he felt right now, he would rip off the shirt, not take the time to release the buttons!

"Samma, you gonna ride 'im?" a child's voice called.

A boy banged out the door and crossed the porch. He leaped to the ground and ran pell-mell toward the corral.

Little Spring? Holden's breath slowed. He eyed the boy with speculation. Black-as-night hair straggled below his ears. He clambered up the fence on sturdy legs, agile as a bear climbing a tree.

Holden's gaze wrenched to the woman, who looked over her shoulder and said something. He failed to catch her words; only a husky timbre registered. *Samma,* the boy had called her. Perhaps this was Bubbling Water's Samantha.

Could be, he thought, counting backward. Twenty-four, maybe twenty-five by now. More than old enough . . .

He shook his head. No. Samantha Timberlake had nursed Bubbling Water. She deserved his gratitude, not his lust.

"I don't know that I'll ever ride him," the woman said.

"Geez, Samma—"

"Guy," she interrupted, her voice stern. "You know what Pa said about your mouth."

"I know't. But 'geez' ain't 'Jesus.'"

Holden smiled at the boy's feisty retort.

"Isn't," she corrected, and argued further. "Pa draws a fine line."

A whinny shifted Holden's gaze to the handsome black that stood on the far side of the corral, distancing himself from the humans by the fence. Ears alert, the stallion eyed them, the boy in particular. The animal lowered his head, snorted and pawed the dirt. Dust billowed up to coat his fine head.

"Ain't he sum'pin," Guy said, clearly disregarding Miss Timberlake's admonishment.

The boy laughed and clapped his hands when, for no apparent reason, the stallion reared and pawed the air. He dropped to the ground, pranced one way, whirled and trotted in the other direction, prowling the fence, looking for a way out.

Holden's interest snapped back to the conversation when he caught the man's words.

"I been breakin' horses a lotta years, Samantha. There's only one way a cantankerous stallion is gonna accept a saddle. Blindfolded, hogtied, and thrown."

Samantha listened to Oscar's arguments and grew frustrated. "You could break his legs!"

"Them's the chances you take ever' time you break a horse. You knew that goin' in."

"If we can't do better by him, then let him go."

Oscar snorted. "That's all-fired loony, Samantha.

We winded three good horses catchin' that critter. Now you're turnin' lily-livered over breakin' 'im?"

"Not lily-livered . . . exactly."

"Don't know what else to call it," Oscar snapped.

Sighing, she stared morosely at the best-looking horse she'd ever seen. Blessed heaven, how she had wanted him. How she *still* wanted him. "There must be a better way," she murmured. "There has to be."

"There is," a voice said behind her.

At her side, Oscar turned and Guy looked over his shoulder.

"Says who?" Oscar challenged.

"Walker. Holden Walker."

His deep voice vibrated along Samantha's nerves like a cat's purr. She was glued to the spot as if a tub of thick, sticky honey had been poured over her head. For some insane reason, she wondered if she dared look at the man with the extraordinary voice. Deep inside, heat coiled in her belly, flashed through her veins. At the same time, inside, she was on fire, and gooseflesh erupted on her skin. She shuddered.

Holy moly, what's wrong with me? This Holden Walker was only a man, for heaven's sake. Not . . . Well, she didn't know what. Taking a deep breath, she steadied her shaking limbs.

"You got a lotta experience, I suppose," Oscar further challenged, sounding as though he thought the man had taken leave of his senses.

"Enough."

She was being ridiculous and rude. *Turn around, you ninny!*

Squaring her shoulders, she turned ever so slowly. A buckskin-clad chest met her gaze. Delaying the inevitable, she glanced down and inspected the man from the ground up. He wore black boots and black trousers that hugged muscled thighs. Two belts circled his narrow waist. One was black; the other, his gun belt, was brown, tooled leather. A six-gun's long barrel rode his lean thigh, a rawhide thong anchoring the tip of the holster to his leg. Like a shootist usually wore a gun. Samantha was certain he could use the weapon—with deadly accuracy.

Even at her height, she was uneasily aware that this man towered over her. His buckskin shirt looked surprisingly clean. Ax-handle-wide shoulders filled the soft leather. Lines bracketed wide, well-defined lips curved in a slight smile. His face was burnished and clean-shaven. Backlit by the morning sun, gleaming sable-brown hair dusted his shoulders below a black hat whose low brim left his eyes in deep shadow. Until he nudged up his hat brim with a thumb.

God in heaven! Gold-centered, circled by greenish gray, his eyes seemed to glitter with inner light. She swallowed. *Cat . . . No.* Only once before had she seen eyes like his. And they weren't human. Wolf's eyes. Dangerous. Compelling.

Befuddled, Samantha could say nothing. Caught by his gaze, she was unable to look away.

He was so still that he appeared not to breathe, while his rude, intent gaze roamed over her as hers had over him. Her lips tingled with a burning sensation when his perusal lingered on them for what seemed like forever. Then he refocused on her eyes.

Her breath was labored, but she forced herself to speak. "I don't believe we've met. I'm Samantha Timberlake."

"It is my pleasure."

While the greeting sounded ridiculously formal coming from a Texan's mouth, his brilliant eyes promised . . . what?

Tremulous with disquiet and wonder, she felt her heart thump with undeniable excitement.

SAVAGE HOPE
CASSIE EDWARDS

Chief Bright Arrow is proud of the quiet, peaceful life he led with the Makah Indians. But his idyllic world changes the day he passes by a frozen pond and sees a golden-haired angel dancing across the ice as if by magic. Yet Bright Arrow can see that the recent rains have caused the ice to melt, and after a loud crack, the young woman falls into the frigid water.

When Kathia Parish is pulled from the grip of an icy death by the strong arms of an Indian brave, she has no idea how she can ever repay him. But as the coming spring continues to thaw the frozen land, she feels her love bloom. Kathia hadn't planned on falling in love; all she can do is have faith that her heart will guide her safely to her destiny.

SAVAGE TRUST
CASSIE EDWARDS

For beautiful, golden-haired Yvette, the train ride west to a new beginning brings only death and disappointment. First her father is killed by renegades, and then the man she promised to marry is revealed as a reclusive cattle baron more than twice her age. When still another derailment lands her in the muscular arms of a very different suitor, Yvette doesn't know what to think. Tall and lithe, Cloud Walker is sought after by all the women of his tribe, but his midnight-dark gaze says the blue-eyed beauty is the only one for him. Though their love is forbidden, though their passion might bring heartache, she knows her life is on track at last.

SAVAGE LOVE
CASSIE EDWARDS

Monster bones are the stuff of Indian legend, which warns that they must not be disturbed. But Dayanara and her father are on a mission to uncover the bones. Not even her father's untimely death or a disapproving Indian chief can prevent Dayanara from proving her worth as an archaeologist.

Any relationship between a Cree chief and a white woman is prohibited by both their peoples, but the golden woman of Quick Fox's dreams is more glorious than the setting sun. Not even her interest in the sacred burial grounds of his people can prevent him from discovering the delights they will know together and proving his savage love.
